BANSHEE

BANSHEE

Mythological Irish Women Retold

Edited By
AILBHE MALONE

Stories By

Jane Casey
Naoise Dolan
Salma El-Wardany
Wendy Erskine
Nikita Gill
Anne Griffin
Sarah Maria Griffin
Jess Kidd
Megan Nolan
Sheila O'Flanagan

JOHN MURRAY

First published in Great Britain in 2026 by John Murray (Publishers)

1

Introduction and chapter introductions © Ailbhe Malone 2026
'The Changeling' Copyright © Jane Casey 2026
'The Swans' Copyright © Naoise Dolan 2026
'Dirty Laundry' Copyright © Salma El-Wardany 2026
'plus she can drive your getaway car faster than any' Copyright © Wendy Erskine 2026
'A Most Deceiving Woman' Copyright © Nikita Gill 2026
'Woman and Wave' Copyright © Anne Griffin 2026
'Woo' Copyright © Sarah Maria Griffin 2026
'Boann' Copyright © Jess Kidd 2026
'Diarmuid and Gráinne' Copyright © Megan Nolan 2026
'Diving for Pearls' Copyright © Sheila O'Flanagan 2026

The right of the Authors to be identified as the Author of the Work has been asserted by them in accordance with the Copyright, Designs and Patents Act 1988.

Chapter ornament design by Aoife Cawley.

All rights reserved. No part of this publication may be reproduced, stored in a retrieval system, or transmitted, in any form or by any means without the prior written permission of the publisher, nor be otherwise circulated in any form of binding or cover other than that in which it is published and without a similar condition being imposed on the subsequent purchaser.

All characters in this publication are fictitious and any resemblance to real persons, living or dead, is purely coincidental.

A CIP catalogue record for this title is available from the British Library

Hardback ISBN 978 1 408 74935 7
ebook ISBN 978 1 408 74934 0

Typeset in Electra by Hewer Text UK Ltd, Edinburgh

Printed and bound in Great Britain by Clays Ltd, Elcograf S.p.A.

John Murray policy is to use papers that are natural, renewable and recyclable products and made from wood grown in sustainable forests. The logging and manufacturing processes are expected to conform to the environmental regulations of the country of origin.

Carmelite House
50 Victoria Embankment
London EC4Y 0DZ

www.johnmurraypress.co.uk

John Murray Press, part of Hodder & Stoughton Limited
An Hachette UK company

The authorised representative in the EEA is Hachette Ireland,
8 Castlecourt Centre, Dublin 15, D15 XTP3, Ireland (email: info@hbgi.ie)

For Aoife.

Contents

Introduction	ix
Boann by Jess Kidd	1
Diving for Pearls by Sheila O'Flanagan	27
The Swans by Naoise Dolan	65
The Changeling by Jane Casey	97
A Most Deceiving Woman by Nikita Gill	123
plus she can drive your getaway car faster than any by Wendy Erskine	151
Woman and Wave by Anne Griffin	175
Diarmuid and Gráinne by Megan Nolan	201
Dirty Laundry by Salma El-Wardany	229
Woo by Sarah Maria Griffin	269
Further Reading	293
Acknowledgements	295

Introduction

'Fadó, fadó' is how Irish fairy tales begin. It's the Irish language version of 'once upon a time', a way to signal to the listener (because these are stories to be told aloud, and remembered, and passed on) that they are about to go on a magical journey, full of druids and demons, fairies and fighters. But this phrase is also something of a trope – it places the telling firmly in the past, and sets up the archetypes of the tale before it even begins.

Irish mythology is a tapestry of characters and 'cycles' that seep into everyday life in Ireland, from the Fianna of the Fenian Cycle (a band of mighty warriors from which Fianna Fáil – one of Ireland's main political parties – gets its name), to the mighty Cú Chulainn or Setanta of the Ulster Cycle (from which Ireland's sports TV channel – Setanta Sports – is named), we have adopted these names into the most common cultural language. Legend is woven into the landscape and into our childhoods: away for the summer at the Gaeltacht in the Aran Islands, I sat by a Stone Age wedge, known locally as Diarmuid and Gráinne's bed; at my Irish-language school, my brother was in a modernist musical retelling of the Táin. Despite the choices presented to these women in these stories, it seems like they are driven by the actions of the men around them and by fate – but where might they have agency too? In the stories my friends and I have learned, these women have no interiority, even though they are often the titular characters. In *Banshee*, I'm simply asking: why not let the women lead?

There is a long historical tradition of women writing (or rewriting) Irish fairy tales – one of the first collections of myths and legends is Lady Gregory's 1902 collection, *Gods and Fighting Men*. Part of the Celtic Revival (she was a contemporary of W. B. Yeats and J. M. Synge), it was a reclamation of Irish fairy tales, albeit through an Anglo-Irish lens. Seventy years later, Sinéad de Valera (the wife of former Irish president Éamon de Valera) wrote several collections of Irish fairy tales for children, similar in style to Roger Lancelyn Green's retellings of Greek myths. Growing up in Ireland in the '90s, I devoured these fairy tales – and hungered for more. I can draw the cover of Sinéad de Valera's *Irish Fairy Tales* without having to open my eyes, and I still feel the sparkle of the scales of the salmon of knowledge, as described by a seanchaí in Connemara National Park. And, to be frank, this is not the first time these stories have been rewritten through a new lens. While some of these tales – including sections of the Fenian Cycle – have been written down, others shared in the oral tradition were altered with the arrival of Christianity. In stories like the Children of Lir, this edit is not hard to notice – there is an abrupt moment where a monk, or Saint Patrick, appears and blesses the characters. Equally, as Irish myth is part of an oral tradition, modulations such as adding flourish and ornamentation, and changing elements to suit the circumstance or listeners, are to be expected. As part of my work researching which legends to include in this collection, I sifted through the Schools Collection (a collection of folklore compiled by Irish schoolchildren in the 1930s). The entire archive is online, and you can read scanned handwritten retellings, but I also recommend John Creedon's *Irish Folklore Treasury*, in which the best are reproduced. It was fascinating to see the beats of a story rippling through the water, differing but the same (in the Merrow – which is retold by Sheila O'Flanagan, for example, the sea woman's red cap appears each time, despite other differences in the text). Meanwhile, Credhe and Cael (The Battle of White Strand) is one of the few retellings I saw that has the same line come up again and again ('The most deceiving woman in Ireland'); it felt only right to assign this story to a poet (Nikita Gill). Another element that's worth knowing is the concept of dinnshenchas – the importance of how places get their names. You can see this expertly explored in Anne Griffin's contemporary take on Clíodhna's Wave, as well as Jess Kidd's otherworldly version of How the Boyne Got Its Name. Some of these legends I have never known in English – when I was researching translations of Diarmuid and Gráinne, I wondered what the translation for tóraíocht ('the hunting') would be – 'pursuit' doesn't seem to capture the terror at the heart of the legend. But Megan Nolan's version has a beating heart of fear and dread – like a hare being chased through brambles. Other legends I know so well I could recite by heart – yet Salma El-Wardany's re-imagining of Deirdre of the Sorrows in an Ireland ruled by the Catholic Church, rather than a pre-Christian society, surprised me with every page.

The authors in this collection represent the cream of contemporary Irish writing. There are writers I know personally, and those whose work I have grown up admiring. There are writers for whom a short story is their metier, poets who are making their short-fiction debut and novelists who were excited to test the challenges of a new format. You don't need to be familiar with the original text to enjoy these stories – but for some context, I've added a line or two of précis for each retelling. I've kept these deliberately oblique; I'd like the stories to stand on their own – if you'd like to read more about what came before them, there's a list of selected reference books at the end of this collection. My brief to these authors was simple: rewrite these legends so that the women are the fulcrums of the stories rather than the levers. In the Children of Lir, why must Fionnuala be both mother and sister to her siblings during the exile? Naoise Dolan revisits this story that she had grown up learning in school, and slants the narrative. The stories of a fairy snatching a young child and leaving a dupe in its place are numerous – but at the heart there is a real fear, something Jane Casey uses to sinister effect in her story. Sarah Maria Griffin grapples with how to parent an eternally reincarnated being in the Wooing of Etain, and in her take on the Labour Pains of the Ulaid, Wendy Erskine's Belfast is both ancient and new – a strange land where curses and half-magic still exist. My goal with this collection is to loosen the ties of the past on these fierce – sometimes frightened, sometimes ferocious – women. Like all fairy tales, these myths and legends have depth and danger. In these worlds, desire and domesticity collide.

AILBHE MALONE, EDITOR

How the Boyne Got Its Name

Boann, a goddess, tries to use a holy well, but it goes wrong. In her attempt, she transforms into the river Boyne.

The Merrow

A man finds and catches a mermaid. He hides her red cap so that she can't return to the sea. They live together, and have a family. She finds the hidden red cap and returns to the sea.

The Children of Lir

A powerful witch casts a spell on four siblings, as a result of which they must spend nine hundred years as swans. The swans are doomed to travel to three different locations for three hundred years at a time.

The Changeling

A fairy snatches a baby, and replaces it with a fairy child.

Credhe and Cael

(The Battle of White Strand)

The story of two lovers – one mortal, one a god – and the mortal woos the god with poetry. When the mortal dies (at the Battle of White Strand), the god's lament rings out.

The Labour Pains of the Ulaid

A goddess seeks help when giving birth but the king refuses. She curses everyone who hears her give birth to suffer labour pains for five days and five nights. All the Ulaid are affected, and their descendants for nine generations after.

Clíodhna's Wave

The goddess Clíodhna is killed by a wave while fleeing the sea god. She transforms into one of the three great waves of Ireland.

The Pursuit of Diarmuid and Gráinne

A doomed couple go on the run, chased by a powerful warrior.

Deirdre of the Sorrows

A young woman is prophesied to bring death to men that love her. She embarks on a doomed romance.

The Wooing of Etain

A god falls in love with a young goddess. His jealous wife turns the goddess into a bluebottle. She is then drunk by a chieftain's wife in a glass of wine and born to that wife in a human body.

BOANN

Jess Kidd

How the Boyne Got Its Name

Boann wears a mantle of gold and a robe of silver. She has slippers of fine leather. Her step is light but never skittish. Her face is handsome but severe. Gems gleam in her hair, which she wears long and fair in her eternal youth, although her harsh eye belies a crone's wisdom. Her mind is as keen as a whetted axe. But like the stabled stallion or the tethered hound, cleverness, unexercised, creates its own havoc. Queen Boann has pride of place in the mead hall and King Nechtan's bed. To her the choicest dishes are served. To her the sweetest poetry is spoken. She takes it all as her due and without visible pleasure. She seeks no confidant and has no friends. Her enemies say she is heartless, and her supporters believe she is shrewd. It is common knowledge that if Boann had a heart she would give it to her little black dog. Dabilla the keen-sighted and sharp-eared sleeps on her pillow, eats from her plate and shadows her every step. Her serving women say that when Boann is alone she tells the dog her woes.

 Chief of which is boredom.

King Nechtan's halls are vast and beautiful, his roof high and fires bright, his floors polished and walls vivid with tapestries. His grounds are green and blooming, kept perpetually at the height of spring. Food is plentiful and servants prompt. For those that haunt these halls in this golden eternity, life is easy but dull. They must do what they can to make their own fun. While Nechtan and his men ride forth on their predictable adventures, the women, whether high ranking or low, have their deeds curtailed by the boundary wall.

The court relies on the ebb and flow of guests to enliven them. They are like deathless crabs in a rock pool sifting through the gifts of the tide. In this, Boann is no different and the court watches closely for intrigues. There are young warriors who catch the queen's cold eye; Boann's heroes are favoured with a rare smile but no more, much to everyone's disappointment. Boann's smiles are true blessings, for she never smiles unless she means it, and consequently almost never smiles. Some say Boann is too discerning. Some say it is fear of her husband that stops her. Others still, that King Nechtan is a hen to her fox. Either way, his persecuted eyes trail her about his great house. As well they might, for here is a woman who lay with the Dagda, chief of gods, time's controller, granter of life and death by the two ends of his magic staff, owner of the plentiful cauldron. Her three serving women tell one another the story of the queen's infidelity, whispering and laughing behind their hands. Their tattle turns circles, mouth to ear, ear to mouth, starting off lurid, ending up profane. They add scandalous embellishments: the look in the Dagda's eye, his personal endowments, the act itself. They are less interested in the magical gestation of a poet and Boann bravely giving birth to her son alone. Then there is the delicious part about the cuckold Nechtan, sent off by the Dagda on a day-long errand. The king left in spring and couldn't understand for the life of him where the new leaves had gone as he rode back to his halls in the depths of winter. The women take sly glimpses at their mistress. This was the woman for whom the Dagda rolled nine months up into one night. For whom he stopped the sun and halted the moon. For whom he fell, faster than a stone to the bottom of a well. They try to fathom Boann's peculiar mystery. The spell she weaves over men. It's something to do with her dark blue eyes, like deep water, with a coolness to them and that bit of insolence. That's likely what drove the Dagda wild.

Boann knows what they think of her. She catches their pointed glances as they help her out of her robe and into her bath. She hears the stifled laughter as they wash her feet. Dabilla reminds her daily not to trust them. He sees them off with a nip to their ankles, or a rent to their hems, or with his sharp bark, which is pitched to shred nerves as easily as fine cloth. Dabilla is loyal like no man or woman has ever been to Boann. He would follow her through fire and water, but he valiantly keeps the king from her bed and that is enough. The little dog reserves a locked-eyed, hackles-raised, deadly antagonism towards Nechtan. Should the king dare visit his wife's chamber, Dabilla reveals a set of surprisingly wolfish teeth. Boann laughs to think of the king usurped by a lapdog. Nechtan doesn't share her amusement; he has long plotted to have the creature poisoned. Knowing this, Boann feeds her pet from her own plate and never lets him out of her sight.

Nechtan must resort to summoning her to his own quarters. His messengers she can ignore but the king's own presence in the great hall is harder to slight. Deny him for too long and he becomes unbearable. Then the courtiers and the servants, the visiting heroes and venerable druids, the harpists and jesters, all become victims of the king's louring brow and putrid temper. In low light, when his eyes are bright with mead and his paunch hidden beneath the banqueting table, Boann can trick herself into believing her husband is still desirable. When she denies him, the king shows himself to be the pettish old man he is. Then Boann cannot help but notice his thinning locks and sweaty lip, his swollen knuckles and hairy ears.

She was reared to be his wife. No one said anything about loving him.

At the start she liked him more because she knew him less, but Boann cannot contemplate their eternal future together. The thought of it fills her with a dark and swarming panic.

With the king's displeasure in her comes a marked downturn in comfort. Milk curdles and strung instruments cannot hold a tune. Knives blunt and wine sours. The fire smokes and meat spoils. The corridors fill with whispers, the heroes ride away and the great hall becomes a morgue. Then the king's wisest advisors visit the queen. Ancient men teetering on staffs and smelling vaguely of sulphur, the scent of difficult magic. Dabilla receives them with a low growl. Boann is icily courteous. They bow and scuttle. It is not a pleasant interview for anyone. Following this visit Boann will down enough sweet wine to drop a carthorse, lock her dog in a trunk and pay her husband the briefest of visits. Afterwards, he will call for feasting, song and perilous sports. Now Nechtan's smiles are limitless, for his wife, his household, his guests.

Tonight is such a night. Boann catches her reflection in a polished salver. Her face, a mask. Blank and lovely. When she eats, it could be ash. When she drinks, it could be air. Her husband, teary-eyed with merriment and relief, takes her hand. He is peering at her palm, drawing a circle there, some druid trick, some fortune-telling antic from their first days together. It's an empty, unsmiling woman he is trying to charm. He pats her hand and returns it gently to her lap. Turning to the kinsman beside him, he gives a meaty laugh.

The only thing Boann can feel is Dabilla, his small warm body against her leg like an anchor, lest she's swept away. She sips air, eats dust and looks about her, careful not to catch anyone's eye, for that might invite conversation. Since she first came to Nechtan's halls as a young bride she has studied his people. Trying to understand their words and gestures. The expression on this one's face. The promises from that one's mouth. She has long come to realise that it is all a performance. The players are interchangeable; only some things remain constant. Druids love incantations. Poets love a lineage. Heroes love a contest. Kings love flattery. But what about a queen, what does she love?

Freedom.

Out beyond the great hall and the well-tended stables, the high stone wall and the sleeping guards. Beyond the polished floors and gold plates, strong doors and high rafters. Beyond the music and dancing, the glad eye and the stacked spears, the sheathed swords and the stories unfurling. Beyond the echoes of laughter and cursing. There is a forest and Boann slips into it, like an otter from a rock into a river, with the same fugitive bliss.

This is the reason why Boann visits Nechtan. Not to appease his wise men, nor mollify his courtiers, nor even to obey the king himself. She couldn't care less about harps and milk and sour tempers. Tonight's festivities will pave the way for her escape tomorrow.

For now, Boann sits by Nechtan's side, watches and waits. The wine is drunk, and the songs are sung and the legends recited. The woodsmoke curls and mugs in the high-beamed room. The tapestries that line the walls come alive by candlelight, rich with colour, showing old conquests and half-remembered heroes. The king and the queen retire to their bedchambers before dawn, and the courtiers disappear into the shadows. Dogs and servants curl up by the fireside in the mellow warmth of the embers. The druids drift to tree-top or cave to conjure and scry. Heroes slumber where they fall, lost to the green-fielded battlegrounds of their dreams. The guards, propped in alcoves, risk a doze.

Now is the time for Boann and her little dog to slip away. Her three serving women slumber on a pallet outside her door, sour-mouthed and tangle-haired, flushed and snoring. Made insensible by the drink and a draught of her own design. Outside, dawn comes light-fingered, pocketing the darkness. Dabilla trots to the door with a questioning gleam in his eyes. Boann unlocks her chest and takes out the weatherworn cloak she hides for this purpose. It covers all of her, falling to her feet, skimming the floor. She pulls the hood up over her head, disappearing into the cloth, which smells of leaf mould and the mineral wind that comes in off the far sea. She picks up her dog, drawing him under her cloak. He lets her, knowing that they cannot risk the patter of his paws rousing the king's wolfhounds. Boann moves through wide corridors, lightly, quickly, avoiding the grand state rooms, with their polished stone floors, long feasting tables and fine wall hangings. She leaves her husband's house by the servants' ways, narrow, rough-hewn passageways leading to wooden outhouses. She crosses the courtyard and slips behind the stables, where the king's fine horses sleepily swish tail and ear. Behind a bank of thorny bushes lies a forgotten gate found by Dabilla on a squirrel chase and opened by a bribed blacksmith. Boann possesses the only working key, having had the lock remade. Every time she turns the key she does so with a feeling of hot dread knowing that some day Nechtan will find her out and the gate will not open. What then? She cannot think.

Boann lets in the sunrise and a colder rush of air. Stepping out over the threshold into golden light she sets down her dog and closes the gate to Nechtan's realm, locking it behind her. The first time she strayed beyond the wall she was struck by the seasons. How could she have forgotten them? It is Nechtan's custom to girdle his house with soft weather, the high wall making the air in his gardens pleasant and temperate. The trees and flowers are carefully tended, the paths swept. Out beyond the wall and Nechtan's fussy discipline, the forest grows wild. The trees intertwining, some dead and fallen, climbers winding, in the frost, rain or biting winds. Boann finds it exhilarating, clambering over the knotted tree roots, finding crops of vivid fungi like disembodied ears, discovering new routes through the chaos. That others may also walk in the forest occurs every time to her. But the paths are reassuringly overgrown and Dabilla will alert her to the presence of another.

It is late autumn and there is a brisk breeze. Boann revels in the changing colours of the leaves. The sun is honeyed through the tree canopy, the trunks and branches silhouetted. The moss on the ground green yet springy underfoot. Dabilla runs into view, his mouth open in a white-toothed smile, one ear up and the other down, so comical in his joy that Boann laughs too. It is during moments like these that she considers never going back. Moments of dizzy fancy before she returns to her right senses. Boann is no fool, well she knows Nechtan's reach. She might dream of living secretly, deep in the forest, as a doe, a bird, a woodcutter. She would need strong charms indeed to hide herself from Nechtan. For the king, she knows, will never let her go. Not because he loves her, but rather because she belongs to him, like a jewelled sword, or a gold shield, something rare and precious, which serves no purpose other than to make its owner seem more important. She shudders to think of the king and his men issuing out from the gates, some mounted, others on foot with sticks and traps. Druids following, holding keen-eyed hawks and muttering incantations to undo the canniest witchcraft. Nechtan would turn every leaf, poke every burrow, interrogate every caught creature. He would tirelessly track his vanished queen, fearing bewitchment, betrayal – theft! Would it even occur to him that she might leave of her own volition? Boann cannot bear the thought of being hunted down, of this quiet place being invaded, branches broken, mud churned underfoot, the shouts of armed men. Besides, she has been reared for a noble life, to take a throne and hold it, not to run away like some wounded creature.

Dabilla bolts out of the undergrowth. He digs, raining soil. He jumps onto a log and runs lightly along it. Suddenly, he stiffens. He's harking to a noise, ears pricked, turning to face the threat. He gives a low warning growl. Boann looks through the trees. Someone approaches.

Grabbing Dabilla and bundling him inside her cloak, she ducks behind the log.

The man is old, thin, dressed in the simple tunic of a servant, but the cloth is finely woven. His beard is brushed but his feet are bare. His bearing, upright. A nobleman then? He moves with steady grace through the forest, holding a wooden cup carefully with both hands, like a child. Boann need not have hidden, for the man's eyes are riveted to the contents of this cup. His expression is one of concentration; he must not spill a drop. As he advances, the trees draw back their branches and retract their roots. Moss flattens and stones skid away. The forest clears a path before him.

Boann has never seen this man before but instantly knows who he is. He is a servant of King Nechtan's well. So the myth is true. The king has never divulged its location, let alone confirmed its existence. And knowing the propensity for magical wells to disappear and relocate at the slightest provocation, Boann has never asked, assuming that since the king made no reference to it, the well had long ago taken umbrage and disappeared.

Boann feels a sudden thrill, low down, at the base of her spine. A flame kindles, the same bone-deep excitement she felt when she lay with the Dagda. She is in the presence of an old and powerful enchantment. A force with the power to bend reality, far beyond her own witcheries. A force that cannot be held or harnessed by kings, queens or druids.

Whispering words to blunt her beauty, Boann sets down her dog and follows. Now her lush golden hair grows sparse and ashy, her smooth skin pocks, her teeth fur and rot, her spine twists, her legs buckle and ankles bloat. The dog at her heels, which makes her so recognisable, has transformed too, into an old bedraggled hare. Now for all the world Boann is a crone with her familiar, her hand outstretched in an attitude of begging. As such, she is dangerous to bait and impossible to deny.

'I am lost in the forest.' Her voice, although croaky, is commanding.

The cup-bearer stops, glances over his shoulder and frowns.

'I am a stranger in need of sustenance.' Boann continues. 'Whose lands are these?'

Reluctantly, the man turns to face her. He knows better than to ignore an alms-seeking witch. 'You have strayed onto King Nechtan's land, Old Mother. Continue up to the high wall and the guard will help you.'

'I have a great thirst,' answers Boann. 'What is in your cup?'

The cup-bearer throws her a look of panic. 'This water is not for drinking.'

'Indeed? Why else would you fill a cup?'

The man bites his lip. Narrows his eyes. Here's a quandary. It may be a hag standing before him, or a goddess. It may even be Nechtan himself, testing the loyalty of his most secret of servants.

'I am Flesc, servant of the king's well.'

Boann smiles. 'The king's well, is it, Flesc? Doesn't a well belong only to itself?'

Flesc hesitates. 'The king tends the well. Three noblemen he employs, to draw off the water for purposes obscure.'

Boann fixes him with her cold crone's eye. 'Does the king visit his well often?'

Flesc's pale eyes are wary. 'Rarely.'

'You take that cup to the king?'

'To his druids.' Flesc sniffs. 'It is not for me to fathom why.'

'The ways of druids are puzzling indeed,' Boann says. 'I should like to visit this well. Show me the way.'

Flesc frowns. 'It is forbidden. Only King Nechtan and his three servants may approach it.'

'Will you refuse a stranger's request?'

Flesc studies her for a moment, weighing up the risks. Then he nods with determination. 'I will. For your own good, Old Mother.'

'Then let me peer into your cup.'

He looks at her in dismay. 'I cannot—'

Boann holds up her hand. 'Then tell me more about the well, or risk my wrath.'

Flesc reddens, contemplating the vessel in his hands as if awaiting further orders. Boann waits, hoping her charm will hold. Dabilla the hare sits back on his long haunches, watching the cup-bearer through prominent amber eyes.

Flesc raises his gaze and lowers his voice. 'The well is tricky.'

'Like all wells.' Boann nods.

'It is a terrible, cursed variety of place. The well itself is stone-built, inauspicious-looking, set in a shady clearing, unremarkable, so that you'd pass it by. A dank hole it is, surrounded by nine overgrown hazel trees that overhang a circle of water, black as pitch. Now and again these trees drop their ripe fruit. Pat, pat, pat, onto the water.' He shudders. 'Within moments ancient malevolent salmon come to feed on the nuts. The water roiling as they fight for their food, silver bellies flashing. Each speckle on the back of these dreadful fish marks a fallen fruit from the trees consumed. As they eat, they grow long and fat with wisdom, their scales dented, their fins tattered.'

'The well has great power?'

'Of a villainous kind.' He glances fearfully at the cup, his voice no more than a whisper now. 'I approach it with caution and do not look long into its dark heart, however much it goads me.'

'The well goads you?'

Flesc's face takes on a harrowed, gaunt aspect. 'Awake or sleeping – I cannot escape it. The burble and hiss of it. It is a cauldron of bitter curses.'

'What would I see if I looked into the well?'

The cup-bearer brightens, finding firmer ground. 'If you looked into the well, there would be a terrible price to pay.'

Boann feels that burning thrill again, flaring up from the root of her spine, firing her heart, setting it pounding. 'Tell me: what price?'

'You would gain an unstoppable flood of wisdom. A torrent of truth. A deluge of secrets. It would knock the sense from your mind and burst the eyes in your head. It would blast your soul and dismantle your body. Even the king himself will risk only the smallest of glances into the water.'

Boann nods. 'A great price indeed.'

The cup-bearer raises his haunted eyes. He looks at her intently before returning his gaze to his cup. 'Whatever you are, that well would alter you in ways you cannot imagine.'

Boann wraps herself in her cloak and sits down on a log, her form returning with the departure of the well's servant. Her hair falls about her shoulders, gold again, the skin on her face and hands smooths and her back straightens. Dabilla has no trace of hare about him. Now he is prick-eared, sturdy, ebony-furred. He lies at her feet crunching sticks, no worse for his mistress's witchery. Boann has half a mind to wait for the man's return so that she may follow him to the well. For such is the curiosity growing inside her.

Dabilla looks up from his stick, the low growl again. Boann hardly has the words of her charm said before a second man comes into the clearing. He goes barefoot, wearing the same finely made servant's garb as his precursor. Gaunt of face and thin of limb, this man holds a silver cup. He is younger than Flesc but with the first frost of age on his hair and beard. He steps lightly and the forest makes way for him.

Boann positions herself in his path. Dabilla, long of ear now and reddish brown, sits on scrawny haunches at her swollen ankles. When the cup-bearer is nearly upon her, he looks up. His eyes are kindly, warmed by some private joy.

'Old Mother, are you lost?'

'I was, until I met your fellow cup-bearer.'

'Flesc, was it? I am Lam.'

Boann gives a creaky bow. 'He told me of the well you tend. That it is a woeful place. Dark and dank.'

Lam smiles. 'Each to their own. I see only beauty there.'

'The water doesn't goad you?'

Lam laughs. 'Not at all. It lulls.'

'I would look upon it.' Boann throws him a wry look. 'If not for the bursting of the eyes and all the rest.'

'It's a deterrent.'

'Then how do you see the well?'

'As a perfect circle of shining water, a mirror for the sun and moon.'

'Is that right? And there are nine hazel trees?'

'As ancient and twisted as your good self. Dropping their fruit into the water, a gentle sound like the patter of raindrops, down into the well where the salmon dance.'

'Flashes of silver from their bellies as they turn?'

Lam's eyes are lit. 'The brightest you've ever seen, set against the deep black water.'

'Flesc says the well is malevolent.'

'Benevolent, I'd say.'

'That it brews evil secrets?'

'If it does, it hasn't made me privy to them,' says Lam evenly. 'I hear only its song.'

When the third cup-bearer approaches, Boann is ready, knuckles gnarled and hair thinning and her growling companion a raddled hare again. Unlike the well's previous servants, this man is armed with a scabbard and sword. He carries a golden cup with martial pride. The forest seems to shrink back from him. Boann sees he is much younger than the first two, sturdier and quicker to react.

He casts a suspicious glance over her. 'Old Mother, for what reason do you haunt King Nechtan's forest?'

'Alms, son.' Boann feels her charm waver under his shrewd eye; she must be direct. 'I have met your fellow cup-bearers—'

'You no doubt kept them talking half the day in the manner of all old crones. Don't try that trick on me.'

'They told me about the king's well.'

'They shouldn't have.'

Boann watches him closely. 'Do you fear the well like Flesc, or love it like Lam?'

The young man is piqued by the question. Boann sees the swell of pride in his chest. She wonders how many eternities it will take for him to become weary like Flesc, or generous like Lam.

'I neither fear nor love the well. It is my duty to tend it, no more.'

'You are a loyal servant to the king. I will commend you to him.'

The cup-bearer's laughter is cynical. 'Be sure to praise Luam when you beg for scraps at the back door, old woman.'

'Tell me something,' says Boann, her tone beguiling. 'Must you be brave to tend to the well?'

Luam glances down into his cup. 'Not brave, only wary. It is an angry bull. An unbroken horse. Only approach it clockwise, stop your ears against its nonsense and don't look it directly in the eye.'

Dabilla-as-hare gives a sharp bark and dives into the nearby bushes.

Startled, Luam drops his cup. It lands on the forest floor.

He watches with horror as water snakes from the vessel and undulates over the ground. Lengthening to a glossy whip, encircling Boann, before bursting apart into a mist of bright raindrops. In panic, Luam scrabbles after the bright pearls. Boann stoops to pick up the cup as a crone, straightening as a queen. She hands it to the scarlet-faced bearer.

'I will not speak of this to the king,' she says, 'if you take me to the well.'

Luam is surly, pursed-mouthed, resentful. He will not permit her beyond this point, but this is enough, she knows the way now. Twin silver birches mark the entrance to the clearing. Now and again, Dabilla can be heard barrelling through the undergrowth, giving chase to some forest creature. Barking with glee. Luam must return to the well, he says, to fill the cup to the brim for, despite his best efforts, water was lost.

On parting, he turns to Boann, narrowing his eyes. 'Queen or goddess, mother or hag, you women are one and the same. Only an exceptional fool would disobey a cup-bearer's warning.'

Boann watches him as he walks away. When he is through the trees, she unfurls her fist. She smiles. There, in her palm, a perfect bright jewel of water.

It behaves like no other droplet she's ever seen. There's a weight to it, a sheen. Back in her chamber, it hangs from her fingertip as she gazes into it, trying to divine its secrets. She sees her face reflected. A girl again, eyes bright, peering, curious. She shuts the droplet in a box and locks it in her trunk. But then finds she cannot bear to be away from it. She takes it out and circles it with gold thread and fastens it around her neck. It rests next to her skin, where she feels it throb in answer to her heart. Dabilla watches her with his tail low and his ears down. He does not like it when she's distracted.

Boann visits the well nightly in her dreams. She sees it from above. A raven-eyed view. A shining circle lit by the full moon. A fierce blue mirror by midday. She witnesses the hazelnut trees dropping their small bounties, the fish revolving below the overhanging branches, breaching the bright skin of the water. In her dreams she walks around the well widdershins, trailing her hand along the stone wall of it. Dabilla follows her steps, tail wagging serenely, eyes soft, as beguiled as she is. The cup-bearers stand by, offering no challenge, their heads bowed. Boann stops. Planting her two palms on the wall, she leans over to look into the water. A sudden rush of breeze, bringing with it the scent of autumn woods, rich loam and fresh soil and the faintest mineral smell of the faraway sea.

Awake, Boann imagines that she sees the well everywhere. In her goblet of wine, wise salmon circle. In her bathwater, arcane secrets swirl. She hears the rippling call of the well from afar. It sets the droplet at her heart eagerly echoing its correspondence. Soon enough Boann learns the well's watery language. The urgent drips, the sudden, joyful bubbles, the persistent eddies, and she understands: a bottomless love is waiting for her. A love that is transforming.

Dabilla stays closer than ever; sometimes he paws her, often he whines.

Boann visits her husband. Nechtan is surprised to see her, for the milk is not sour and the harpists are playing in tune. They sit together by the open window. He takes her hand gently and she lets him. He traces a circle on her palm. Now she understands it is the sign of the well. She does not take it as his tacit permission. Nechtan would give her anything she asks for, but never the thing she truly wants.

The queen has demanded of her husband a great feast. Such a diversion would usually be welcome, but the courtiers are nervous. Her serving women no longer whisper about their mistress and laugh behind their hands. Now they fear her. One remarks on the devilish brightness of her eyes, another the gauntness of her cheekbones, another draws attention to the queen's restless, drifting manner. Even the king notices. He consults his wisest advisors. They have seen it before; the queen is eaten up with yearning, for whom, they cannot tell.

The morning after the great feast finds the king's household buried in sleep. This time, Boann takes no chances. She has dosed her husband's wolfhounds and bewitched his guards. It is just as well, for Dabilla refuses to be swaddled in her cloak, instead he bears his teeth and wriggles out of her reach. The little dog hangs back as Boann takes the servants' ways through the quiet halls and corridors. The gate opens without fault. She finds easily the route to the well. She has walked it a thousand times in her sleep. There is no sign of the king's cup-bearers on the path. Around Boann's neck her hidden droplet sings.

As soon as she steps through the twin birch trees, Boann feels the air change. It is just like her dreams: the golden dawn light, the mysterious clearing. The well is smaller than she expected, but otherwise all is as she imagined. Dabilla hesitates to follow, standing out beyond the trees whining. But as she advances the little dog is left with no choice but to follow his mistress. He cringes into the clearing, tail between his legs.

Boann listens. She can hear the faint rustle of leaves in the hazel trees. They hang heavy with fruit. She sees that each of the cup-bearers told her the truth. That this place is dark and beautiful, sinister and lovely.

She reaches up to her neck and loosens the stolen droplet, which circles her palm with a touch far gentler than Nechtan's fingertips. She sets it on the ground and watches as it travels over the clumps of bright leaves, the mossy stones, climbing the wall of the well and catching a spark of dawn light as it falls, shining, over the edge.

She calls Dabilla to her. The small dog drags his paws, his belly low to the ground. Never has he been so unwilling. His terror finds answer in the fear that blooms inside her. For all this she will not return to Nechtan's hall. An eternity where serving women will smirk and her husband will sulk, where wise men will scrape and bow resentfully, courtiers will snipe and heroes will seek her favours. She will no longer preside over all of them, icy and friendless but for a little black dog.

She hears the rushing song of the well. She tries to fathom its mood. It is faintly mocking, yearning, affectionate.

Boann knows this for what it is: a test.

The well sent her the cup-bearers one by one, to teach her to feel love and fear and pride on her approach. But it is her choice, whether to gaze upon the water or to look away.

She slowly begins to circle the well, walking widdershins, as she did in her dreams.

In Nechtan's house the dogs wake as a pack and start to whine. The slumbering guards come to with a start. The king has been pacing his chamber since just after dawn, filled with a terrible foreboding that something is very amiss.

Boann walks widdershins.

The sound of rushing water gets louder. A booming noise from a great depth. A building pressure.

Boann keeps walking.

The pitch of the water rises. Now it is screaming.

Boann stops and plants her two hands on the wall that circles the well.

The serving women raise the alarm. Three sets of light-shod feet running through Nechtan's halls. They sob and shout. Scream and yell. The queen has gone.

Boann leans over the wall and looks down into the well.

There falls all around her a terrible hush. A sudden deep silence. The breeze stops blowing and the birds stop singing. Dabilla freezes too, showing the whites of his eyes in terror.

The king and his men issue forth from the gates of his great house. Some on horseback, others armed with sticks and axes. Grizzled druids among them, narrowing their eyes, from their fast-moving lips spittle and incantations.

What does Boann see?

In a perfect black mirror is the reflection of a peering woman. Her hair a bright halo. Her reflection scatters, distorted by a strong tail perhaps, a delicate fin, something moving in the deep. The surface of this water is thick and undulating, as unctuous as oil. Boann baulks with sudden fear, and the well, as if in answer, starts to churn. But she cannot look away now. She is mesmerised by the rippling patterns in the dark water. So that she grows calm and lulled, and by degrees the surface of the well stills again. Boann smiles and the woman in the well smiles back.

The first jet knocks Boann's left eye out of her head. She reels, holds out her hand and the water takes that too, cleanly at the wrist. The well erupts, pouring out into the sky, a cone of twisting water, bright at the core with Boann's blood. With her remaining eye she sees the fine big salmon streaming into the air, leaping high above her. She can hear Dabilla's terrified bark. She scoops him up and runs.

The well discharges after her, snaking down through the forest. Boann uses every charm she can remember, for speed, for strength. She runs faster than the king's best charger, hearing the thunderous waves fall and crash behind her. She changes direction with the agility of a deer. Feeling the spray on her back. A wave reaches out to circle her ankle, ripping the foot from under her, snapping it away. Boann slides forward on the swell. Fighting. Cursing. Dabilla is swept from her, she sees him carried away in the flood. Tiny, wide-eyed, bobbing, drowning.

In this moment Boann lets go.

She gives herself to the water's embrace. It fills her ears and plugs her nose. When she smiles it takes her teeth.

When she stretches out her arms it pulls them from her torso. No matter. Boann lets her mind feel outwards through the darkness as she rushes over a new parched land. Past Dabilla, who has broken apart and been planted as two round rocks. She caresses him in passing. Boann loses her leg on the river bend. Her heart stops when she reaches the sea. Her skull is dashed on the seabed and her mind, unanchored, finally washes free. It is everything she ever dreamed of.

DIVING FOR PEARLS
Sheila O'Flanagan

The Merrow

The gentle rain pattered against the windows of the classroom, a soft lullaby for the children seated at the low tables, who had folded their arms and were currently resting their heads on them, their eyes closed. They were on their sos, the short mid-morning rest period that was as much for Miss O'Reilly's benefit as theirs. Some of the children had already fallen asleep, and apart from the rain and the soft sighs of the children's breaths, the only sound in the room was the steady tick of the large, white clock on the wall.

Helen O'Reilly slid a slim book from the drawer of her desk. Like all her textbooks, it was neatly covered with plain brown paper. The word *sos* was neatly printed on the label on the front, but inside, the title of the book was *His Wanton Wife*. It had arrived that morning as part of her monthly Mills & Boon subscription and she'd covered it in brown paper immediately.

Helen knew that as a well-educated woman and schoolteacher, she should be reading George Orwell or

Ernest Hemingway or John Steinbeck, but her guilty secret was a love of romantic fiction with girl-next-door heroines and heroes who possessed strong jawlines and steely blue eyes. After all, she had no hope of finding the real thing in Carnrath, where most of the men were farmers or fishermen and, in her opinion, wouldn't know how to woo a woman if you gave them written instructions and a detailed diagram. It might well be the 1970s, she often told herself, but romance hadn't made it to the west of Ireland yet.

The door to the classroom opened and she swiftly replaced the book in the drawer. The children lifted their heads, instantly alert. The sound of twenty-five chairs scraping against the tiled floor echoed around the room as they stood up beside the tables, their eyes fixed on the statuesque figure of the nun who had walked into the classroom, followed by a young girl.

'Dia dhaoibh.' The nun looked at them.

'Dia is Muire dhuit, a Mháthair,' they chorused in reply.

With the customary greeting over, Helen signalled to the children that they should sit down again. As they did, their gazes slid from the nun in her black habit to the girl standing beside her. She was taller than most of the children in class 2A, with limbs that seemed too long for her body, sticking out at all angles from beneath a sky-blue dress that had seen better days. Under the intensity of their scrutiny, she folded her arms across her chest and fixed her own gaze in the mid-distance, as though she was somewhere else entirely, unaware that her shabby dress didn't reach her knees and that her brown shoes were scuffed and worn. Her flame-red hair was tied back into a plait and held in place by a green ribbon that matched the colour of her eyes. The girl's hands were broad, though her fingers long and slender, and around her wrist was a bracelet of small pink shells threaded onto a piece of twine.

'This is Mary,' said the nun. 'Mary Muldoon. She's joining us here at St Theresa's. I expect you all to make her feel very welcome. You will, won't you?'

'Yes, Mother Martha,' chanted the children.

'Mary. This is Miss O'Reilly. She'll be your teacher.' The nun put her hand on the child's back and propelled her forward.

'It's lovely to have you in our class,' said Helen. 'We'll find you a nice seat.' She looked at the children in front of her and called one of them up.

'Carmel Dunne,' she said. 'I want you to look after Mary.'

'Mery.' The girl's voice was low but clear. 'My name is Mery. Not Mary.'

The nun exhaled sharply.

'Mary in this school,' she said. 'Like God's Holy Mother. Not a Christmas greeting.'

Mery said nothing but Helen saw a spark of rebellion in her eyes.

'You go with Carmel now,' she said. 'I'll talk with Mother Martha.' She turned to the nun. 'I didn't know about this,' she said as Mery followed Carmel and sat down at an unoccupied desk. In her peripheral vision, Helen noticed that she sat ramrod straight and ignored the other children, who continued to scrutinise her with interest.

'Nor did I until yesterday.' The nun's words drew her attention back from the girl. 'Father Clarke called me. The family is from the island.' The flicker across her face showed what she thought of people who still lived on the island. 'The mother died. Fell from a boat and drowned. The father and daughter moved here a few weeks ago. He wasn't an islander originally so they targeted him to return.'

'There must be very few people left there now,' said Helen.

'Less than a dozen families,' said Mother Martha. 'Older people mainly. Harder to move. It's best for the girl. She needs a good Catholic education.'

'Indeed.' She glanced again at the child and then out of the window. It had stopped raining and she could see past the trees and towards the coast. The sea was rough, the waves topped with white foam. The island, however, was invisible, shrouded in mist as it so often was, keeping itself hidden from those who didn't live there. Very few from the mainland ever made the journey across the water, and even fewer from the island came to the mainland. The mainlanders knew of its barren landscape, the land too poor for growing crops, the few remaining houses in need of repair. Only wild folk lived there, they told each other. People who hadn't moved with the times, who didn't know about running water or electricity or telephones or any of the conveniences of modern living. Away with the fairies, they'd remark. Strange folk. Not like us.

'Can she read and write?' Helen looked towards the girl again and then back to Mother Martha. 'She needs to be able to read and write. This isn't an infants' class, after all.'

'She seems competent enough,' said the nun. 'But she's stubborn. Like all the island types.'

'I'll look after her.'

'Excellent.' The nun gave her a perfunctory nod and then raised her voice to say goodbye to the classroom of children. Once again they stood up at their tables and chorused 'slán leat' to her.

'Well now,' said Helen when the nun had closed the door behind her, 'we've all had our sos and we have a new friend in the classroom. Why don't we introduce ourselves to her and then she can tell us about herself. You start, Cormac Dillon.'

One by one the children stood up, said their names and a few words about their families. Eventually everyone had spoken.

'Now you, Mary,' said the teacher.

'Mery,' she said.

'Most people will call you Mary,' said Helen. 'It sounds almost the same.'

'I won't answer them,' said the girl. 'Mery is my name. It's short for Merrow. That's the name my mam gave me.'

She looked defiantly at the teacher, her stare steady and fearless.

I'll have to be careful with her, thought Helen. She could be trouble.

She recalled a meeting in the pub the previous year. Half the village crowded into the smoke-filled lounge. Talking about the islanders and the government-funded programme to resettle them on the mainland. The villagers weren't keen. They said it wasn't fair on them, or the islanders either. They had their own ways, their own customs. They were different. The villagers agreed that the plan wouldn't work because the islanders would never adapt. And indeed, after further consultation, it was eventually and quietly dropped and nobody spoke of it again. Yet somehow it had been reported as a victory for the islanders over the government rather than a win for the villagers themselves.

Now Helen smiled at the young girl in front of her.

'You're right,' she said. 'We need to call you by your own name. So tell us about yourself, Mery.'

'We moved here because my mam . . . died. I didn't want to leave the island but they told us we had to.' Her voice held a subdued undercurrent of anger.

'We're all very sorry about your mam,' said Helen. 'Tell us about your dad.'

'He's a carpenter,' said Mery.

'That's a great job,' said Helen. 'Sit down there now and share Carmel's book for the moment. I'll get you one for yourself tomorrow.'

Mery did as she was told. She looked at the pictures

in the book that was open in front of her. But she wasn't seeing the words beneath them. Instead she was seeing her mother, standing on the prow of the boat, her long hair streaming out behind her before she stepped into the water and was lost for ever.

Mery's first week at the school was challenging for Helen. Despite trying to involve her in classroom activities, the girl kept to herself, although Carmel Dunne did as she was asked and tried to help her fit in. But aside from her status as an islander, there was an air of solitariness that set Mery apart. She was an observer rather than a participant, and her literal interpretation of the questions the children asked her made them look at her in bemusement. They played the same tricks on her as they always did to new children, although she mostly ignored them. Cormac Dillon tied her plait to her chair. Maggie Lynch hid her schoolbag. Pól Ó Murchú called her names, including cat-eyes, carrot-head and smelly-fish. He hurled the last insult at her in the playground, and this time she reacted, knocking him over and throwing herself on top of him, pummelling him with her fists until he started to cry. In a fury at his own tears, he reached out and pulled her bracelet, which broke, the small, polished shells scattering across the asphalt like pink pearls.

Mery screamed and hit him even harder.

Helen ran over to break up the melee, hauling Mery to one side and then checking that Pól was uninjured.

'You can't do this,' she said to Mery when she confirmed that the boy had suffered a grazed knee and hurt pride. 'It's not how we behave.'

'He started it,' Mery said. 'He called me names and broke my bracelet.'

'You shouldn't have been wearing it,' said Helen. 'I told you before, we don't wear things like that at school.'

'It was my mother's,' said Mery.

'Even so—'

'I will fix it and I will wear it.' Her voice was determined.

Helen sighed.

'They're stupid children,' said Mery. 'And rude. I hate them all.'

Helen decided to walk the young girl home after school. She wanted to have a word with her father and she thought it would be easier to do it informally at the house rather than the school. The Muldoons lived in An Teach Beag, a small stone cottage about a mile from the schoolhouse. It was previously owned by Seamus Brophy, a farmer who'd emigrated to America five years earlier, and it had been lying derelict until the arrival of Mery and her father.

Helen exchanged the fashionable platform boots she wore in the classroom for a pair of sturdier walking shoes, then she and Mery set off along the road together. As usual at the time of year, it had been raining earlier in the day, but now the sun was filtering through the hazy clouds that veiled the sky, forming a large, vibrant rainbow.

'It looks like the end of it is in your garden,' said Helen. 'If we walk quickly we might find the crock of gold.'

'That's a fable,' said Mery. 'There's no gold at the end of a rainbow.'

'Maybe not,' said Helen. 'But it's a nice story. And we all need nice stories to brighten up our lives.'

They walked on in silence. Helen felt as though she should be talking to the girl but she wasn't sure what to say. Despite the altercation in the playground earlier, Mery was far more composed and self-contained than most of the nine-year-olds she knew. But that could be because of her mother, Helen reminded herself. It was hard on a child losing a parent so young. Having to leave her island home would have been hard too. She could understand the girl's solitary nature. Even though she didn't approve of fighting, she also liked that Mery had reacted to that little gurrier Pól Ó Murchú. It showed spirit.

Helen O'Reilly liked children with spirit. Even when they caused her trouble.

The rainbow had faded by the time they reached the small house. It was a single-storey building with a flaking red door between two deep-set windows also painted red. Mery unwound a piece of string from her neck and used the key on the end of it to open the door.

'Isn't there anyone here?' asked Helen.

'Of course not,' replied Mery. 'My dad is working.'

Without being asked, Helen stepped inside and found herself immediately in a kitchen and living room. The kitchen area contained a wooden table covered by an off-white oilcloth, four wooden chairs set around it. A naked light bulb hung from the ceiling. There were two cupboards on the wall, their doors a faded yellow. Beneath the cupboards was a small fridge. On the draining board beside the Belfast sink were two bowls, two spoons, two cups and a plate. Behind the sink, a large glass jar filled with pearl grey and pink seashells stood on the deep windowsill.

At the other end of the room, a rather battered armchair was placed beside the unlit fire in the grate. There was a smaller armchair on the other side of the fire, along with a coal scuttle and a poker, and a dark wooden dresser whose shelves were bare except for a Bush transistor radio and a small pile of books. There were no curtains at the windows and no pictures on the walls.

Mery took the shells of her broken bracelet from her pocket and let them drop into the glass jar on the sill behind the sink.

'What time does your daddy get home?' asked Helen.

'When he finishes work.'

Helen noticed that Mery wasn't wearing a watch. Nor was there a clock in the kitchen. She looked at the Timex on her wrist. It was almost three.

'Isn't anyone coming to look after you?' she asked. 'An auntie? A granny? A friend?'

'I don't have an auntie. My granny lives far away. I haven't been here long enough to make friends. I don't want any of them in my class as friends anyway.'

'What will you do for lunch?'

'We had sandwiches at school.'

There was a lunch break at midday, but Helen couldn't imagine the unappetising cheese sandwiches Mery had brought all week were enough to keep her going until the evening.

She opened one of the wall cupboards and saw a tin of Bird's custard, two tins of Libby's fruit cocktail, six packets of Knorr oxtail soup, a half-eaten sliced pan with the waxy paper carefully folded to keep it fresh and a packet of Marietta biscuits. There was also a half-finished packet of tea and an unopened jar of coffee. The fridge contained a pint of milk and a pat of butter along with some rashers and a couple of eggs. She was pleased to see the fresh food, not, she thought, that rashers and eggs were exactly a substantial meal, but they were better than oxtail soup from a packet.

Mr Muldoon was clearly a father who didn't know how to parent his child. Helen was glad she'd decided to come to the house to talk to him about his daughter. It was obvious she needed to discuss Mery's care with him too. It wasn't that she wanted to interfere, she told herself, but it wasn't right to abandon a nine-year-old girl to look after herself.

'Are you making tea?' asked Mery, who'd been watching her.

'A cup for you and one for me.' Helen took the packet of Lyons Green Label from the cupboard shelf. 'And a biscuit each.'

'I'm not allowed tea,' said Mery. 'I drink milk. Half a glass. I can have two Marietta biscuits with butter too.'

'OK.'

Helen made the tea and dried the cups on the draining board. She poured milk into one of them for Mery, then spread butter on the two biscuits and stuck them lightly together.

'Do you do this all the time?' Mery squeezed the biscuits more tightly so that thin strands of butter emerged through their tiny holes. She licked the butter then bit into the biscuits before taking a gulp of milk.

'What?'

'Come into people's houses and make tea?'

'Not usually,' admitted Helen. 'What will you do until your dad comes home?'

'I'll go for a swim,' replied Mery.

'A swim?' Helen stared at her. 'The water's too rough and too cold for swimming. And you can't go by yourself.'

'There's a cove on the other side of the hill,' said Mery. 'It's not cold and it's nice to swim there. You can come with me.'

'Yes, but I wouldn't be in water with you.' Helen was horrified. 'It's not safe. Anything could happen.'

'What sort of anything?'

'I . . . don't know.' Helen didn't want to say that Mery could drown. Not after what had happened to her mother. Actually, she thought, it was strange that Mery wanted to go near the water at all given the tragedy that had befallen Mrs Muldoon.

'I swim every day,' said Mery. 'My dad lets me.'

'But—'

'I have to lock the house when I go out,' said Mery. 'Do you want to be locked in or out?'

'Mery, I really don't think—'

'I have to go!' Mery's green eyes flashed with anger. 'I do.'

'OK. OK. I'll go with you.' Helen emptied her unfinished tea into the sink. 'Get your things.'

Mery went into her room again and emerged a couple of minutes later dressed in an unflattering brown tunic and carrying a plastic bag that seemed only to contain a thin towel and a red bathing cap.

'What about your swimsuit?'

'I'm wearing it underneath.'

Helen sighed and then left the house with her. Mery locked the door carefully and hung the key around her neck again. She led Helen along a small track across the stoney field towards the sea. Mery strode ahead, each step determined, until they reached the cove where, as she'd promised, the water was surprisingly calm.

'I didn't know this was here.' Helen looked around in surprise. 'I always thought the headland . . .' Her voice trailed off as she squinted into the sun. The island was closer than she'd expected from this vantage point, thrusting out of the water, its steep cliffs black against the silver-grey waves and the calm blue of the sky.

Mery ignored Helen, put the plastic bag beside a rock and then tugged her tunic over her head. Her swimsuit, an iridescent green, fitted her more perfectly than the dress. She reached into the bag and took out the bright red bathing cap which she pulled over her hair. Helen noticed that she was wearing another shell bracelet on her wrist.

'Stay close to the shore where I can see you,' she warned. But Mery ignored her, running to the sea and then diving into a breaking wave. Helen watched anxiously as the girl's slender body sliced through the water, her bathing suit seeming to merge with the shifting colour of the sea, first grey, then green, then blue, then aquamarine. If it weren't for the red bathing cap, Helen wouldn't have been able to distinguish her from the water. And then the cap disappeared. One minute Helen had her eyes fixed on it, the next it was gone.

'Oh, God,' she whispered. 'Where is she?'

She began to call then, loudly and increasingly frantically as she raced along the water's edge, scanning the waves in the hopes of seeing Mery, feeling her panic rise with every passing second.

She removed her shoes and jacket and raced into the sea herself, the water cold on her stockinged feet.

'Please,' she said out loud. 'Please, please, please.'

But there was no sign of the girl.

Helen stood with the waves breaking over her body and began to cry, the salt of her tears mixing with the salt of the sea.

She didn't want to leave the cove but she had to get help. She ran to one of the small houses on the headland, where a middle-aged woman, her plain dress covered by a white apron, opened the door and listened as Helen gasped that there was a child in the water and needed help.

'Mother of God.' The woman blessed herself. 'It's a good thing I had the phone put in last week. I'll call the guards.'

It was out of Helen's control then. The police arrived and she followed them back to the cove, where the coastguard's boat was already coming into view. She watched as the boat criss-crossed the cove and her heart sank even more with every pass it made.

It was thirty minutes later when a tall man in an Aran jumper and dark corduroy trousers arrived. His hair was a thick mop of black, his eyes a flinty grey in a weather-beaten face.

'Seán Muldoon,' he said. 'Mery's father.'

'She wanted to swim. She insisted.' Helen could hardly hold back her sobs. 'I couldn't stop her, and the water seemed calm.'

'She's a child. Of course you could stop her.' It was the woman from the house, who'd also followed them to the cove, who spoke. 'You're an adult. A teacher, I hear. You should be able to control children.'

'I . . .' This time Helen couldn't stop herself. The sobs erupted from her, heavier and heavier until her shoulders were heaving.

'There's no need for this.' Seán Muldoon put his hand on her arm. 'It won't help.'

'I know. I . . . I'm just so sorry. She's right, that woman.' Helen lifted her tear-streaked face to him. 'I should've stopped her. I wanted to. But . . .'

'. . . you couldn't,' he finished for her.

'In my head I was saying no, but my voice was saying yes.'

'She has that effect on people,' said Seán.

The coastguard's boat had moved further out into the open sea where the swell was heavier.

'She said she was a good swimmer,' Helen told Seán. 'She certainly seemed to be at home in the water.'

'She *is* a good swimmer,' he said. 'She got that from her mother.'

Helen felt her heart break for him. First his wife, now his daughter. How could anyone live with that?

Dusk was falling. The guards said that they would have to call off the search for the day. That they'd resume in the morning. That it was possible that the girl had been swept into one of the many other inlets along the coast. That they weren't giving up hope yet.

But Helen had already given up hope. She knew she'd seen Mery swimming on top of the water one minute and disappearing beneath it the next. And she knew for certain that the young girl hadn't resurfaced again. She was somewhere in the deep. And it might be years before her body was found.

The following morning she was at the cove just as the thin line of the coming dawn began to form in the sky. She looked out for the red swimming cap, but nothing was visible in the dark, turgid water of the sea.

'Why are you here?'

She whirled around at his voice. The tall, solid body of Mery's father loomed in the darkness.

'I was looking for her,' she replied.

'You won't find her.'

'The coastguard said not to give up hope.' Her voice faltered.

'She knew what she was doing,' said Seán Muldoon.

'She was – is – a child!' cried Helen. 'She didn't know at all what she was doing. I think she was looking for her mother. And I'm not surprised. You left her alone all day in that house. That's neglect.'

He stepped closer to her.

'I didn't want to leave the island, but I was told she had to come here. To go to school. You were the one in charge of her when she got into the sea.'

'I know.' Helen couldn't hold it together any longer. 'I know and it's all my fault and I can't . . . I can't . . .' She began to cry uncontrollably. 'I'm so, so sorry.'

He stood beside her, unmoving.

'She knew what she was doing,' he repeated.

His voice was flat.

They called off the search that evening. There had been no sighting of Mery anywhere along the coastline. Nor on the island, which had been visited and searched by the Gardaí.

The girl was an islander, after all, they told themselves. She might have tried to return, even though to swim from the cove to the island against the current was impossible. In any event, there was no sign of Mery, either in the small whitewashed cottages or any of the narrow coral bays.

The people of the town held a vigil for her. They came to the Muldoon house and prayed, the women murmuring decades of the rosary in front of the fire that Helen had set in the grate after spending the day tidying the cottage. Seán Muldoon hadn't objected to her being there but he hadn't spoken to her. The others avoided her too, knowing that she was being questioned by the Gardaí. Helen had already told the police everything she knew and they'd been outwardly sympathetic. Nevertheless, she'd felt them judging her, asking themselves why she'd let a nine-year-old swim in the treacherous sea, and why she hadn't managed to save her.

The local women brought food for Seán, filling up the tiny fridge with perishable goods and putting the rest of the food in the small pantry. There was enough to feed him for a couple of weeks at least. Helen was glad of that. Seán's face had hollowed out in the last forty-eight hours and he looked exhausted. At the edge of the group of people, she saw Dr Sullivan and asked him to keep an eye on him.

'We'll all keep an eye on him,' he said. 'It's a dreadful thing that's happened.'

A dreadful thing that was all her fault. It surprised her that there wasn't more gossip about her. Although maybe there was and she hadn't heard it yet. Helen was well aware that simply because it hadn't happened in the school, it didn't mean she wouldn't be blamed. This was a village after all.

She stayed in the house until everyone had gone. She asked Seán Muldoon if there was anything she could do for him.

'No.'

'I'll be going then.'

He didn't look at her as she left.

That night she dreamed of the sea. She was standing on the shore with Mery beside her, looking out at the tumbling waves. And then the young girl took her by the hand and dragged her into the water. Helen protested as she felt the waves lap at her ankles, reach up her legs and finally envelop her. She looked down at her body and was surprised to see that she was no longer wearing her wool jacket and practical skirt and jumper. She was in a bathing suit like Mery's, green and shimmering, and there was a red cap on her head.

She felt herself being pulled deeper and deeper below the surface. Sea creatures floated past them, some dark and barely visible, others vibrant blues and greens. They were suddenly surrounded by an enormous shoal of silver fish and Helen felt Mery's grip loosen. The girl kept steady and upright in the water as the fish swam around her. Helen felt that she should be frightened, but she wasn't. Mery touched the fish with her free hand, moving her body to their rhythm, swaying slowly while the shells on her bracelet gently clicked off each other like an underwater code.

It was then that Helen saw Mery's tail, the same iridescent green as the swimsuit she'd worn. Her hair was now free of the bathing cap, floating like tendrils of seaweed in the deep water. Mery pulled at her again and they went even deeper, where it was too dark to see. Helen closed her eyes.

When she opened them again she was in her bed, and the alarm clock was ringing.

The children at the school forgot Mery very quickly. She had, after all, been there for less than a fortnight. But the Gardaí didn't immediately stop the search for her or the investigation into what had happened. At the centre of their enquiries, Helen worried about her own culpability and what effect that might have on her career. Already she felt a shift in the way people treated her. It was in the tight-lipped nods of the mothers when they dropped their children off at school, the quiet hush when she walked into the staffroom and the tense silence in the grocery store where she did her weekly shop.

In the end, Sergeant Duffy said that no charges were being pressed. When she heard those words, Helen cried with relief. But she knew the guilt would never leave her.

She went again to see Seán Muldoon. Although it was now the end of May, the weather was colder than usual and a small spiral of smoke drifted upwards from the chimney of the cottage. She knocked on the door and waited, looking over the hill towards the sea as though some knowledge of what had happened to Mery would come to her. The dream of swimming with the girl was still sharp in her memory, and although a part of her wanted to forget it, another part found it comforting.

The door opened. Seán Muldoon stood in front of her, wearing his dark corduroy trousers and a cotton shirt with the sleeves neatly rolled to above his elbows. His grey eyes looked at her enquiringly.

'I wanted to see how you were doing,' she said.

'Well enough,' he told her.

She hesitated, looking past him into the house. It seemed cleaner than before, she thought. Less dusty. More cared for.

'I wondered if you needed anything.'

'Like my wife? My daughter?' He seemed to look right through her.

'I don't know,' she said.

'Come in,' said Seán. 'Have tea.'

The house had definitely been thoroughly cleaned by someone who knew what they were doing. The patterned linoleum floor was shining. The table was clear of crockery, as was the sink. The throw on the back of the armchair by the fire was neatly arranged. The once grimy windows now sparkled, allowing light to enter the room unfiltered. A second glass jar of pink and pearl seashells was placed on the sill beside the one she'd seen when she'd first visited An Teach Beag, the contents shining in the sun.

She closed her eyes for a moment, and heard the click of the shells on Mery's bracelet again.

Seán filled the kettle and put it on the gas hob. He took tea from a small caddy on the shelf and spooned it into a new ceramic teapot. He shook some bourbon biscuits onto a plate and put it on the table along with two mugs and a pint bottle of milk.

'No milk jug,' he said. 'Sorry.'

'It's fine,' said Helen.

He poured the tea.

They sat in silence.

'You're doing well with the house.' Even as she said the words she knew they sounded all wrong.

'People come.' He shrugged. 'Women mostly. They bring me food. They tidy up. Like I wouldn't be able to do these things for myself.'

Remembering the state of the cottage when she'd first come with Mery, Helen made a sound that could have meant anything.

'It must be so hard for you.' She blurted out the words after another silence. 'Losing your wife and your daughter to the sea.'

'I was always going to lose them to the sea,' he said. 'They were island people. Sea people.'

'But for them both to drown.' A tear leaked from her

eye and slid along her cheek. 'It's too much for one man to bear.'

'They were a gift,' said Seán. 'They enriched my life. I'm grateful for them.'

'But still no sign, no news . . . of Mery?'

He shook his head.

She thought of telling him her dream but she knew he wouldn't want to hear it.

So she went home.

The following day in the staffroom she told the others that she'd visited the Muldoon house. Since the closing of the enquiry, the atmosphere had thawed slightly, although she still felt the weight of their judgement on her shoulders and was looking forward to the summer holidays when she wouldn't have to interact with them every day.

'You're behind the curve,' Eilis Matthews said. 'Everyone's visited Seán Muldoon. All the women are taking care of him. Especially the unmarried women.'

Helen registered the tone behind her colleague's words.

'There aren't so many good-looking eligible men in town that we can afford to overlook him,' Eilis continued.

'But he's a widower. And he lost his child.'

'Even more to find attractive,' said Eilis. 'A certain amount of house-training from wife number one and, tragic though the loss of Mery is, at least the prospective second Mrs Muldoon doesn't have to worry about a stepchild.'

'I never heard anything so callous in all my life.' Helen was shocked.

'You're an awful innocent eejit,' said Eilis. 'Life isn't like those books you like to stash in your desk. You can't wait for Prince Charming to sweep you off your feet. You have to go after what you want.'

'I don't want Seán Muldoon,' snapped Helen.

'Good. There are plenty of women who do.'

A year after Mery's disappearance, Helen went to the cove by herself. There was to be a remembrance ceremony later, but she didn't want to be part of that. She wanted to remember Mery in her own way. She stood on the shore and looked towards the island, barely visible through the swirling mist. The sea was calmer than she'd ever seen it, the waves breaking gently against the shingles on the shore. She recalled in detail the moment Mery had run into the water, the flash of her green swimsuit as she plunged beneath a wave, the moment the red of her bathing cap disappeared. It was as though she were actually seeing her again, moving effortlessly in the water, at one with the sea.

She gazed at the island, reliving the moment of Mery's disappearance over and over, wanting it to stop, but punishing herself by continuing to let it spool forward and back in her head.

At first she thought it was her imagination, but then she realised that there was a young woman wearing a red bathing cap standing waist deep in the water. For a moment she thought it was Mery and her heart leaped, but the woman was at least ten years older and her swimsuit, though the same shimmering green as Mery's, seemed to be positively translucent, so that she appeared almost naked in the water. As Helen watched, the bather removed her cap and her long hair fell around her shoulders.

She was beautiful.

Mesmerising.

Helen found herself walking towards her, not noticing that her feet, in her soft moccasins, were getting wet. She walked deeper and deeper into the water until she was a few metres from the woman.

'Mery?' She had to say the name because she was looking at an older version of Mery, impossible though that was.

'Hello, Miss O'Reilly.'

'It can't be you,' said Helen.

'Why not?'

'You're all grown up.'

The young woman smiled.

'And you drowned.' The words came out of Helen's mouth as a sob. 'I was there. I saw you. One minute you were in the water and the next you were gone. It's all my fault. I'm so sorry.'

'Nothing is your fault,' said the woman.

'You were in my care and I allowed a tragedy to happen.' Even as she spoke, Helen realised that whatever was taking place now wasn't real. That she had somehow conjured up an image of an older Mery. Perhaps so that she could have this conversation with her. So that she could stop blaming herself.

'You did what I wanted you to do,' said Mery. 'You brought me to the cove and you let me go.'

'I shouldn't have.'

'You had to,' said Mery. 'I couldn't go by myself and I couldn't go with my father. Someone else had to bring me.'

'Why?'

'To set me free.'

'You're dead!' cried Helen. 'You're a figment of my imagination. You're not free. You drowned. Just like your mother. And you've left your father broken-hearted.'

'How can I be dead when I'm so very much alive?' asked Mery. 'And how can I have drowned when the sea is my home? Just like it's home to my mother.' She drew herself up out of the water and Helen gasped as she saw Mery's enormous green and blue fish tail.

'I'm having a psychotic episode,' she said to herself. 'It's all too much. I can't—'

'You have to forgive yourself.' Mery's voice was calm and soothing. 'My father understands. He always did. He knew this would happen, although he thought my return might be delayed by moving from the island. But we've always been from the island. And from the sea that surrounds it. Me, my mother, others like us.'

'Stop it!' Helen closed her eyes and put her hands over her ears. 'You're not real. None of this is real.'

She stood motionless in the water, waiting for whatever it was to pass. And then she felt a sudden swish nearby and a large wave almost submerged her. She gasped and struggled for breath as she tried to hold her balance. As she felt herself fall she thought that perhaps it was fitting that she too would drown in the cove. That she would be forever linked with Mery Muldoon.

She felt the strong arms lift her up and carry her back to the shore even as she coughed salt water from her lungs.

'You're all right,' said Seán Muldoon. 'Take a minute. Catch your breath.'

She didn't have the ability to ask him why he was there. She only knew she was grateful that he was.

He set her down on her feet. The water squelched from her shoes and she shivered. He took off his heavy tweed jacket and wrapped it around her shoulders.

'Thank you.' Her teeth were chattering.

'You need to come to the house. Dry off.' He didn't wait for a response but took her by the hand and led her along the sandy track to the cottage.

There were new copper pots on the shelf above the sink. Framed prints on the white walls. And yet more jars filled with colourful shells on the windowsill.

Helen thought of the women who came here to look after him. And their motives.

He handed her a towel and showed her into the tiny bedroom that had been Mery's. The bed was neatly made but there was no sign that she'd ever occupied it. Helen took off her shoes and her tights as well as the patterned cambric skirt she'd been wearing. Thankfully, although her shoes and tights were still wet, the skirt seemed to have dried on the walk back to the house. She rubbed her hair briskly with the towel and then ran her fingers through it to tidy it. By the time she'd finished, her shoes were nearly dry. She didn't bother with her tights but instead shoved them into the small leather bag she'd carried over her shoulder.

Then she saw the key hanging from the handle of the narrow wardrobe. The house key on a long piece of string.

Seán had made tea and buttered a couple of slices of brown bread.

'To warm you up,' he said.

'Thank you.'

'Why were you there?' he asked, when she was sitting with her hands wrapped around the big white mug.

She explained about the anniversary. About wanting to remember Mery. And about trying to assuage her own guilt.

'People tell me not to blame myself, but I do,' she said.

'You left the school,' he said. 'You're no longer a teacher there.'

'I was cleared at the enquiry, but in the end I couldn't stay. My new job suits me well enough.'

'Not what you dreamed of doing,' he remarked.

'Are any of us living the life we dreamed of?' she asked.

'Some of us are.' He looked thoughtfully at her. 'What made you go into the water?'

'I thought I saw her. And then I thought she spoke to me. Only it wasn't her. It was an older her. It was . . .' She shook her head. 'A hallucination,' she said.

'She talks to me. Her mother talks to me. They bring me with them sometimes.' His voice was matter-of-fact.

'Bring you where?'

'Beneath the waves. Where they belong.'

'Jesus, Seán, you know that's not possible. You're hallucinating too. You need help. I need help.'

'Mery's mother always told me she'd go back,' he said. 'I didn't want to believe it, but I knew. And Mery . . . well, I knew about her too. She was like her mother. Different.'

'I thought she was a mermaid!' cried Helen. 'How insane is that?'

'There have always been mermaids around the island,' said Seán. 'All the island people know about them. They made a home there. The water suits them.'

'Ah, Seán.' She sniffed. 'Those stories are nonsense. They're from olden times when people made things up to make sense of life. But we're living in a modern age. Old legends are simply tall tales. You're saying these things because you can't believe they're gone. I'm sorry if that sounds harsh, but it's true.'

'They can come to land and live as normal people.' Seán continued as though she hadn't spoken. 'Muriel, my wife, did. But eventually the pull to go back is too strong.'

'She jumped off your boat,' said Helen. 'She killed herself.'

'I knew she'd only be with me for a time, that one day she'd have to go home. I knew Mery would too. I accepted that.'

'Mery isn't – wasn't – a mermaid,' said Helen. 'She was a little girl. A normal little girl who drowned.'

'Her mother is from the sea and she is also from the sea,' said Seán. 'I hoped she'd stay longer, but she missed Muriel too much. I couldn't care for her like she could.'

'This is all crazy.'

'Why is it crazy?'

'You've constructed a world to comfort you. But it's not real.'

'What about today?' asked Seán. 'You walked into the water. You talked to Mery. Wasn't that real?'

'I talked to a vision of someone who was a lot older than Mery would be,' retorted Helen. 'I talked to a figment of my imagination.'

'I'm sorry you think that,' said Seán. 'Mery trusted you and I trust her. I'm surprised you're not open to other possibilities.'

'Have you spoken to Father Ryan?' asked Helen. 'He's going to say a Mass for her this Sunday.'

'He believes what he believes. I believe what I believe. Do you think I'd be able to function if I thought my wife and daughter deliberately drowned themselves?'

She said nothing.

He refilled her cup.

She glanced behind him at the jars of shells on the windowsill. There were some she'd never seen before, brightly coloured, clearly not from Irish waters. She wondered where he'd got them and then, to her shame, wondered if Mery or her mother had given them to him. She thought again of the key in the bedroom, hanging from the wardrobe door. It wasn't possible. It wasn't. He was delusional. Unwell. It was understandable, but sad.

He got up from the table and returned with a plastic folder that contained Polaroid photos. He shook them onto the table.

She stared at them.

The photos were blurred but she could see the young woman from earlier and an older, very beautiful woman by her side. Both waist deep in the water. Both in the cove. Laughing and smiling. Happy.

'She came to land because we fell in love,' said Seán. 'She warned me that one day she would leave. When Mery was born, she reminded me that Mery would leave me too. And when that day came for both of them, I had to let them go.'

She couldn't process it. He truly believed his wife had come from beneath the sea and had returned to live beneath the sea. If a woman – a mermaid – fell in love with a land person, they could live with them. But not for ever.

'You mean, Mery could return if she met someone from the land and fell in love with them?'

For his sake, she tried to sound as though it could be true.

'Yes. It will only be for a time, and they measure time differently from us.'

'I told you the girl I saw – I thought I saw – was much older than Mery could possibly be.'

'They grow faster in the water and then begin to age more slowly,' he told her.

'I find that hard to believe.'

'So did I, at first,' said Seán.

He'd faked the photographs, of course.

She wasn't an idiot.

She stayed away from the cottage. She knew that women continued to call on him, to check on him, to make sure he was eating properly. She heard about the rivalries among them. She thought about him a lot, but she didn't try to contact him again.

The following year she went to the cove once more. She stood at the shoreline and waited to see if Mery or her mother would appear. But even though she was there for over an hour, there was no sign of either of them. She told herself that she was relieved.

She met him as she walked back up the track.

He looked well, she thought, less gaunt than before, although his hair was beginning to show signs of grey and there were wrinkles around his eyes that she didn't remember.

He smiled at her and wished her a good day.

'I didn't see them,' she said.

'They've moved from these waters,' he told her.

She wondered if therapy would help him, but when she told him the name of a woman in the city who specialised in trauma, he laughed.

'I'm perfectly well,' he said. 'It's you that needs the help, Helen. Let me take you out in my boat. Let me share with you the joy of the water. Maybe then you'll understand.'

She went out in the boat with him. It was something she needed to do, to put all this nonsense out of her head. The sun was high, the sea smooth. The breeze was warm on her shoulders as she inhaled the mixture of salt and tar rising from the wooden slats of the boat.

Seán steered the craft expertly out to the deeper water between the mainland and the island and then paused, allowing it to drift parallel to the shore.

'Look down,' he said.

For a heart-stopping moment she wondered if it was all a trick. If he'd murdered Muriel. If he'd somehow enticed Mery into the water to drown her too. If he was going to murder her now.

She moved away from him and looked over the rail. Her eyes opened wide. There were hundreds of fish – fish she'd never seen before and didn't recognise – all swimming beneath the boat. And at the edge of the school of fish, a shimmering green tail gracefully moved from side to side, orchestrating them.

Seán whistled slowly, and the owner of the tail moved closer to the boat and rose out of the water alongside it in a single flowing motion. Helen recognised her from Seán's faked photographs. Muriel. His wife.

The mermaid smiled, kissed Seán on the mouth, then, before disappearing beneath the waves again, dropped a pink shell into the boat.

Seán picked it up and handed it to Helen.

'Now do you believe?' he asked.

She stared at the shell, real and substantial in the palm of her hand. She rubbed her finger gently across its pearlescent surface, It was cool from the water, smooth and polished. Like the shells on Mery's bracelet.

'She won't be back for another year,' said Seán. 'She's moved across the ocean with Mery. Mery is making a new life for herself. She's happy. Muriel's happy. And so am I.' He smiled at Helen. 'I like being here with you,' he said. 'I'd like to do it more often.'

She looked up from the shell and stared at him.

And then he kissed her.

She could taste the salt on his lips.

*

IRISH WOMAN CLAIMS FREE-DIVE RECORD

23 August 1980

Mery Mikimoto, a native of Ireland, has claimed the free immersion free-diving record, diving to a depth of 103 metres in under four minutes at an event in Okinawa, Japan. Ms Mikimoto is the wife of Hisashi Mikimoto, a Japanese free diver and descendant of Kokichi Mikimoto. Kokichi Mikimoto Sr employed the famed Ama divers to collect oysters as he developed his business of cultured pearls a hundred years ago. The pair met while participating in a free-dive competition also in Okinawa. Ms Mikimoto moved to Japan in her teens and has not visited Ireland in some time.

THE SWANS
Naoise Dolan

The Children of Lir

1

Aoife had two inborn qualities that could be accommodated well enough within a rural Irish childhood: ruthlessness and a dash of megalomania. Broadly her early experience of life was that she decided what she wanted, then got it. School was easy and sports were easy, and even her parents were easy enough. So when, aged seventeen, she declared her intention to be an actress, it seemed to her that this would come easily too.

In primary school, she had made up games and stories, and your option as a fellow child was to go along with what she'd invented or stay out of it altogether; no collaborative input was possible. She made up plays to perform with her cousins for their aunts and uncles, and later as a teenager she wrote scripts secreted away in copybooks once it became apparent that the adults in her midst lacked the capacity to appreciate her vision. But she didn't want to write; she wanted to be seen.

'I need to find drama things,' Aoife told the guidance counsellor at the start of sixth year.

Ms de Spáinn rotated her lumpy office chair and considered the present case. Before her was a fidgety Leitrim schoolgirl of below-average height, crooked teeth, acne and a slight lazy eye. Visually, nothing much about Aoife commanded respect. But the voice, yes, there was that: the voice was something else. None of the young ones knew how to enunciate – it was a frequent complaint – you heard it everywhere – they swallowed their words. Here was one whose lips never touched her teeth. You could put a pencil in her mouth and everything would still come out clear. Ms de Spáinn was not among life's thespians, and in fact was unsure she'd ever seen a play, but she was under the stubborn and mysterious impression that the main requirement was to talk like the ones who did audiobooks.

'There's a youth theatre group in the town,' she told Aoife confidently, then checked the leaflets on her desk to ascertain if this was true. In fact there were four stacks of leaflets telling students to work smart *and* hard, one stack about cold sores and two about abstinence-only contraception, which a Catholic organisation had insisted be displayed in exchange for funding a desperately needed twenty-three square metres of astroturf. 'There's no youth theatre group in the town,' Ms de Spáinn continued, as if unsheathing someone else's brazen lie.

'I'll found one,' Aoife said.

'There's the risk it'd distract you from your Leaving Cert.'
'But if I found something, I can put "founder" on my CV.'
Ms de Spáinn could find no further objection.

Aoife had got her way once again, and she kept getting it over the following few months. Her newly founded youth theatre group – she used the verb 'found' amply in public communications lest future employers google her – grew in numbers and strength. Eventually they amassed as many as six members, only five of whom she'd personally black-mailed into joining. The sixth was her.

The group put on shows in October (*Hamlet*), November (a one-act play about swans that Aoife had scrawled out in three hours, her decision not to write any more temporarily overturned after smoking weed stolen from her cousin Tadhg) and December (*Hamlet* again). After a sustained campaign of PR emails to national and local papers, the company gained two paragraphs of coverage in the *Leitrim Observer*, just under an article about potholes.

Aoife wore her triumph lightly. She did not advertise her next intention: to train as an actress at the Lir Academy in Dublin. The application deadline was in February, and she couldn't have anyone else in the group getting ideas. None of them posed any obvious threat, but competition was competition.

Come February, while everyone else was cramming for their mock exams, Aoife rewatched her self-taped video, read through her application one last time and pressed send.

It was only the beginning. There would be auditions and callbacks and callbacks on the callbacks, and nearly everyone got rejected; that's what she'd heard. But people were always going on like that, that you couldn't do this or that, that nobody could manage such a thing. She'd never listened before, and she always wound up glad she hadn't; if you waited for other people to give you the go-ahead, you'd never try anything at all. So she would be patient and see the process through.

Two weeks later, she got a three-sentence rejection letter without even the chance to audition in person.

It was not in Aoife's nature to give up. But to redirect herself? Yes, this she could do.

'There are other drama courses,' Ms de Spáinn told her in a guidance-counselling session the following month. 'Or take a year out and—'

'My parents haven't the money.'

'And work, I was going to say. Audition again with more experience.'

Over the past few months, Ms de Spáinn had grown invested in Aoife's enunciatory powers, and ever more convinced that they would lead her to stardom.

'I'm not doing that,' Aoife said. 'I'm not pathetic.'

Her choice of phrasing threw her – had she really meant to put it like that? – but in the end it was true. This was the first time in her life she'd heard the word *no*, and she didn't fancy hearing it again. They'd already said they didn't want her. She wouldn't make them repeat it.

Instead she decided, immovably and within the space of about twenty minutes, that she'd really always wanted to be an agent. To book jobs for actors, foster their careers, prod for upward nudges on their pay. It was the sort of thing a founder would do, an entrepreneur, a woman of action, and her penchant for such words had not left her.

That evening she wrote dozens of emails to agencies, offering to work for free. What she'd told Ms de Spáinn was true: her parents didn't have the money to be funding unpaid internships. But she'd get another job too or she'd make it work somehow. Above all, she would not fail.

That summer she photocopied and chased invoices for three different agencies in Dublin, taking extra hours in a call centre to pay the bills. The accommodation she found was one lower bunk in a four-person room, with twelve in total sharing the kitchen and bathroom. The landlord claimed the €800-per-person rent reflected the grandeur of living at the top of an inner-city townhouse. 'This is objectively a tenement,' Aoife remarked to one of her new flatmates, Dara, and they shrugged and said that was just how things were.

It was fine as long as she did literally nothing in the apartment, not even sleep if she could help it. Her sexual standards lowered with each month spent in the building. Soon enough she would go home with anyone who had hot water.

'I'll need a better living situation before I'm sure if I'm bisexual or just need to maximise my options,' she told Dara at the end of the summer.

'There's no way you're straight,' Dara said.

'I know,' Aoife said. 'It's men I'm in doubt of.'

'Who isn't?'

'Straight women.'

'They can't be helped,' Dara conceded.

Whatever other side gig was going, Aoife took it. Cleaning at Trinity College during the summer break when they let the student rooms out as tourist accommodation, dog-sitting, realising she hated dogs and instead cat-sitting, realising she hated cats too and instead selling her few possessions on Depop. A mercenary glint alighted in her eyes when she chanced on any avenue to ready cash.

And so it was with gleaming interest that, in the last week of August, she noted the email in her agency inbox: EMERGING PLAYWRIGHTS COMPETITION.

She was supposed to forward it to any clients who also wrote. But none of them needed the €1,000 prize as much as her.

The small independent production company running the competition had forwarded it to Aoife's agency as an afterthought only two days before the deadline, highlighting that women 'and other minorities' were welcome to apply.

There would be no time to wring out something from scratch. All she had on file was the swan play she'd written in school while stoned off her tits.

Over the next forty-eight hours she lost sleep and fell behind on work, trying to refashion the script into something decent. Her lazy right eyeball twitched by the end of it, her left one was bloodshot and her thumb clicked from the repetitive strain of typing. By the end she had given it her all, though she had no energy left to determine if the result was even legible.

Twenty minutes before the deadline, she sent it to the production company with the comment:

If women are a 'minority' in your talent pool, I can only assume it was assembled by Fianna Fáil.

They'd not dare send her a form rejection after that. If only to avoid looking sexist, they'd have to afford her what the Lir Academy had withheld: the dignity of direct feedback.

Nonetheless she submitted the play under a pseudonym. Since she could not be sure if it was any good, she preferred to keep her distance.

Three years later, Aoife was on the rise.

At the end of her internships, during which she had been so diligent as to frighten people, one of the agencies offered her an assistant position. They couldn't quite stretch to the Dublin living wage, though they provided a thoughtful few sentences in the offer letter on how they wished they could; it was a pity her landlord didn't accept adjectives, just cash. At least it was enough money to move to a better apartment, shared with only three other people, whose proprietor was committing only the milder forms of tax fraud. There was no other option, anyway. She couldn't go to college. Her Leaving Cert results had been abysmal, which didn't sting her because she hadn't tried in the first place, an excellent mode of avoiding disappointment really. Intention mattered, just as it did in criminal law. Desire distinguished murder from manslaughter; it made all the difference, too, when it came to success. You could be bad at something, plenty of things, but you'd only failed if you'd been trying to be good.

In any case, she wanted to be an agent. She'd decided to want it and she'd keep on wanting it, and that was how she'd handle the matter.

She settled into her position and was good at her job. Everyone liked her. Each year they gave her more things to do.

And she was about to become a published playwright, albeit under the pen name Nora Barnacle.

She still winced when she remembered the congratulatory letter. Despite having read it hundreds of times, she still could not recall an entire sentence, only isolated phrases that made her every muscle clench in shame.

Parody of self-serious would-be avant-garde. Melodrama with a wink. Masterclass in so-bad-it's-good.

Besides the €1,000 advance on royalties – warmly accepted and promptly passed on to her honest, hardworking landlord as recognition of his labour in continuing to own property – the prize consisted of the production company putting on the play. It would take a while, they warned in the letter, to get funding together and all the rest of it. How involved did she, Nora Barnacle, wish to be in the process?

She replied saying she would take no further part in it, that they were welcome to put the play on if they liked, but that they were not to contact her any further about the matter. Then she did what was natural and comfortable and self-protective: endeavoured to think of the thing no more.

2

During this same period in her life, after years of Aoife paying her dues at the agency, her boss Bodb delegated her the care of four new clients.

'They'd be my pick of the new class,' he told her without preamble at her desk, handing her a thin stack of CVs.

'What cl—'

'There's too much talent in this country, almost,' Bodb interrupted. 'It's a problem, the amount of Irish talent. Could you believe it's something I tell people every day.' Aoife could believe it, since one of those people was her. 'It's not finding talent that's the problem,' he continued, and then, as though spontaneously arriving at a startling new conclusion: 'It's that there's too much talent.'

'You're dead right,' Aoife said. 'So who exactly are these—'

'But these four,' Bodb said, 'if I wouldn't of signed them, London would've.' He tended to say 'If I wouldn't of' when he wished to sound like a hard-nosed man of business. 'They're just after finishing drama school,' he added. 'Now they're my clients, mind you, and it's my commission, but you can take care of them day-to-day. You're ready for the responsibility.'

'Are you sure?' Aoife said, because it was the expected response. 'I don't know am I ready at all.' Of course she was.

'Listen, Aoife, look, look, see.' When Bodb needed time to think, he gave you meaningless strings of physical directions. 'You're with us a year now, is it?'

'Three,' Aoife said.

'And over this year—'

'Three years and three months, if you count the internship.'

'—you've made your mark, etched your stamp, if you will—' Bodb continued.

'I think "Made your stamp, etched your mark" would work better.'

'—and the impact on the agency is around us to see, provided of course we've the eyes for it—'

'Though I guess you can etch a stamp.'

'—and trust me, Aoife, when I say that everyone in this building has eyes.'

'But not to stamp it.'

'What?' Bodb said.

'You can etch a stamp, but that's separate to actually stamping with it,' Aoife elaborated. 'So if you say I've etched my stamp, you mean nothing's been stamped yet.'

'This is the kind of positive thinking we need,' Bodb said, wholly satisfied. 'Now. Have a read of their CVs.'

'I wanted to ask—'

'Would you have any questions, by the way?'

'I was actually wondering—'

'It's an open-door policy here, if you ever do have questions, though at the same time don't go thinking you've to pretend to have questions or we won't think you're interested enough.'

'I do have questions. I've one, anyway. What drama school did they go to?'

Bodb took a moment to register that he was being spoken to, then said, 'The new clients?'

'Yes.'

'There's the four of them. Three lads and a girl. The lads are Aodh, Fiachra and Conn. I'm on to Aodh about whether Hugh might work better, you know, internationally. Fiachra and Conn, there's no English for that, can't be helped. And the girl would be Fionnuala, even worse.' Bodb shrugged, martyred as he was by the unhelpful cultural preferences of Irish parents.

'But my question,' Aoife said, 'is what drama school did they go to?'

'The Lir,' Bodb said. 'Am I not after saying?'

There was no time to go through the CVs during the work day, so she took them home and read them sitting on her single bed. She did have a private room now – there was that at least – but there was a patch of mould on the ceiling so vivid that it seemed on the cusp of acquiring sentience and voting rights. Someone was always leaving hairballs in the shared shower drain, someone else – or potentially the same person – believed the toilet cleaned itself, and anything you left in the fridge was treated as a donation to the general public from a Samaritan heart.

Reading the CVs on this miserable little bed, whose mattress had given up on life and could you blame it, Aoife saw that all four new clients were exactly her age. They'd grown up in south Dublin and taken private drama classes since they could barely talk, gone to summer schools abroad, interned in Los Angeles. By sixteen, they'd all been in films. When Aoife had applied to the Lir Academy with her hastily patched-together credentials, these people had been doing real acting for years.

And yes, some of that was choice, wasn't it, and working harder maybe, and knowing earlier than her what they wanted. But they'd been framed to want acting, set up to regard it as an option.

Well aware that she would hate herself for doing it – this depressing and humiliating ritual, purely symbolic when she already knew the answer – she plugged their surnames into Wikipedia. Sure enough, all their parents had pages with extensive bibliographies and flattering headshots. At this point in the arts, she'd developed a sixth sense for it. You met someone gratingly young who seemed oddly self-assured, weirdly convinced that it would all work out for them. You locked eyes with them, and you got an itch that said: they're of Wikipedia family, so they are.

Aodh O'Wikipedia, Fiachra O'Wikipedia, Conn O'Wikipedia and not forgetting dear Fionnuala. Fuck them absolutely to the ends of the earth.

'Thank you so much for trusting me with them,' she told Bodb the next day.

3

Fionnuala had been an object of public scrutiny since her mid-teens.

The mistake was using her real name. She'd go back on it now if she could. It wasn't that she'd got astonishingly famous from *Spliffs*, the teen drama she'd starred in while still in school. But she did get recognised, especially in Ireland. If she'd made up some other name for her acting, it could have bought her a little privacy. But it was too late for that. Now her personal history was on the internet for anyone to see, and it would remain there until the end of time. Even if she gave up acting and spent the rest of her life doing completely normal things, anyone she went on a date with could google her. They'd know where she grew up, how many siblings she had and which childhood traumas she'd disclosed under pressure to be 'vulnerable'. They'd read whatever deranged things she'd come out with during her tenth back-to-back interview and believe that it had represented her then and, worse, still did now. Long after the money had run out, the things she'd had to do to earn it would remain. Because you couldn't say no to the interviews, could you, or say I'm not answering that, or be difficult in any way. Everyone knew you were supposed to be grateful. There were hundreds of people on the other side of that door, beating it down to take your place, and so you sat still and were a nice girl.

'Learn to enjoy it,' her mother had always said. But she didn't understand. She was an art historian who appeared on the odd documentary. Nobody actually cared about her in any way. And like most people whom nobody actually cared about in any way, she couldn't imagine the possibility of it kind of sucking when they did care.

The problem was, Fionnuala loved to act.

And she did love the audience right there in the theatre, or the idea of them when she was filmed. Having the performance itself engaged with – yes, this much she wanted and needed. It was only the need to offer a self outside the role that drove her mad.

Hence the Lir Academy. She hadn't needed to go; she'd have found work without it. But she'd wanted classical training so she could move into theatre. It probably wouldn't earn her enough to live on, but if she did plays and TV adverts and nothing in between – one for love, the other for money – then she would escape the worst of the publicity junkets.

There'd been a certain scepticism of her at drama school initially, an assumption that she hadn't earned her place.

But she'd got on well with the best three lads in the class: Aodh, Fiachra and Conn. It was no surprise to any of them when the legendary agent Bodb O'Flaherty had offered to sign them all after their end-of-year showcase. They'd kept themselves to themselves during the BA, had been friendly enough to everyone else but intimate only with each other. The boys didn't have as much professional experience as Fionnuala, but they all came from similar families and they understood each other. You could call that elitist if you wanted; frequently enough, their classmates did. Still, there was no malice in it. They liked each other, simple as that, and now they'd stay together at the same agency.

'There's a girl who will be handling things for you day-to-day,' Bodb told Fionnuala on the phone after she signed the contract. 'You're as well come and meet her.'

Fionnuala agreed, and arranged to get coffee with Aoife the following day.

'The theatre,' Aoife repeated.

She wasn't the aggressive, will-to-power sort of ambitious young agent that Fionnuala had been expecting. Instead she had an impenetrable calm about her and enunciated each word with an assured clarity.

Fionnuala waited for the usual reaction to her saying she wanted to move to the stage: don't be doing that until you're famous enough that you can afford to treat it as a vanity project. By which point they will, of course, pay you some obscene amount for it anyway, the number-one rule in the arts being that money can exclusively be found for those who don't need it.

But Aoife didn't say any of that.

Instead she said: 'The theatre could be a good move for you.'

'You reckon?' Fionnuala said, wary of this unexpected concordance.

'You'll have no trouble getting parts as it is,' Aoife said, 'but I wouldn't say many of them will offer you really good character work. So if you get that stage foundation in now, then further down the line you'd have a better shot at the film and TV work that really interests you.'

'Unless they forget I exist,' Fionnuala said, wanting to be convinced otherwise.

'That would have been a risk a few decades ago,' Aoife said. 'But we don't have a monoculture now. We've no new movie stars, not really. Nobody is famous for longer than two seconds. You can't perpetually maintain that level of attention anyway, so you might as well do what you want.'

'And you could find me that kind of thing?' Fionnuala said. 'Something in the theatre? Or would I have to—'

'There's actually something after coming in just today,' Aoife said.

'Stage work?'

'Yes. One question though.'

'What?'

'Can you sing?'

*

The Aoife one wanted all four of them to try out for it. She made the argument to Fionnuala that she'd have a better chance of being cast herself if she had good chemistry with the three male leads, and for a first job after drama school, a bit of camaraderie would help them all. Fionnuala quite agreed. After her meeting with Aoife, she got to work on the boys.

Aodh's first response was simply: 'I don't do musicals.'

'They're more respected these days,' Fionnuala said.

'As *if* everyone would actually go around singing and dancing in perfect unison.'

'You're not meant to take it literally. Just like a Shakespearean soliloquy doesn't mean the person is actually talking aloud.'

'You do it if you want,' Aodh said. 'I'm not.'

'I'll sort your Wi-Fi for you.'

Aodh paused, and Fionnuala knew she'd found his weak spot. For three weeks he'd been complaining about having to get Wi-Fi installed in the studio apartment his parents had just bought him. He was not, he claimed, cut out for that sort of thing: the task of it all, the logistics.

Next came Fiachra. He needed no convincing on the musical front, having always been the best singer and dancer in the class. But he wasn't so sure of the concept.

'Swans?' he said. 'Really?'

'Noble creatures,' Fionnuala said. 'Also vicious. Depth to that, don't you think?'

'Which swan would I even be?'

Fionnuala consulted the script. 'Enigmatous Swan would suit you best.'

'Is that even a word?'

'Aodh wants the Enigmatous Swan, but between you and me' – Fionnuala smiled insinuatingly – 'I think you'd get it over him.'

Fiachra had always begrudged Aodh his sharper bone structure and his marginally richer parents. The second swan was in, if only out of spite.

The third swan was the hardest to win over.

'I'm grand with musicals,' Conn said. 'And I'm even grand with swans. But the libretto—'

'We can ask for edits in rehearsals.'

'It's shockingly bad.'

'If we get cast, that is.'

'Listen to this, Fionnuala,' Conn said, and held up the script. '*The Dermatitic Swan is of problematical skin/But his rashes cannot hide the magic within . . .*'

'They said it's not a final version.'

'It doesn't even scan.'

'Conn,' Fionnuala said, 'I'm asking you as a friend. You don't even have to take the part. But since the three of us are going for it, after all we've been through together, if you could just do the audition with us . . .'

'I'll come along and watch,' Conn said.

'No, you've to try out with us. We've always done everything together.'

He'd always been the most sentimental one of the group, the most attached to its cohesion. After Fionnuala, he'd done the most acting as a child, and she suspected it had alienated him at school. Being one of the four at the Lir Academy seemed to be the first time in his life he'd had friends.

She'd found the right lever to pull. The last swan agreed to audition too.

A month later, the Aoife one called all four of them into the office.

'I wanted to tell you in person,' she said.

Fionnuala looked in turn at Aodh, Fiachra and Conn.

'I've just had a phone call with the casting director of *Swans: The Musical*,' Aoife continued, 'and you got it. All of you. You all got a part.'

The boys seemed genuinely happy. The start to their careers hadn't been as simple as any of them had anticipated; it had been a month of rejections, often without even a callback. The senior agent Bodb had phoned them all from his current stint in New York and had made a comment both wise and true, something along the lines of there simply being too much talent in Ireland. The musical Fionnuala had strong-armed the boys into trying out for had come to mean more to them in this context. She'd seen them getting tenser in the weeks since auditions, more hesitant to even talk about *Swans*.

But they'd done it. They'd all been cast. Their worries were at an end.

'Now, the producers want to get moving quickly on it,' Aoife said, 'and since Bodb's away, he's given me the go-ahead to handle the contracts so you can start rehearsals.'

She gave them each a twenty-page document and told them to have a read of it, leaving the room so they could do so in their own time. Of course none of them did; they skimmed the first few pages and gushed to one another about their great relief. 'I was not expecting to care this much,' Conn said, 'but it felt like bad luck, all those auditions going nowhere, and now isn't the curse after being broken.'

'They said it might go to the West End, even,' Aodh said.

'We know,' Fiachra said. 'We were all there.'

'The West End,' Aodh repeated. 'Imagine.'

'It won't happen,' Conn said. 'But happy days if it does.'

When Aoife came back, they told her they were satisfied with their contracts. In unison they signed.

4

Aoife basked in her triumph until Bodb returned from New York.

The casting call was the first news she'd heard of her play since accepting the €1,000 advance. It still stung to think of the script and the feedback too closely, that her earnest attempt to write well had been taken as absurdist satire. A new, graver wave of horror had seized her when she realised they were adapting it as a musical. To add insult to injury is one thing. To add not only insult but show tunes . . .

Still, she was not without pragmatism – indeed the fairer question was whether she was *with* anything else at all – and she saw an opportunity to get rid of the four new clients for however long the production lasted. The four of them would be bound to *Swans: The Musical* throughout the duration of its lifespan; they couldn't do so much as a toothpaste advert on the side. Ideally this period would be something in the region of nine hundred years, but she'd take whatever respite from the four of them she could get.

When Bodb flew back in, he was furious.

'What's the one thing I always told you about exclusivity clauses?' he said.

'Don't sign them,' Aoife conceded.

'And if you do sign them?'

'Make sure it's for a lot of money.'

'And is this a lot of money?' Bodb queried.

'No,' Aoife said. 'It's a pittance.'

'I would fire you,' Bodb said, 'except that no one else knows how to use the iPad.'

So her tasks were simply downgraded: less contracts, more handling devices that the digital non-natives struggled with. Truthfully, her prospects at the agency had never been glowing enough for it to particularly be the end of the world for her. The greater responsibility they'd given her over the past few years had not come with any meaningful pay rise. Since there was no real progression in sight, she was happy enough to go home earlier and less tired.

But Bodb wouldn't stop complaining.

Every day now, parts came in that would have been perfect for the four new clients. That they were contractually bound to this swan nonsense caused him unspeakable grief. It was always like this, he lamented: the moment you signed an exclusivity clause, you came into far greater demand. 'If I would of been there . . .' he said over and over, and Aoife learned not to listen to the rest of the sentence.

He couldn't bear to see the musical. Nor could Aoife, both because of how far its interpretation had strayed from her original ambitions and because it would give her pain to see these beautiful people recite her car crash of a script and somehow pull it off. She'd signed them away; she'd constrained them; she'd held them back somewhat, it was true. But in the end, they'd still be onstage, not her, fully arrived at an age where you were meant to be barely starting.

The four of them frequently moaned to Bodb about the exclusivity clause, she knew. She heard him on the phone, telling them that, yes, it was Aoife's fault, that she should have spotted the condition and warned them. Which told you everything you needed to know about the protective bubble they'd grown up in, really – the protective bubble they'd never left. You can't sign a contract without even reading it and then complain about what it says. Maybe they'd learn a lesson from it all. Maybe they wouldn't. She washed her hands of them in any case.

For as long as she could, she avoided thinking about them.

But the musical was starting to take off.

*

Swans opened in Dublin to rapturous reviews praising it as an instant camp classic. 'The libretto is dreadful, there is no plot to speak of and nobody involved can tell you in one sentence what it's even about; we predict a massive hit,' said the *Sunday Independent*. 'A biting crystallisation of the vanities of our age,' claimed the *Irish Times*. Aoife wasn't sure how a crystallisation could bite, but the quote wound up on the posters all the same. The general public hate-watched it, hate-sang the lyrics back to one another, hate-went to see it for the dozenth time. Clips and quotes went viral, so that soon Americans with too much time on their hands were flying in to post their contraband swan footage online. It was that rarest of entities, that most striking of lightning bolts: an Irish thing that non-Irish people cared about.

Without fail, the reviews highlighted the remarkable freshness of the cast, their dewy skin and limber movements. 'So young as to seem immortal,' claimed an RTÉ radio critic.

Their contracts were extended three months at a time. All four of the leads wanted out at various points, but none of them could ever quite bring themselves to do it. It was hard to walk away from a sure success. The longer they stayed, the more associated they became in the public eye with, specifically, the swans.

Nor could they say no to touring in the rest of Ireland, nor to the West End, nor to continental Europe, and especially not to the Yanks.

Decades passed. *Swans* remained. It became the longest-running Irish musical of all time.

There was talk backstage of the mysterious playwright pocketing the royalties without publicly taking credit. They weren't even on the posters – by their own request, apparently. 'I googled the name,' a producer mentioned once in passing, 'and all that came up was filthy modernist love letters.' No one knew what he meant and no one wanted to.

5

By any reasonable metric Aoife had won the game of life.

Cash-bought Dún Laoghaire apartment, another heap of money invested with good enough returns that she'd never have to think about bills. Resignation tendered at the agency job. All the time in the world to do whatever else: act, or even write. All she'd have to do was announce herself as the enigmatic Nora Barnacle and the world of the arts would be at her feet.

Aoife did not leave her apartment except to walk on the beach just outside. When she returned indoors, she closed the shutters and lay on the couch in the dark. She had groceries delivered though there were supermarkets a five-minute walk away, and claimed on the app each week to be sick, that they should be left at the door so as not to infect anyone. And wasn't that true, in a way? Wasn't she altogether contagious?

For many years she talked to no one and let whatever it was fester inside her.

She denied it as long as she could.

But there was no avoiding the reality.

Only one thing she'd created had ever made it to public attention. Everyone had seen it besides her.

She searched online for the next Dublin performance of *Swans*.

6

'Look at us,' Fionnuala said in the dressing room. 'We've been eaten alive by the swans.'

It was true. Their bodies were breaking down from the inhuman choreographic demands placed on them night after night. They were losing their voices; audiences complained when an alternative cast appeared, so that the original swans were made to tour non-stop. Their make-up took longer each season, with deeper wrinkles to cover, darker eye-bags, more elaborate contouring to mask that their faces were falling in on themselves.

They had taken to sharing swan dreams during downtime. Some of them flapped but couldn't fly, others fell down a well or got crushed by a barge along the canal or screeched and screeched and woke up screaming. None of them could remember whose dreams were whose any more. Once shared with the group, a swan vision would descend on one of the others the following night, so that a private and violent collective narrative developed running adjacent to the actual show.

In the shower Fionnuala heard things, saw things. She could not put words on it to the others exactly: a combination of water and the texture of her own feathers and hissing and stretching her neck.

There'd been a special anniversary performance in London the previous month where they'd condensed the show to its essentials. The four came onstage and each sang a song about what kind of swan they were. Then interpretative dance, with little clue as to what in fact was being interpreted. Next there was a subplot – which, in the absence of any other storyline, became de facto the main plot – about the Villainous Swan seeking to drive the four from their resident lake. Finally a few more numbers about the value of friendship, further dancing and the accidental gay anthem 'Can You Cygnet?'

Then a final number where they all died.

The London concert marked the nth year of *Swans: The Musical*. They knew the actual number but said nth to one another, or 'thousandth-or-so' on occasion.

The original exclusivity clause was no longer binding. Nobody was forcing them to keep renewing the contracts or to keep accepting such strenuous conditions when they did. Occasionally, for as long as a week at a time, one of them would resolve to withdraw. But it was never all four at once, and so the others who were committed to the swans in that moment would override the dissenter.

The swans had given them so much. A loyal fanbase; money, even. Their salaries had risen and they got a cut of the merchandise. There was talk of a film adaptation, which would mint them for life if it came about.

Provided they weren't too old to play the swans. They observed their crows' feet with mounting inquietude and policed one another's brows for the first signs of Botox. Aodh took to barging through doors and dropping heavy things to check the others could still spontaneously emote.

They'd had no life outside *Swans* since it began; the nieces and nephews they'd met as infants during the first few years on the job were now adult strangers.

The musical could not exist without them. The producers reminded them of this whenever they asked for some alleviation of their working conditions. 'You are *Swans*,' they would say. 'We're all counting on you. Don't let us down.' Nobody else depended on them. None of them had partners, let alone children, and their extended families had learned not to expect too much. Anyone in their lives with any tendency to be needy had long since been pushed away. They'd thought they wanted that; they'd thought it would free them. But when you got up each morning and asked yourself what to do, the answer was ultimately to go where you were required. Years of *Swans* had made it so that *Swans* alone had a use for them. Without the musical, they were nothing.

Now they were about to perform the second *n*th anniversary performance, in Dublin. The venue had offered them two free tickets each – 'For loved ones,' they'd said. Fionnuala hadn't been able to think of anyone in her personal life who'd want one. She spoke to her parents once a month, if even, and her siblings were married and living abroad. She'd ignored so many texts and taken so many rain checks that the most stubborn of her former friends had given up. The lads were in a similar position, and so in the end they'd all given their tickets back to the organisers.

'We don't have to keep doing it,' Fionnuala said.

They cradled their coffees in the dressing room, the other three of them, and waited to see if she'd explain.

It wasn't that the statement itself was unprecedented. Of the four of them, Fionnuala was the one who said it most often: that nobody was forcing them, that no one could detain them, that they could walk free tomorrow if they liked.

But this evening there was something different in her voice. She seemed to truly mean it.

'One last *Swans*,' she said. 'Tomorrow morning we quit.'

'And then what?' Aodh said.

'Maybe nothing,' Fionnuala said. 'But we can't keep going.'

They knew it was true. Their limbs would collapse and their faces would melt right off them and they'd be pushed out sooner or later. Today everyone loved them, but tomorrow or the day after or at some inevitable future point, *Swans* would be done with them like everyone else already was. They could wait for that moment, or they could walk out now of their own volition with some scrap of dignity still attached.

They shook on it there in the dressing room and proceeded onto the stage.

The audience appeared before them as it always did, an anonymous blurry field.

Swans arrived autonomously from their bodies by this point; nothing they did was a decision. They moved as a unit through the structure that came more natively to them now than any language could. Not even the knowledge that this was their last performance could change their delivery: they could not give more or less of themselves to any particular performance of *Swans*, because this would require agency. Instead they surrendered every night and the musical ran itself through.

Until the last song, the death song, the shuffling off their mortal coil. This fate had ceased to alarm them. It was how the musical went.

But tonight, as their familiar death subsumed them, a face in the front row of the audience became clear.

Aoife watched the four of them sink to the floor, heard their warbling last chords. The instruments from the pit fell off in gradual succession until only a shrill violin remained. They were alone now, nearly, she and them.

A change seemed about to come over her features, something like an opening crest of catharsis. But before the four swans could ascertain her expression, the script called for them to close their eyes. They were powerless against their roles. They succumbed to the dark.

THE CHANGELING
Jane Casey

The Changeling

He walked with a brisk step along the cliff path, whistling. It was a clear day and warm, though a blue haze hid the distant mountains from view. The sun was sparkling on the waves below: thousands and thousands of tiny lights that dazzled him and made him look away, inland, across the narrow stone-walled fields that patchworked the island. In the distance they were cutting hay, scythes glinting in the sun, the bend and sweep of the arm following a rhythm as precise and measured as a dance. He was staring at it, distracted, so he nearly collided with his neighbour who was strolling in the opposite direction.

Tomás removed the pipe from his mouth and nodded. 'You're in a hurry, Conor. What's the rush?'

'Ah, no rush. Bríd's been on her own all morning, that's all.'

Tomás nodded, his face puckering into wrinkles that might have been a twist of worry, or a smile. 'How's the little one?'

'Grand, grand.'

'And Bríd's getting on all right?'

'Not a bother on her,' Conor said easily.

'I'll tell Máire to drop in on her again.' Tomás hesitated. 'It can be hard on them. The first weeks.'

'You'd know if anyone did.' Máire had given Tomás eleven children in quick succession, eight of them boys, and all fine, healthy babies who had grown and thrived. His neighbour's wealth was in his children.

Conor often imagined himself with a troop following him to save turf on his trips to the mainland. They walked behind him to work the fields he had inherited from his father on the island: boys with blue eyes and dark hair and broad shoulders like himself. They watched how he handled a sleán and tried to do the same.

This is how you do it, look, with a turn of the wrist . . . and he would carve out a neat sod of turf with a flourish for his invisible, invented audience who would nod, impressed.

'After what happened last time,' Tomás began, and stopped as Conor turned his head sharply, like a dog about to snap. 'Ah – I only mean it's natural she'd be nervous.'

Conor pulled his face back into an expression of bland friendliness. 'I'd better be on my way.' A touch of his finger to his cap, and he was gone, swinging through the long grass, still whistling although he was no longer listening to himself or feeling anything but cold, dark rage.

After what happened last time.
Tomás should know better than to bring that up.

The house stood a little apart from the others in the village, but that was all right; they were as close as a deck of cards there, pressed up against one another, the women and children in and out of each other's homes all the time. He liked that there was open ground to cross between the last house and their own, with a few hens scratching in the dirt and a lean black-and-white dog waiting for her owner's call. He wished the house was further away, if anything.

. . . you're here.

With a critical eye he examined the thatch as he walked towards it, pleased to find it neat and secure against the wind. The chimney was smoking and that made him pick up his pace. He was hungry but he felt strong, vital, in his prime, his body barely complaining from the effort he had expended that morning in the fields. He wasn't bent and worn like Tomás. He was a man who had everything he could want: a wife, a house, land of his own to work, a child.

The thin weak cry drew his shoulders up around his ears as he bent his head to step through the door. He saw the cradle first, sitting near the fire, woven from close-drawn wicker that seemed to protect the tiny occupant like a hedge around a field. The cradle was sturdy. It stood on two wooden rockers, carved by his grandfather for the baby who had been his father and for his father's brothers (one gone to America in '47, fleeing the Great Hunger, and one dead). Conor had slept in it himself. He had presumably stared up at the lattice of thin branches over his head like the infant that belonged to him now. It was hard to imagine that he had ever been as intent as the baby, with her black, unblinking eyes. She seemed mysteriously focused on tracing the patterns his grandfather had woven, as if there was some meaning in them he couldn't quite read.

He waited for the feeling of pride to return and found only irritation.

'Can you not stop her from crying?'

. . . if I could stop her from crying don't you think I would do it without you telling me I should? Don't you know I would do anything to keep her from pain and heartache?

Don't you know I would do anything to keep her from you?

'It's been like that all morning. The noise.'

His wife's voice came from the far corner of the room. She was sitting with her knees drawn up to her chin on their narrow bed, her face a pale blur in the darkness. The walls were whitewashed but the smoke from the turf fire had turned them dark grey. The chimneypiece was black where the smoke was strongest. He should paint it white again, he thought, and knew he wouldn't bother.

He wasn't the only one who had lost heart. When they'd

first married, she would pick flowers and put them on the small deep windowsill. Now there was nothing decorative at all in the place, apart from a few pieces of delph on the shelves in the corner. There was a mark where a small wooden cross had hung, over the bed, and he frowned as he noticed its absence.

'What are you doing over there?'

'It won't stop crying.' Bríd put her hands up to her face, pressing them into her cheeks. 'It won't stop.'

'She's probably hungry.' He strode across and took his wife by the arm, pulling her up. 'Feed her.'

'I can't.'

'You have to.' He gave her a nudge towards the fireplace, misjudging how much force he needed to use, so she gasped and fell in a sprawl on the hearth. It always shocked him how fragile she was, how slight compared to him. It made him feel awkward beside her. 'Get up.'

... *as if I care about what you do to me. Anything physical can be endured.*

He drew her to her feet, his fingers meeting around her thin upper arm. His nails were dirty from the work he'd been doing, his hand shockingly tanned compared to her pallor. He felt his heart twist with love that almost made him gasp. 'You're all right? Not hurt?'

She shook her head, her red-lidded eyes fixed on the floor. He couldn't read anything into her expression – not resentment, not anger, not disapproval. Not even distress. Her face was blank, remote as the stars. The baby cried on.

. . . even from the start it took nothing to provoke you. The first time you tried to kiss me I pulled away, laughing, thinking it was a joke, and you hit the smile off my face and then you . . .

'For God's sake, Bríd, talk to me. What's wrong with you? What did you do with yourself this morning? Lie on in the bed?'

She shook her head, her hair hanging in strings around her face. 'I cooked a meal. I cleaned the place. I washed your shirts.' They were strung on a rope over the fire, drying.

'Why didn't you hang them outside, and it a fine day?'

'I thought it might rain.'

'No rain today,' he said. 'The sun is splitting the stones.'

She tucked her hair behind her ear and said nothing and he remembered with a squirm of shame that they had argued once – well, he had berated her – for hanging the shirts out on the line in the sunlight. He'd thought he saw that red-headed witch Fionnuala Ní Mharcaigh laughing at the places where the linen had worn. The shirts were good quality, with plenty of life in them, and when he was dressed he looked smart, but the scars of Bríd's neat stitches were visible when light shone through the fabric. They told a tale that he would prefer to keep to himself.

. . . because you told me I wasn't allowed to hang them outside and, yes, you're remembering that now, aren't you? You were ashamed of the rags you wear, and rightly so. You're puffed up with your own importance in your finery, a cockerel with a ragged tail perching on a dunghill. Fionnuala laughed because she'd seen me mending your flimsy, cheap shirts. They tore because there's no grace in you, awkward and clumsy as you are. A beast of a man. Nothing makes you happy. Everyone knows what you're like.

Everyone knows why we married.

'You made something for my dinner?'

'In the pot.'

'And the baby? Did you look after her?'

Her face was sullen, her mouth turned down. Defiant.

'It's not.'

'What? What does that mean? It's not what?'

'A baby.'

The silence between the adults filled the little cottage. She stood with her head bent, her body braced, ready for him to argue with her.

There.
I have said it.
Now.

He took a step back instead, and another. He felt cold, scared, as if something incredibly ancient had entered the house. It seemed to stand between them, darkening the air. 'What do you mean, it's not a baby? It's your baby.' A big effort. '*Our* baby.'

'It's not.'

'Did she not come out of you two weeks ago? Yesterday you were telling me you were still sore.' She had cried as she said it. She was his wife and he wanted her, and if she wouldn't let him have her she was no use to him, but he had been gentle.

... when I begged you to leave me alone you hurt me anyway, like the first time, like every time.

All of them had been after her – Liam Óg, Seán Rua, Micheál who had played the fiddle for her when she danced. That was what had attracted him in the first place. The sight of her with her hair bouncing, her red skirts lifted so her fine legs showed; he would never forget it. She had life to her, a gleam in her eyes, colour in her face, and she had laughed when he approached her. He'd thought at first she was laughing at him and the rage had almost choked him, but then he'd realised it was surprise that made her laugh. He was known for keeping himself to himself as much as he was known for being a handsome man, and she felt special because he had singled her out.

... you followed me when I went out for some air. I was hot from dancing, and giddy, and I ran outside to fill my

lungs and stare at the sky. It was a clear night, the heart of summer, and the sky wasn't fully dark even though it was late, but the stars were stitching themselves into view. I heard a footstep behind me and it was you, and I wasn't scared enough to run.

I barely knew your name.

I had never heard you speak.

I thought you were awkward and strange. It wasn't that you were ugly – no one ever said that about you – but the girls couldn't stand to look at you. There was something missing from you. Something wrong. Something I couldn't name.

But then I was little more than a child myself.

She had been shy with him and that gave him confidence he didn't ordinarily possess. He'd asked her to go walking with him along the strand to look at the stars.

. . . and you dragged me down to the sea. No one heard me crying for help. No one heard me scream.

Conor had been in Galway for a year before that, finding his feet in the city. His life in a boarding house was bleak and his job in the city – delivering milk – was brutally hard and boring. He was lonely, even though he was never alone.

Then his father had died and he came back to the island to work the farm and live the life his father had known, and his grandfather, and the nameless men who had gone before them. There was no pang of regret as the currach nosed through the waves, the spray stinging his face, the mainland fading to a smudge on the horizon. He had returned but not as a failure, as he had feared. This was natural, the proper order of things, to go back at the right time in the right way. He embraced his new, old life.

And then he saw Bríd.

Every time he saw her he felt a shock of pleasure. She was beautiful. Long dark hair, delicate skin, narrow wrists and ankles, the arch of her neck, the curve of her waist: perfect. That night, by the sea, she had agreed to marry him.

. . . and that night, by the sea, you forced yourself on me and I—

His mother hadn't been pleased. She had wanted him to stay in Galway and marry well instead of going back to the island. She had wanted him to sell the land. She had cleared out of the family home, leaving it to his new bride. She had gone to live with her sister in Clare, back where she was from originally, glad to be on proper land instead of a scoured spare knot of rock with the sea on all sides. She had never fitted in there. Unless you were born on the island, of island stock, you were always an outsider.

. . . your mother knew what you'd done and so she wouldn't stay on the island. My mother said it was hard for your mother when she first arrived as a bride. The women tried to

help her where they could. She had a difficult time with your father. There were rumours about him, and the things he did to her, and I believe them. He taught you well.

Conor's mother had always been wary of the local customs, so he hadn't been brought up to believe in the same things as everyone else, whatever you called them: the Old Ones, the daoine uaisle, the Sidhe. He had been brought up mumbling prayers but not to the fairies. To him, a tall stone in a field was a stone. A mound of earth was nothing to fear. He didn't hear the music others heard, or claimed to. He didn't see what others saw. He wasted no time placating the island itself. He owned the land, not the other way round.

So he didn't want to listen to Bríd.

'I hope you don't mean what I think you mean.' Fear made his voice harsh and she flinched. Her face was still mutinous though.

'That's not my baby. That *thing*.'

He walked over to the wicker cradle. The baby was grizzling, her fingers reaching and stretching with tiny seeking movements. She was red in the face, small and shrivelled and unlovely. Her eyes were black in the dim light from the fire, shining and liquid. The wooden cross was wedged into the cot near her feet.

'She looks the same to me.'

'I wanted to put it on the fire.' Bríd's voice was low, a monotone, and it made his skin feel as if it was going to crawl off his body with horror. 'All day I've been thinking of it. My grandmother always said if *they* took your baby and left another in return, you should put the changeling in the fire and then they would come back to rescue it.'

'Bríd.' His voice cracked on her name. 'That's enough.'

'Or the sea. Take them into the sea and let the water carry them away to their own kind. Then your baby comes back on the next tide. All you have to do is wait on the shore.'

'Stop it now. You're scaring me.' He twisted to look at her and her eyes were empty, like those of a sleepwalker, a ghost. 'Promise me you won't do anything like that, Bríd.'

'I don't want this in my house.'

'It's your baby.' He bent and stripped the coverlet off the tiny body, showing her. 'Look. Really, look at her.'

. . . you think you understand but you're as thick as a block.

'I heard that you cleared away a fairy ring in one of the fields. Is it true?'

He opened his mouth to say no and then remembered that he had, back in the autumn, around the time Bríd had realised she was to have another baby. He had gone down one morning to dig potatoes, in high spirits, and found the mushrooms had appeared overnight. He remembered them, a pale and perfect circle in the soil. It had been the work of moments to walk around kicking the heads off them, scattering them to shrivel away into nothingness, and he hadn't thought anything of it.

Now a cold sting of doubt made him uneasy. 'How did you know that?'

'Someone saw you.'

'Who?'

'I don't know.' She backed away from him as he turned to look at her. 'I don't! It was the talk of the village.'

He didn't like that – being the subject of people's criticism. Their scorn. Sweat broke out across the small of his back, his upper lip, under his arms, and he shifted his weight.

'That's nonsense.' He struggled to articulate his defence. 'They were only mushrooms. Nothing strange about them.'

'Everyone knows not to interfere with a fairy ring.' Her voice was flat. 'You should have left it alone. The fairies are punishing us.'

He took a step towards her, his shadow falling on her. 'You're blaming me for something that's not even true. The baby hasn't changed.'

'That's not my baby.'

'Is this because of what happened last time?'

'Last time?'

'With Órla.' He raised his hand and rubbed the back of it across his mouth, as if he could wipe the word away.

'Órla.' Her face softened at the memory of the tiny scrap of human life that had been her firstborn, with a mop of black curls and a pointed chin. 'No. That was different.'

Different. One way to describe it. He shivered at the memory of the scream she had let out of her when she found the baby dead in the cradle. That ashy look on the child's face, like the dawn. She had held the small body until he made her put it down, and in minutes it was cold.

Bríd hadn't spoken, after that cry, for six months. All of her words had died with the baby.

Plenty of words spoken in the village, and beyond.

The anger surged up. It wasn't unusual to lose a baby or two: the island cemetery was full of them. Hadn't he given her another? He hadn't complained that it was a girl again. He had kissed her as she lay there after her long labour, exhausted. She had barely looked at the baby. What he remembered was that her face had been anxious as she looked at him for approval.

What more did she want?

. . . I can't let it happen again.

He cleared his throat. 'Have you a name for this one yet?'

She shook her head.

'Name her. Then you'll start to care for her.'

'How can I care for a changeling?'

'Do you not want it?' He made a move towards the cradle and she stepped forward, one hand outstretched.

'Don't.'

He reached into the cradle anyway and lifted the baby, settling her on his shoulder. The infant was so small his hand covered her entirely, her soft fine hair tickling his fingertips. Her body was hot against him but the skin on the back of her neck was cool enough; she wasn't sick. It was the ferocity of her determination to live. She was still curled up as she had been in the womb, a new leaf yet to unfurl.

He glanced at Bríd, wary. He couldn't talk her out of it, so the only alternative was to indulge her. 'I've heard if you take care of what the wise ones leave you – look after it like your own – they give you back your own child.'

'Do they?' A slow blink.

'What do you want to name her, Bríd? Everyone is asking.' The baby wriggled against him, her head butting him in search of milk, her hands working. A wavering, thin cry. He shushed her, patting her back, watching his wife.

'I don't know.'

'You can't call her "it" either. Promise me you won't say any of this to anyone else. Promise, Bríd.'

Slowly, she nodded. 'I told Máire.'

'That can't be helped. Sit down there in the chair.' The baby's nails scraped the soft skin of his neck, where his collar kept the sun off him. He winced. 'Take her. Feed her.'

Bríd took the baby from him and held her, pulling the shawl around her to hide the child as she fed. She looked away, her lips moving although he couldn't tell what she was saying. Conor watched her for a moment longer, then went to the fire and the iron pot where stew was bubbling.

He needed to eat too.

That night, in the darkness, she whispered to him.

'Síofra. I'll call her Síofra.'

He was more asleep than awake, half-aware of her

holding the baby. Bríd was patting her back, coaxing the air out of her, humming under her breath.

There, that was normal, he thought, congratulating himself on his insight. A name for the baby. It was like a sheep rejecting its lamb; there were ways to fool the animal into cherishing it once again. You could skin a dead lamb, he thought hazily, and drape the soft skin over the back of an abandoned one, and put it to the mother and she'd mistake the new lamb for her own even though hers was dead.

But this baby was as much Bríd's own as little Órla had been. She was tired, that was what it was.

He went to sleep happy, and woke up happy, and his good mood only faded the next day when he ran into Tomás's Máire outside the house.

'Bríd has a name for the baby.'

She shaded her eyes as the sun dazzled from the dusty road. 'What did she call her?'

'Síofra.' He said it with pride.

'Síofra? Is that so?'

'What of it?' He felt something tighten within him.

'You know what it means, don't you?'

He hadn't thought anything more than it was a nice name, pretty, unusual on the island but no worse for that.

'It means "of the fairies",' Máire said with a touch of pity in her voice that scalded him in shame like boiling water. 'She hasn't forgotten this notion that the child isn't hers. She's more convinced of it than ever.'

For weeks he watched Bríd with the baby, out of the corner of his eye. In the night he stirred when she did. He woke early in the morning when she fed Síofra in the chair by the window. She would stare out at the lightening sky, her eyes on the horizon, never looking down at the infant in her arms. She did enough to keep the baby clean, fed and quiet, tending to her with silent competence, but she never remarked on the baby's looks, or how she was growing and changing.

Gritting his teeth, he asked Máire and a couple of the other women to keep an eye on Bríd and Síofra while he was in the fields. They were only too pleased to help. Bríd spent her days with a big group of them, all laughing and telling stories. He didn't like it – and didn't like the silence that fell when he came to speak to Bríd. He could hear them thinking about how he looked and what he said.

. . . you're right to turn red when you come to get me. If only you knew the things they say about you.

If only you knew what I say about you.

The women understand why I don't coo over Síofra, why I do what I must for her without love, why I never smile when I look at her. They know more than you ever will.

It was Bríd's implacable serenity he found troubling. He dreamed of an empty cradle, of a dead lamb in a field surrounded by a ring of mushrooms, and he woke up crying. He felt as if each day was edging towards something terrible.

The baby, on the other hand, was thriving. She was a beautiful child, everyone said. The image of her mother.

And Bríd smiled, but when he asked her outright she shook her head.

'That's not my baby. My baby is gone. This one isn't mine.'

The fine weather didn't last. In place of the long bright days came squally wind that bent the grass and whipped yellow foam out of the sea. Rain beat down on him as he worked in the fields, but the hay was saved and the wheat was harvested, so the weather didn't matter. He could dig potatoes in the rain, the spade sliding into the wet earth with pleasing neatness. His imaginary children crowded around him again. He felt better when it rained, obscurely: it was as if everything was normal again. The year was turning for home, for long nights and frosty mornings and the warmth of his wife's body under the blankets. Come winter, he would edge Bríd out of the group of women that gathered in the sunshine to spin and gossip, and take her back to himself, to the cottage set away from the others, where they could be alone once more.

On the day he came back from the fields and found the cottage empty, he didn't worry unduly. He walked down through the village until he heard the sound of voices and laughter from Tadhg Mac an Bhaird's house. He pushed the door open and the women who were gathered there looked up, interest fading to wariness.

The woman of the house, Gráinne, got to her feet. 'Is it yourself, Conor? You're welcome.'

He sketched a greeting, barely polite as he searched for one particular face among the many. 'Is Bríd not with you?'

'No. She hasn't been here today.'

The other women nodded, their hands still, work forgotten in their laps.

'I saw her on my way here.' Máire got to her feet with a wince. 'She was walking down the shore road with the baby, not long ago. I thought she might be meeting you.'

'No.' He tried to smile, as if it didn't matter. 'We must have missed each other. I'll go and find her now.'

'I can come with you.'

'There's no need.' He was halfway out the door now, anxiety making his mouth dry. 'You stay here in the warm. The wind would cut you in two.'

Not a day for a walk, he thought, half-running back the way he had come, his stride rushed and jerky now. Not a day to go to the shore, unless you had some reason. In spite of himself, not wanting to, he remembered what she had said before.

Take them into the sea and let the water carry them away to their own kind . . .

And that distant, otherworldly look she had on her face when she said it.

The baby didn't matter – there would be another child, a brace of them – but his wife, the most beautiful woman he'd ever seen, the reason he was the envy of men across the island . . . he couldn't bear to lose her.

He began to run in earnest, stones rattling under his boots, the wind pushing him back like an invisible hand. At the bend in the road, high above the beach, he saw her. She was alone on the shore. Her hair was loose, blowing behind her like a dark flag, and the wind plucked at her skirts. She was holding the infant close, bundled in a shawl. Her head was bent as if she was whispering to it.

'Bríd!'

The wind ripped her name out of his mouth and threw it away. She couldn't hear him, he knew with a sick kind of impotence. She was oblivious to him.

. . . I could feel your eyes on me before you shouted. I knew you'd be there. I knew you'd come looking for me and the women would tell you where I was.

He threw himself down the path that led to the beach, careless now, close to stumbling as he went, cursing under his breath or praying or some combination of the two. He called her name again and again, his voice raw with fear. She heard him at last and turned. He caught one brief flash of her face, like the inside of a bird's wing, before she faced the sea again.

'Stop!' he yelled hopelessly. 'Wait.'

She took a few steps and the water swirled around her feet, darkening the hem of her skirt, weighing it down so it clung to her. The water was knee high, and in a few more steps it rose to her thighs.

He ploughed through the surf, the spray flying up around him, and caught her just as the water reached her waist. 'Bríd, what the hell do you think you're doing?'

She swung around and he glimpsed her face: white, set, her eyes staring. Then she swung the bundle in her arms at him – the child! – and the world exploded into pain and brightness that sparkled around him like the night sky in a hundred pinpricks of starlight. For a crazy, dizzy second he was back on the beach, panting, savage and desperate as he held her down that first time, the stars spread above them.

And the world faded to darkness.

Waves pulled at Bríd's clothes, wrapping them around her, dragging her off her feet. She stood as still as possible, staring at her husband. He was face down in the sea, small tremors racking his body. A low groan rose from somewhere deep within him, and he began to turn his head, instinct driving him to seek the air even though he was fully unconscious. Quickly, trembling, she reached out and threaded her fingers through his hair. She pushed him under the surface, keeping clear of his arms and legs as he began to thrash.

. . . because I paid too much attention to the baby, the last time, and you had to remind me who mattered most. You made me put Órla in the cradle, even though she was hungry, so I could lie down for you. That was my first duty,

you said, and you hit me when I tried to argue, and the baby cried and cried. I was used to a raised fist by then. I could bear that. What truly scared me was the way you looked at Órla as if you hated her. As if you were jealous of the love I felt for my child.

As if you wanted Órla gone.

You were never anything but a cold, cruel imitation of a husband. A changeling. A monster, not a man.

Bríd held on to Conor's head until her muscles ached, waiting as his movements became jerky, then stilled completely. She was gasping for breath herself. The water was cold but she no longer felt it.

She felt nothing at all.

. . . then early one morning I woke with the dawn, to find you standing over the cradle, leaning into it.

Your big hand on the baby's face.

I leapt out of the bed and tried to pull you away. You shoved me aside, focused on what you were doing, until it was over and the tiny body lay there, and she was gone.

I couldn't stop you.

I can stop you now.

She held on until it was impossible that he could still be alive. Then she shoved him away from her and let the body ride the waves out to sea.

... and on the day the new baby was born I found you staring into the cradle with the same look on your face – a kind of cold appraisal, like a farmer might have for a weak little lamb or a runt of a pup. A girl was no use to you, you said the first time. I knew what would happen when they told me it was another girl. I turned my face away and wept, not for disappointment, but for fear.

The tide seemed to push her back towards the shore, the cold making her gasp and shudder. In one hand she held the shawl that she had wrapped around a heavy stone. One blow was all it had taken: one unexpected swing to the side of his head had felled him to helplessness. She searched her conscience for guilt and found none.

The water streamed from her clothes and ran from her hair as she dragged herself up the beach on leaden legs. The air felt warm, as if the island was welcoming her back. The women came to meet her, straggling down the hill, the younger ones running through the grass with their skirts pulled up, the older ones holding their shawls against the wind.

'Is it done?' Fionnuala asked, her face white and pinched, and Bríd nodded as they gathered around her.

'Thank God,' Gráinne whispered. 'We'll say nothing.'

'An accident.' Fionnuala looked around. 'Agreed?'

Nods and murmurs around Bríd and no sign of dissent. They knew what he was.

'Where's the baby?' That was Máire, who had come to see her the day after Síofra was born, and held the child while Bríd wept, then spoke over the small downy head in a soft, rapid whisper.

Tell him she's a changeling.

Make him think you're neglectful of her. Let him think you're planning to do something to her.

Lure him to the sea.

Let the waves take him away.

Bríd pushed through the women and went straight to the place where she had left Síofra. The baby was in a hollow in the grass, staring up at the sky. When she saw Bríd, she kicked her legs, once, and smiled for the first time in her short life.

'Oh you darling . . .' Bríd picked her up and pressed her wet face against the baby's soft cheek, her perfect ear. There was nothing at all in her of her father, Bríd thought. She was a child with no father, a gift from the other world. She must never know about him. She must never know what he was really like.

Bríd sat down, holding the baby close to shield her from the wind as the women moved to surround them. Síofra stared up at her, entranced.

'Let me tell you the story of how you came by your name, my child of the stars,' Bríd began.

A MOST DECEIVING WOMAN

Nikita Gill

―――――――――

Credhe and Cael

I was not born goddess. Goddess is what I became. There are those who will tell you my tale crafted another way. But stories hold more than that. They are made of the never-ending ivy of time, the ancient spellwork of nature, the gristle of blood and bone. What glitters in the sunlight was forged in a mountain at the very end, all so that it glints like a silver wreath donned with emeralds in your hands. Pretty. Perfect. Powerful, perhaps. But not the whole tale. We, like the rarest of diamonds, are all fashioned from coarseness and darker things.

My mother, all-seeing, a true child of the Tuatha Dé Danann, knew precisely what I was the moment she held me in her arms, my cries still fresh to the world. If I close my eyes, I can almost see it. Her favourite azure gown edged with gold as she rocked me in her arms that very first time, her long, golden hair perfect. Unlike mortals, the aos sí were ethereal even in the primal art of bringing life into this world. My mother had not cried out, my birth itself mere moments long. When I was swaddled in soft, fine cloth and brought to her, she was already recovered, her waist trim. She held me close and looked into my already open eyes. Eithne, who nursed me, told me that never had a mother looked so beautiful after birth, but I suspect that this was because Eithne was my mother's biggest admirer and her greatest confidant. It was only after I had asked after my mother a thousand times as a child that Eithne confessed how much my mother had cried after I was born, her sorrow ringing through my father's palace. The cries of an immortal are a bitter blade, one that draws blood across all of time.

She saw something in that moment that she held me. Her eyes had widened as they looked into my own violet ones, the serenity on her face broken by what she saw in my newborn features. A prophecy. A fate. A destiny. Name it what you will, but it was in that moment that my mother knew well that I would suffer in ways no child born of an immortal should.

Perhaps this was also the moment that she realised the gods had seen fit to make me mortal. For my mother, realising that her firstborn daughter would know death was a curse beyond measure. It was no wonder then that, after this, our relationship was fraught with equal parts frost and fire.

Fortunately for my parents, they had other children. Immortals, unlike me. And their attentions were distracted permanently by raising children that would not die.

For my own sins, I was left mostly with Eithne – my first memory will forever be of the babbling brook in the palace grounds glittering in the moonlight, the sapphire and ruby wildflowers that grew around it and Eithne's warm and comforting hand holding my tiny one as I pulled at her, begging to get closer and closer to the water. The nights back then glowed with the cool of the moon, the midnight of the skies filled with a dozen stars dancing, singing to us. Eithne would laugh warmly at my attempts to reach the creek, but I would feel her fingers imperceptibly tighten around mine. She was my aunt after all, a distant relative of my mother, a lesser immortal in a hierarchal structure I grew to know later, but an immortal none the less.

The others in the palace, whether man, woman or child, avoided me.

I noticed it in the way my parents would refuse to let me eat with my siblings. The way I was kept in my own wing of the house with Eithne as my sole source of comfort and my guardian. The way the servants would do their work without ever looking me in the eye. The maid who would bring my food never lingered longer than her duty. The guard outside the door never spoke to me. Eithne was left to handle bathing and clothing me while my sisters were aided by an array of handmaidens.

I only saw my two brothers and two sisters when our parents required us to make a court appearance. And this was very rare. I could count on one hand how often we were together in a room. It made for a solitary childhood.

It is strange to have spent a childhood lonely in a bejewelled palace that glittered with white marble, windows so wide and welcoming, walls encrusted with jewels, its golden ballroom frequented by fae of every nature, from high courts to low courts. There was always a giggling gaggle of immortals around every corner. And yet, I had not a single ally, no one to name friend. I was a small ghost that haunted my family and their home.

It occurred to me as I got older that they thought my mortality was like a sickness. One that could be passed to them if they were not careful.

Perhaps, then, it was for the best that I learned to love stories so much. I can still recall Eithne's dulcet tones as she would read to me from ancient texts in those evenings before I fell asleep. She would bring me milk mixed with lavender and honey and I would settle under the furs on my bed for a story about the elders. Sometimes there was the tale of a war, sometimes one of a warrior, but my favourite tales were always the ones with a woman or goddess who was cleverer than a freshly crafted sword.

These stories were rarer than the others. Often the tales were of gods and mortal men, half warning, half prayer. But the stories where the women outwitted them all, they remained the ones that I asked for every night. Until one day Eithne told me, 'Credhe, I know why you ask me for these tales always.'

At the time I was seven years old and I had feigned a look of as much surprise as I could on my young face. 'I just like hearing them.'

Eithne had watched me carefully for a long time before saying, 'As you age, child, you will see that this otherworld we live in – and the world of mortals – does not work the way these stories work. Women . . . goddesses . . . we do not wield power the way men and gods do. If we do snatch it, it is not for long. Your mother learned this lesson. Pray you do not have to learn it too.'

She touched my chin, making me look in her eyes. 'You have a cunning face, child. They do not like women with faces like yours. Learn to soften your features. Hide them the best you can. Once your mother learned to do this, she became queen.'

Before I could ask what she had meant by these words, she had returned to the story. But an image of my mother's face, sorrowful when she looked at me, came to my mind's eye and I held my tongue, and shut my queries within a treasure chest of unending questions I knew I could not ask. After that day, I was more careful when asking her to tell me stories. I also realised that this was a place where dark secrets hid in the corners of the rooms that were filled with beautiful crystals and gleamed with such light.

It began as a whisper. Those who served us had always had their ears to the ground in a way that none of us realised. In our arrogance as higher beings, we took their loyalties for granted, thought them powerless in their capacities. But knowledge is a powerful thing – powerful enough to bring most kings to their knees.

My father was a king. One of the blessed lands of Kerry, his rule magnanimous and fair, from what I had heard. But even the palaces of the most magnanimous rulers were filled with those who thought they could rule better, who thought the people of that land were getting too used to fair laws and peace. Most wars do not begin in the roads of peaceful villages by those who just about make ends meet or have just enough to be content. They are engineered by those who have too much already. Greed is not just a mortal failing. Power can corrupt any living being. And my father, peaceful as he was, had earned enemies in a court of nobles who thought he was too kind, too good. And then one day they gained what they thought was evidence of his incapacity to rule. Proof that he was too soft.

I was a child of twelve when the whispers reached me. I had been on my way to the gardens, my favoured hideaway, when I heard the voices of two of my mother's handmaidens.

Did you hear about the—

I did but I cannot believe it to be true.

If it is, do you know what this means for the queen?

If it is, do you know what it means for the king?

I dare not think it, I dare not believe it.

But what if—

Shush. We may be endless, but there are still ways to punish us.

I may have been young and shielded from most of the world and what lay beyond the walls of my father's palace, but I understood well enough in that moment that what I had heard was dangerous. The question, of course, was, how dangerous were those words and why were those two handmaidens so scared?

It took me three days to find out what was being whispered in those hallways, the furtive glances I had seen on the beautiful faces seared into my mind. If any sense of danger within me was begging me to let go of this exploration, I was not interested in listening to it. I was like a hound who had scented blood for the very first time. I needed to find out what was happening behind those palace walls.

In the end, I positioned myself outside my father's favoured chambers. There was a way my thin, small body could hide between two jewelled urns that no adult immortal in this palace could, so I stood in secret, and listened.

It took three days of slipping out of my own chambers, where I was meant to be studying our history, our stories, magic, and hiding in this secret place before someone finally opened the chamber doors and forgot to close them properly. I leaned against the wall as I watched the shard of light in the hallway, the sound of voices echoing just slightly in the grandeur of the halls.

And what of our children, Cairbre? Have you considered the consequences of letting her stay here of all places?

My eyes widened. That voice was my mother's voice. It was higher than usual, a slight tremor within her usually confident notes.

I have. The children are stronger than you give them credit for. They will learn how to live under even this.

And that was my father's quiet, commanding voice. I closed my eyes and listened closer, willing every part of my body to still so that I could understand what they were talking about.

She did not even want you to be king, my lord. She said you were too weak. And far too trusting to become the kind of king we need. That is one of the reasons why you sent her away, do you not remember?

I frowned. Who was my mother talking about?

My father's voice, still unwavering like an old oak in a storm, came back to me through the doors.

She is my mother, Caoimhe. I do not understand how you expect me to turn her away when she has come begging forgiveness and asking for mercy.

Each of these terse sentences brought me a missing piece of a mystery I could not see clearly. Why had my father sent his own mother away? Why did she think he was too weak a king? And most importantly, why had she returned? My mother's voice became even higher with her indignation.

If you insist upon her living within our home, I will have to ensure that none of our children are infected with her poison. I will not forget what she did.

My father's voice penetrated through the walls now as he responded to my mother:

Enough! My mother will stay here. Her grandchildren are free to visit her if they wish it or if she wishes it. She is kin, Caoimhe. You will do well to remember that.

After that, my mother did not speak any more. Instead, my father's voice lowered slightly as he relented.

I understand your need to protect our children. And if it appeases you, we shall tell them not to visit her.

My mother did not speak. I could picture her beautiful face hardened now. Even after compromise, she would not find it in herself to soften. My father's sigh echoed as he spoke again, his voice quiet and tired.

My love, I have placed her in the furthest halls. She has brought her own handmaidens. You will see her in the evenings when we awaken if she cares to eat with us. Which she has assured me she is unwilling to do.

I heard my mother's footsteps as she walked towards his chamber doors. Before she opened them and walked through, I heard her hushed voice say:

I hope you do not grow to regret this decision, Cairbre. If there is one thing I have learned from your mother, it is that a wolf never loses its taste for blood. And a hare cannot outrun it for ever.

And with those words I heard her shut the heavy oak and gold doors, her quiet footsteps leaving an ominous shiver within my bones.

*

A part of my affliction, as Eithne and my mother called my mortality, was that, unlike the rest of our kind, I could go walking in the daylight. It did not burn my fair skin, nor did it affect my eyes as it did the other immortals. In fact, I found the rays of the sun soothing on my skin. I discovered this one day when I awoke in the afternoon instead of late evening and lifted back my curtain to look outside my window. The land outside took my breath away. I had never seen the brook glisten this way, nor had I seen the cobalt skies before, so different from their midnight purple hue. Birds, dozens of them, frolicked across a clear sky.

I should have waited for Eithne, perhaps. Gone back to sleep and woken when everyone else in the palace did. But the glimmer and glow of an old world born anew beckoned to me like a siren song.

In my nightgown, I went out to find strawberries and red roses. Everything was so clear in the daylight. I gathered some in the fabric of my gown and brought them back to my room, examining them and tasting them to see if they tasted any different. They were warm, but they tasted much the same. I held this little secret of mine – that I could walk out in the sun – safe in my chest. I did not want to share it with anyone yet. The desire to hold things within me that no one else knew about made me feel powerful in a palace where I was powerless.

Perhaps this was why I went to visit her. My father's mother. It was the same curiosity that led me outside to the sun, and it was a part of me that had given me a beautiful gift for following my own heart. I did not doubt it when it spoke to me again, the whispers large inside my mind. What could my mother be speaking of? Why had I never met this grandmother? What could she possibly be doing here after all these years, and why had my father exiled her?

The palace had been full of whispers since she had arrived a few days before with her own people to serve her. Word was that ravens the size of horses had brought her in a silver and amethyst carriage; staff had come in an onyx carriage. She had arrived at midnight and my father had gone to greet her. My mother had forbidden my siblings and me from going outside at the time.

Children, however, are a law unto themselves. And I was a lonely child, longing for kin to see me and love me despite my mortality. So I waited. I waited until my grandmother was settled in her far wing of the palace. I waited until my parents and siblings and Eithne and all the staff had fallen asleep before tiptoeing through the labyrinth of hallways that would lead me to the darkest wing of the palace. Why would my father, a largely just and fair man, give my grandmother this cobweb-filled, lightless place, I wondered as I quietly moved through the dark passageways. The ebony door stood at the end of the passage, like a yawning mouth of the night sky – eternal. On the front of this door, a large silver wolf emblem gleamed, its ruby eyes a warning for any and all that stood before it.

Those ruby eyes glittered despite the absence of any light to make them glitter. Mesmerised, I moved to touch the wolf's open mouth. But before my fingers could reach it . . .

. . . the door swung open.

A pale face and long, dark hair greeted me. She was a tall woman, her eyes a bright violet, just like my own. None of my siblings had these eyes, and for years they had made me feel even more isolated from my family, from anyone else in this palace. My heart thumped in my chest as I stared up at her. Her features were schooled to a passivity, but those violet eyes blazed in a way mine never had.

'G-grandmother.' I stammered, suddenly deeply unsure of myself and whether being here was a wise plan, 'I j-just wanted to . . .' What had I wanted to do precisely? I did not know.

Her eyes were on me for what felt like an eternity until finally she spoke.

'Come in, child. I have been expecting you.' And with that, she swept back into the darkness, leaving the door open for me to walk in.

I took a deep, slow breath to steady my nerves. Then I followed her into the darkness.

The inside of my grandmother's chambers was very different from the cobweb-covered dark passage I had walked through to see her. An assortment of crystals had been charmed to glow with light, dappling the room with an ethereal glow. Her black gown was covered in delicate silver filigree that captured this light. The motif of the silver wolf was everywhere, along with dark ravens and golden owls. I went to run my fingers along the feathers of one of the owls as we walked past them and had to snatch my hand back in a hurry when it turned to me and hooted in indignation, clearly unhappy at being disturbed.

'Be careful. Many objects in here have a mind of their own,' my grandmother muttered as she led me through to a luxurious room with a large, polished oaken table. It had already been set with two places: lavender and poppy seed bread and honeyed milk at what I assumed was my place and a strange, dark drink in a crystal chalice for her. She sat first, then gestured for me to sit down. I sat across from her as she watched me carefully, those violet eyes so like my own, studying me with an unnerving clarity.

'How old are you now, child?' she asked, her voice sweetened like the honeyed milk in my glass before me.

'Twelve, your ladyship,' I said quietly.

'A teachable age,' she mused. 'Not a child any more, not a woman yet.' Her eyes seemed to be calculating something about me. My eyes followed her hand as she reached for her drink and I reached for my own honeyed milk. For a moment, we sipped in silence. Then . . .

'My mother does not know I am here,' I announced, then clapped my hand on my mouth. I should not have told her that. Why had I said this to her?

She simply kept looking at me, her face unreadable.

I stared at her. She was unlike any other being I had ever met. Her unnerving gaze, her strange blazing eyes, her long, dark hair and her presence that seemed to fill the room. 'I do not know why I am here,' I told her, honestly.

She smiled and her sharp features softened slightly. 'I know why you are here.'

When she did not elaborate any further, I asked, 'How do you know when I do not know?'

She sat back in her ornate chair, making it look more like a throne. 'You would like to know why.'

I carefully took her words in as though they were a conch from the babbling brook that I was rolling in my hand. Within her words was a secret, but it was hidden inside a fog. I could see the shape of it, but could not guess why. She watched me struggle before speaking again. 'You must have wondered. Why you were born so unlike the others. Why you were given the gift of mortality whereas the rest of us are cursed to know life for ever.'

It was the first time anyone had ever spoken to me about my affliction that way. That mortality was the blessing and immortality the curse. I could only stare at my grandmother in silence.

'Why do you think of immortality as a curse?' I almost whispered the question.

My grandmother placed her hands forward and I watched as a piece of parchment began to materialise between her fingers. She lifted it and said softly, 'Has anyone ever read you a poem?'

I nodded my head quietly. Many of the tales that Eithne read to me were written in verse and I far preferred them to a story told otherwise.

My grandmother handed me the parchment and said,

'Most poems in this world and the next are written by those who know death. The beauty of this work rests upon the tension between love and death. The reason why mortals are blessed is because love is not eternal. They have a finite time to love one another before death takes them. This is what poetry is about. Courage, love, sorrow, all encapsulated in a life that must come to an end. Do you understand?'

I frowned and then shook my head. She gestured to the parchment. 'Read it.'

> If I were ever to love again, may it be the raven-haired Medh.
> Bring me the night dipped in moonlight upon which I sang her song.
>
> And upon her berry-red lips my name, in dreams she came to me.
> So I, a humble traveller, was graced with this elegant, dark queen.
>
> We flew within her carriage, beyond glittering star-drenched rivers
> and mountains covered in glistening snowdrops and ice.
>
> And as we flew, she showed me all her secrets and told me
> of every sacred story she knew. And I, no longer weary

from my days of walking, settled into this quiet night.
And raven-haired Medh with her violet eyes held me

till the dew appeared on the amber flowers in the
sunlight.
And then, like the stars, she disappeared, and took her
secrets with her.

Oh, if I were to ever see her again, I would ask her to
never leave.
If I had an eternity to give, then hers for ever I would
wish to be.

But I am to age, whereas she will not. And even upon
my death
as I die weary and old, I will guard the secrets she gave
to me.

If I were ever to love again, may it be the
raven-haired Medh.
Bring me the night dipped in moonlight upon which I
sang her song.

I looked up at my grandmother, her eyes distant now, an eerie quiet in this room. The poem was strange but one I wanted to read again immediately. The words were haunting in and of themselves, unlike any that Eithne had ever read to me, or any that were in our library – the yearning of the one who wrote it wept from every word on the parchment. 'Grandmother,' I said softly, 'who wrote this?'

She shook her head. 'It does not matter. It was long ago now.' She took the scroll from me and within seconds it had disappeared.

We sat together in silence as the words rested heavily between us. I sighed and looked up at my grandmother and said, 'I am sorry. For what you lost.'

My grandmother looked back at me and smiled. 'Astute child. This is why I knew you would be the one who would come to find me.' She reached out carefully and touched my chin. Her hand was cold but I did not flinch. 'To be immortal is to watch everything around you decay. Even love. Even hope. The poets, they know that. Do you understand?'

I nodded carefully. When put this way, it seemed as though my mortality was more of a gift than a curse. At least, if I ever loved and lost, I would not have to be cursed to carry that grief for ever. At least, if someone I loved ever wrote a poem about our love, it would outlast me and not be the last thing I ever held to remember them. To hold the words of someone long dead, and treasure them as the last memory of our love, would be a curse indeed.

My grandmother took another sip of her drink and I followed suit by eating the lavender cake.

'Why did my father send you away?' I asked quietly.

My grandmother turned away slightly as she spoke her next words. 'You read the poem. Why do you think he sent me away?'

She looked down at the milk in front of me and said to me quietly, 'Promise me this, Credhe. You will learn to accumulate power. More power than anyone in this land. No matter the cost, you will become the most powerful woman in all of Ireland.'

I sighed. 'I do not know how to do this, Grandmother. I am mortal. I am young.'

She smiled at me, but this time it was razor sharp and there was a glint in her eye. 'Neither your youth nor mortality will stop you. I will show you how to accumulate more power than you could ever imagine. But you must make me three promises in return.'

I nodded, my own violet eyes meeting hers with eagerness. 'Of course. Anything.'

Her smile widened and for a moment it struck me just how much that smile reminded me of that of a wolf. 'Marry a mortal. Let verse be your guide. And be fearless.'

I visited my grandmother every day from that day. An era passed learning under her. And slowly she turned me from a quiet child who loved flowers into a wily woman who used witchcraft to gain everything I desired. Knowledge, when wielded with a warrior's might, was as powerful as a freshly crafted sword.

'Kings are only as grand as the wealth they hoard, Credhe,' my grandmother would tell me, pressing the flower of the poppy and dragon's blood into my hands as she taught me a spell for dreams. It was under her tutelage that I learned to dreamwalk, the same way I had learned to daywalk.

'Dreams,' my grandmother told me, one night before my sixteenth year began, 'are the doorway between the mortal world and the otherworld. It is how we can walk into the minds of mortals, influence them, grant them premonitions.'

She had shown me how to aim for wealthy merchants first. How their greed would leave their dreams open. She showed me how to find the object of their desires, their greatest wishes, and tell them that I would grant them their boons. And in return I could ask for portions of their wealth. Diamonds as big as my little finger, rubies as large as my fist, sapphires and emeralds that glittered like light was trapped within them, chalices made of gold, horns of reddish gold, a silver bowl for the juice of berries.

It was Eithne who first noticed the accumulation of rubies and sapphires, the emeralds that poured out from inside my bed. She asked me where I had found them. I told her I did not find them, I had earned them. She did not seem happy with my answer, but what could she do?

I began wearing deep blue silken gowns, necklaces that dripped with diamonds in such a way that my own once ash-blonde hair sparkled like it was silver and gold.

The maids would linger a little longer now, touching the jewels I kept in a chest by my bedside. The guards started bowing low when I would walk into the rooms. And soon, the courtiers, who had taken no notice of me before, began to send their daughters to speak with me. I shared these stories with my grandmother, who laughed a strange laugh, full of mirth and the bitterness of old gooseberries.

'Nothing changes in these realms. Power is accumulated over time, but both mortals and immortals are magpies,' she told me. 'Now, my dear, let me show you what the mortal kings and queens can give you.'

Under my grandmother's careful but strict instruction, I learned how to appear in the dreams of mortal kings and queens and find out the things they desired the most in the world. And then I would send them messages to leave me offerings.

My grandmother showed me how to bless them in return, for royalty was always more complicated than the simple merchant. Their dreams were of more power, the need for heirs, the desire to live and reign long. But the returns for those boons were of equal measure. A chair of mahogany covered in Alpine gold made by the finest of craftsmen, a bed made in the east by Turbe garnished in precious stones and gold, a bower made of silver and gold. I had all this and more carted into my wing until there was no more room for more.

Yes, my powers were raw, unlike my parents', who were able to elegantly summon storms or turn water to ice, their elemental powers renowned across the kingdom. My sisters danced with the power of fauna, bringing flowers and ivy and trees to life out of nothing. My brothers could work with water, whether lake or sea or river, and command it at will. But I could walk through the land of dreams, a gift that few immortals had cultivated.

To his credit, my father did not flinch or look surprised when I told him about leaving home. Instead, he raised an eyebrow and asked, 'Do you know what it would take to build a palace of your own?'

I smiled. 'Do not concern yourself with me, Father. I know well enough what I must do.'

My mother's eyes had narrowed in suspicion, but I was too engaged with my own plans to pay her much mind at the time.

It was only when I began to fill chest after chest, room after room, with my belongings that my mother, overcome with curiosity, stayed up until the late hour of noon to follow me.

When my father summoned me, I walked into his throne room with my head held high. It was only when I saw my grandmother there that I faltered.

'Credhe,' my father started, his usually steady and powerful voice quiet. 'Is what your mother says true? Have you been spending time with your grandmother after you were forbidden from going to that part of the palace?'

I looked into my father's cold stare without an iota of fear, just as my grandmother had taught me. 'I have.'

I could see my grandmother hiding a smile from the corner of my eye.

'Why,' my father said slowly, 'would you disobey us?'

Years of repressed anger at being ignored turned into a cold pride as I answered. 'Why should I stay away from the only kin who has given me power, knowledge, everything I could possibly ask for?'

My mother and my sisters gasped at my words. No one ever spoke to my father that way.

My father gritted his teeth and turned to his mother. 'Did you tell her? What you did?'

My grandmother's face was a mask of quiet calm as she looked upon my father. 'I did say to you, Cairbre, that you would have a child more powerful than any in the land.'

'Finish it.' The soft words echoed in the terse hall.

My mother, trembling with rage, was staring at my grandmother with such fury that a slight chill ran through me.

My grandmother sighed. 'Does it matter?'

'It matters.' When my grandmother did not speak, my mother told my father sharply, 'Finish it. Tell her the rest.'

My father turned to me, the anger in his voice barely contained. 'She cursed you. She is the reason you were born mortal. She is the reason why you are so different from us.'

I stilled, my eyes widening as I took in his words. Slowly, I walked to my grandmother, my violet eyes meeting hers.

And then, I sank to my knees and kissed her hands. 'Thank you, Grandmother. For giving me the gift.'

Unlike my sisters or my brothers, I chose my own betrothed. By then, all the land knew me as the woman who had built her own goddesshood. To my own kind, I was a certain kind of terror and wonder at once. A self-made goddess who had shaped her own destiny with her own two hands. The accumulation of my wealth came with a thousand stories. But you know how stories are. They change in each storyteller's mouth. And rarely are they favourable to women.

Instead of goddess of love and spirits, they called me the most deceptive woman in all of Ireland. Said that my wealth could only have been amassed through manipulation and lies, treachery and deceit. Women like me were dangerous. We taught other women that they could do the same – build another destiny.

Medh, my grandmother, chose to stay on in my father's palace. When I visited, I only visited her wing. She stayed for five more years before telling me, 'Credhe, it is time for me to move on elsewhere.'

And I asked her, 'Where will you go? Come stay with me.'

She shook her head. 'I am tired of the kindness of kin. I would like to live on my own terms.'

I could see it in her eyes then. This was her way of saying this was the last time we would be together.

'Do not waste your tears on me, child,' she decreed. 'You have learned all you need from me.'

I had always known one day she would leave my father's palace, but I had thought she would come to my own chalk-walled, earthen, beloved palace. But I respected her enough to know not to ask again and bid her farewell as requested. 'Remember,' she told me, 'marry a mortal. Choose nothing less than a poet.'

I had nodded, tears shining in my eyes as I embraced her for the last time.

I always said that a man who could write me a poem worthy of my attention would be the man who would hold my heart. I saw Cael in my dreams. Tall, broad warrior, his brooding eyes and dark hair, his generous mouth and his hands, which he often used to wield both sword and magic. I knew I wanted him then. The way I knew I had wanted power.

So I visited him in his dreams. I asked him to write me a poem. He was headed for war. I knew this. But he came to me first. The first man to write a poem that did not praise my eyes or my beauty, but instead composed an ode to all that I had acquired in my long quest for power. It was as though he truly saw me. The first man to ever do so. He had stood among his men in my own household as he recited. But Cael was mortal. As mortal as I. It was no wonder that his poem was so honest, so true to who I was that I had taken his face in my hands, kissed him till it felt as though the entire world had stilled for us. Cael was not the first man I had kissed, but he was the first I had ever felt as if my spirit understood. We were joined together in matrimony on that day itself. We spent seven blissful days together, a paradise crafted in this home I had built with my own two hands. Those were the most beautiful seven days I had ever known.

Cael's goodness made a giver out of me. I went with him to the battlefields. I fed his army fresh milk from my own well-tended cows. I fed them stew and cared for the sick and the injured. My generosity won me much praise, but I did not care. All I cared about was the way Cael saw me and I saw him. We knew each other the way a bird knows the sky or the oak knows the earth it is rooted in. Three years we spent together on battlefields, but even through war and bloodshed I held the hand of my beloved, and suddenly the roar of war was simply the din in the distance. All that mattered was the way Cael kissed me, held me, his fingers brushing through my silver-gold hair, and called me beautiful. No one had ever said it the way he said it before.

We spent nights reading poetry to one another, and never ran out of laughter and song, even through the worst moments of war.

I had never known a love like that. I knew in those moments, the few we had, that I would never again know a love like that. My parents had been distant with each other, their love bound with royal duties. But what I felt with Cael was warm and true. It was as though he brought the sun he walked into. When he was away, the whole world felt colder, greyer, more lonely.

He was mortal, but I did not expect the end to be so sudden. And so soon. I had wrapped his armour in my magic, giving him every ounce of power I had to keep him safe far beyond a mortal warrior. I thought my magic gained from the aos sí would keep him safe.

I was wrong.

When they told me he had died, it was as though my own soul died with him. I asked them how it happened. It was a sword blessed with its own magic. Just enough to destroy mine. Just enough to take my Cael.

In that moment, I once again thanked my grandmother. To know an eternity without Cael would have been the most terrible suffering I could ever imagine.

I looked for his body for days and nights, each moment, it felt like my heart was blackening and curdling with grief so strong, it made me want to toss myself from a cliff. I could not keep living like this. I knew I could not. When we found him, and brought him to his grave, I stood and howled the first and last poem I would ever write.

And then I chose to lay down beside him. Hold him in my arms even then, even at the very end.

They will tell I died of sorrow.

I did not.

I died knowing that I was free to die.

I chose to die, knowing I would see him again.

PLUS SHE CAN DRIVE YOUR GETAWAY CAR FASTER THAN ANY

Wendy Erskine

The Labour Pains of the Ulaid

Only Finny left in the place now, along the Loanen. The eldest brother, Concho, killed at twenty-six. The daddy, known as Ol Sexy Blue Eyes, dead a few years back. Ness, the middle one, returned and then left again. Sick face and busted veins, he said he was working on the sites, but what could he have lifted? Not much.

The lot of them, cursed.

Down the Loanen, to where it meets the brae, then along the wynd of the old McStrudder land to get to the town. Three-mile walk, there and back. Finny does every day. This morning the new girl in the shop looked at his hands, ten black crescents. But in Magill's it was old Mary as usual and she said as she always does, well Finny love, what did you see on the road today?

I just saw the morning and that would be the height of it.

In his bag the three giant bottles, plastic. Old Mary says that she'll see him tomorrow. She waves goodbye.

Finny might pause before he reaches the house. Bag's heavy. Its plastic cuts into his hands by the end of the first mile. To tip the heavy bottle, two-litre, without spilling it, is hard. You fuckin bastard, he says when the drink runs down him and onto the grass. Fuckin bastard thing, he mutters, to the wide fields. And then he continues on his way, boots loud on the tarmac of the road, whispery on the grassy sides of the Loanen.

That particular spot though. Place between the old sycamore and the oak, where the hedge dips like a lazy smile. He'll always stop there. That part of the Loanen. In winter when all's skeletal you can see right to the mountains, but in summer, the hedge clotted with white, you can't look further than the ditch. That sheuch could swallow a sheep or calf.

But the Loanen is long and straight. Blind man could drive it.

Blind woman could drive it.

Could only have been deliberate, her coming. Could only have been.

Hinges half attached to air because the wood has splintered and fallen away, he opens the gate to home. Walks past the old car on bricks. Inside, lights a fire, always slow to take, a puny flame. He sits at the big kitchen table and fills a glass from the first bottle. Finny drinks and reads the paper he bought. A woman has been killed. There's an enquiry over a road collapsing into a sinkhole. In the summer there's to be a music festival on the coast.

Upstairs are the bedrooms. Dead and gone, Ol Sexy's door isn't opened but Finny knows the ceiling paper is stained brown. Water getting in from those smashed slates. Finny still sleeps at the front of the house, same single bed for a boy. But twenty-nine now. Twenty-nine. Rattle in the wind from the frame that's always been loose. Come a storm, the chimney whines. Finny when a kid thought of ghouls and tortured souls, alone in the house by himself. Concho away, smuggling, dealing, doing what he did, Ness out in the woods with those weirds, all taking eel. Ol Sexy Blue Eyes was in a bar somewhere, holding court, silver tongue, some barmaid listening to his nonsense as he ran his hand over his thinning black hair.

On the night she came, Finny was ten. Had been alone for two days because they were all at the Hema, in a town forty miles away. An ancient cattle-trading fair had shifted into a week-long bacchanal. The Hema was not for kids. They flocked from around the country, women and men, to that ancient cattle fair that had got eeled up, coked up. That night the rain lashed the windows and the glass in the windows flexed in the gale. Finny thought he heard knocking at the door. And then the screaming sound in the chimney. But again, knock knock knock. Robbers maybe because there was money in the house. Ol Sexy Blue Eyes had recently sold the five fields. The notes were in tartan tins under the sink in the kitchen. They were in the ice box in the fridge. Would robbers knock? There it was again.

Finny slipped out of bed and went down the stairs, the knocking in the darkness and now a voice shouting please. A woman's voice. He listened to hear if there were any men. But he only heard her, so reached up to slide across the bar. The woman's head was bent, her face not visible as the rain fell on her. Her car, she said, had gone off the road. Was in the ditch. Strangers had knocked on their door before. Finny minded the time Ol Sexy Blue Eyes let the boy on the run sleep in the barn. He opened the door for her to come in.

He walked behind her as she went up the stairs, her hair hanging in soaking tartles, leather jacket dripping. When she paused on the landing he opened the door of his bedroom. You can sleep there, he said, pointing to his bed. When he switched off the light, he could hear her breathing from his spot on the floor in the corner.

His thin sleep woken by her teeth chattering, the bed shaking, and he knew she had a fever because he had seen Ol Sexy Blue Eyes like that the winter past, so he went to the bathroom press and the stack of old stuff, pulled out dusty curtains, still with their hooks, put them on top of her. Back again and there were sheets and towels, dressing gowns, skirts and dresses that had belonged to his dead mother. There was a matted fur coat like a bear. Finny kept going, layer upon layer, until he couldn't hear the chattering.

When dawn broke, she was sleeping. Face bone white and had a sick sheen but still, she was sleeping. Finny went out and walked down the Loanen and saw where the car was, dipped in the ditch. Number plate had been ripped off but no tyre marks on the road.

House was a mess then. House smelt of fat, every pan with a solid grey inch of it. The kitchen stacked with boxes of electricals that Concho was storing for someone. Half smoked red beside whiskey in a mug that said Star Bright. Rust on the fridge bled a watery brown. The woman would be away before they got back. They could not say he should have sent her to the barn. Concho had said that the boy who was on the run probably died in a ditch somewhere. His leg was fucked, Concho said. His leg was totally balloxed.

For three nights Finny was on the floor in the corner. Each morning he brought the woman a little food from what they had left him, made her tea. She started not to look that sick way any more. She pushed the sheets and towels and curtains off her. Thank you, she said, and her voice was now a cool drink of water. Thank you. She wasn't young but she wasn't old either. She wasn't pretty but she wasn't ugly either.

The school was miles in the other direction. Ol Sexy had said he should lie low while they were away. No hardship, not to go to the school, with its damp walls and gouged desks, the yap-voiced teacher. But he could walk down the Loanen where he wouldn't be seen. And so he left the house. On the side of the road he came across a dead hare. The flies were settling on its wide, milky eye. He went down to the river at the bottom of the brae, at the part where it was deepest, where the black water moved slowly and you could skim a stone on the surface.

As Finny headed back up the Loanen, past the car still stuck in the ditch, he could see, coming from the house, a thin curl of smoke. When he opened the door, he saw the place full of light. The windows had been cleaned and on the stove was a pot of stew. All of the stuff that Concho was storing had been moved. Things gleamed. On the table was a jug with branches and flowers from the garden. Out in the back yard, a washing line had been strung up and didn't white sheets billow in the wind. And then she came in, the woman. She indicated for him to sit down, then brought bread to the table.

Thank you, she said.

He ate the bread and drank the mug of tea she gave him. He looked at what she was wearing: black jeans, black boots and a black jumper. On the corner of the chair was her leather jacket.

Thank you, she said again, touching his arm.

No bother.

She said that her name was Macha. Macha.

Macha asked why he was alone and he told her they'd be back in another day or so from the Hema.

Concho'll be able to get your car out of the ditch, he said. So that you can get back to where you came from.

She made no reply. Later, Macha said there was room in the bed for the two of them. Well, she was thin and he was only small. She wore her jeans and her jumper. The black leather jacket hung on the wooden frame of the bed. In the morning, Macha washed in cold water, then lit the fire.

Hard brakes! slamming doors! yelps! Ol Sexy Blue Eyes, Concho and Ness had got back. Son of a bitch, motherfucker, he's not going to get a penny from me. Over my fucking dead body! Then Concho laughing. Macha and Finny sat at the kitchen table. Door burst open and in they came – to see polished brass and the table with the white cloth. On the stove coffee, and on the table a freshly baked loaf of bread wrapped in a tea towel.

Holy fuck! Concho said.

Ol Sexy Blue Eyes poured himself a coffee. What kind of devilment is this? he said, looking around him. Fairy magick. A miraculous fucking appearance.

Her car broke down, Finny said.

That's the car on the Loanen, said Ness. How could anyone go off the road there?

Ol Sexy Blue Eyes took in Macha's black jumper, her jeans, her scrubbed clean face, as she began to sweep the floor.

How long is this miracle to reside with us? asked Ol Sexy Blue Eyes, smoothing his black hair.

Concho said that he would get the car lifted. He regarded Macha as she moved across the floor, shook his head at Ness. No fucking ass!

*

Finny's bottles on the kitchen table. If he looks through them, the world is amber. He knew not to ask Macha questions.

When Ol Sexy Blue Eyes started holding court, she used to get up and do something else, something deliberately dull. Of course he let her stay. There hadn't been a woman in the house for ten years and now there was. There was Macha. He called her my dear, sweetheart, darling, cutie pie, the lady of the house, cookie and she made no response. There was Macha. She wanted there to be no talk. It was a condition of her being there. Finny could understand that. She did not want anyone to speak of her. No one. When one day in the school they were asked to draw their family, he put Concho, Ness and Ol Sexy Blue Eyes at the table. Not even a smudge to represent Macha.

The world is thick amber and warm. He knew not to ask Macha questions. He knew not to talk about her to anyone.

Macha made a garden out of the wilderness beyond the yard and Finny can see it yet, even after more than ten years, the arch she constructed for the roses and creepers. He takes a drink. The bed was warm when she was in it and sometimes if he woke, her arm would be over his chest. No possessions beyond her car, clothes and the leather jacket. When Ol Sexy Blue Eyes died, Finny made a bonfire of his stuff, his clothes, his things. Hoped it was going to be a crazy blaze but it just crept and smouldered for days. When there was only ash left, Finny took a stick and wrote her name.

Ol Sexy Blue Eyes had taken to exercising in the barn with rusty weights and this amused Concho.
 Too fucking young for the ol boy. If she even likes men.
 She's a strange one, Ness replied.
 She's that all right.
 She's strange. Maybe she's a succubus.
 Suck a what? Concho laughed. Can't see your woman sucking anything too much, fuck sake.
 Ness shrugged.
 You and your words from books.
 It was true. Ness loved to read. Reading and eel. That's what he loved.

A friend of Concho's called by one day. Ku. Him and Concho were in the money after shifting some gear for a big name. Big name from the south. Concho went to the city with a girl he met and they partied in fancy hotels. He came back with bags of clothes with badges and logos. Ku bought a second-hand sports car. Ku, T-shirt on a cold day, said that he could handle a car better than anyone he knew. Speed was a hard-on. Ku and Concho were in the kitchen and Macha was filling a kettle with water at the time. She switched off the tap. Concho talked about the time as a kid he'd taken Ol Sexy Blue Eyes' car down the Loanen and back. He'd had to take a cushion from the sofa, put it on the driver's seat, so that he could see out. Macha turned on the tap again. When she put the kettle on the stove, she said quietly, I'd be faster.

What was that? Ku asked.

I'd be faster. I'd be faster than either of you.

Concho laughed. The woman who drove a car into a ditch on a fucking straight road?

I'd be faster.

Your head is up your ass.

I'd be faster.

It was agreed that at dawn each of the three would drive Ku's car down the brae to where it met the Loanen, and then they would finish in front of the house. Ness would make sure that each car started at the top of the minute. He'd be in the back seat each time so that he could drive the car to the top again for the next competitor. Ol Sexy Blue Eyes brought the big clock from the hall out onto the road.

First came Concho, flying down the Loanen. He got out of the car, let out a whoop. Beat dat, motherfuckers! he said. And then Ku. Finny's eyes moved from the car to the clock to the car. And then the clock. Because Ku was quicker by six seconds. Ku affected a lack of surprise. He got out leisurely. As I told you, he said. As I foretold.

*

plus she can drive your getaway car faster than any

And then it was Macha. Ku and Concho weren't even watching at the beginning, but as the car began to shoot down the Loanen they looked with alarm at the sweeping hand. When Macha got out, she wiped her hands on her black jeans and went inside. She made a pie that night, with apples. Ku had left by that stage and Concho and Ness were quiet. Macha had shaved eight seconds off Ku's time.

Finny finishes the glass, goes to the cupboard to see if there is any bread left and there is, the heel of the loaf, dry and hard. He moves closer to the fire. Well.

He sighs. Well. Things changed. One time when Ol Sexy came in from lifting those rusty weights he said something and Macha laughed, briefly. Finny had looked up because it hadn't been that funny, Sexy Blue Eyes usually wasn't, although he had started to get lean. He had begun to be polite to Macha. Thanks for the dinner. The best I ever tasted. He stopped talking so much, sat quiet at the kitchen table.

Then one night Finny woke up and Macha wasn't there. He lay there in the dark, waiting for her to return. But she was in Ol Sexy Blue Eyes' bedroom because Finny could hear. Finny didn't speak to her in the morning and he threw in the bin the food that she had made for him. But he had to get used to it. It became the way things were, and anyway, Macha didn't seem any more impressed with

Ol Sexy Blue Eyes than usual, although she slept with him at night. The ol boy, Concho said, he's getting ripped. One time Finny put on Macha's leather jacket. Do I look like I got a motorbike? he asked. It smelt warm and of oil. It smelt a bit like an animal. Where did you get this jacket? he asked. She said she couldn't remember.

Then it happened that Macha started to get tired. After she'd been chopping wood, she had to sit at the table. Her arms looked not so thin and her face filled out. It became not so unusual to catch her asleep on the sofa. She even took to wearing a pair of old tweed trousers of Ol Sexy Blue Eyes because her black jeans didn't fit her any more. The cronies or the wrecking crew or the desperadoes, as Ol Sexy Blue Eyes called his friends, saw little of him. There was one night, dark and stormy as when Macha first arrived, when the family was all there. The fire blazed and Macha had lit candles on the mantelpiece and the length of the table. She had taken willow branches from the garden and arranged them. The food was good. Concho said thank you. He was in a reminiscing mood.

Wasn't it some fucking caper that day with the driving, Macha? You were mighty.

Ness seemed more like he was before the eel habit and hanging around with the weirds. He told them the story of something he had read, set thousands of years ago. As he recounted the old myth, his moving hands cast dancing shadows on the walls. And wasn't Macha, at the head of the table, expecting a baby?

There's a bird that Finny sometimes watches for if he moves to the garden. He doesn't know the name of it and so he just calls it the bird. It comes close enough but always observes a distance. He has put out bread, but if he is sitting there, the bird won't violate its rules. Well, he has his own similarities. He goes every day for the same bottles. Of course he could make changes, if he wanted. Finny has thought about the old rusting heap on bricks next to the house, Macha's old car from the ditch. He has lain underneath it. You can taste the metal in your mouth. If he kicked the bricks it would collapse on him and he would feel the weight on his thorax. He might hear the crack of ribs. He would not die straight away, he reckons. Rather it would be a slow seep, through the dark of the night, to the dawn. Concho died in an alleyway in a city, shot. Concho could have made a run for it, they said, but he didn't. It was strange. Finny unscrews the lid of the bottle again.

It was a year after Macha's arrival. Time again for the Hema, with its singing and drinking and gambling and racing and dancing. Exciting women were being brought in from another land. Ol Sexy Blue Eyes said that if Macha wanted, he would not go this year, even though, since he was sixteen years old, there hadn't been a fair that he had missed. Not a one. Macha had said go. Finny would be there with her. That was enough. But she was clear on one point. He should not mention her to anyone. There should be no talk of her. Well, Ol Sexy Blue Eyes said, why would I not mention you?

Because Macha just told you not to, Finny said.

Yes, said Macha.

Well, said Ol Sexy Blue Eyes, as you wish. As you wish.

So for a few days it was just them again, Finny and Macha, the rain on the roof and on the radio some nonsense. The kitchen was warm and with the rest away there was no hurry to get anything done.

On the third night, they were peeling potatoes. They stood, the pot between them filled with water, Macha with a knife, Finny with a knife, the rhythm of working like that, seeing the creamy white beneath the mud, the piles of scraps rising. It was nice. But then Finny cut too light and the knife moved too quick, slicing through the ball of his thumb. At first it didn't bleed and he gazed in wonder at the gash, the layers within. And then the blood came running, pouring into the water, pluming pink. Needs a stitch most likely, Macha said, and then laughed because they both knew they wouldn't be going to a doctor's. She went upstairs and came down with a sheet from the press that she had torn into strips, winding it tight around Finny's thumb. When the blood seeped through, she unwound it, pressed the wound closed, wound it again.

They were eating when there came a knock at the door. They looked at each other. They've got the wrong house, Finny said, whoever they are. They've made a mistake. Macha settled back again into her chair. But the knocking started again, and the shouting. It was a man's voice. He was shouting for them to open up. When they did, Finny saw a man in his early twenties, eeled out, jaw working, eyes darting into the house. I've been sent for the woman, he said. She needs to come now.

He pushed past Finny and went into the kitchen. Now, he said to Macha. You need to get in the car.

Macha sat where she was.

She's not going anywhere with you, Finny said.

Wanna see the old guy lose his legs, because he's gone run up debts with the Gallens. And the Gallen brother-in-law, who usually steps in to make the peace, well didn't the fucking old guy do something to piss him off the other day and so he said, the brother-in-law, let him be beat to fuck, I don't care.

The man asked if he could have a drink of water, which he finished in quick gulps. People were in the bar, he said. The best one in the town. And big Gallen says how the best type of woman never lets a man leave the house hungry or horny. Hungry or horny. And Ol Sexy Blue Eyes starts sniggering, like he's got some big secret, and big Gallen notices this and says, have you got something you want to say? And Ol Sexy says no, but he's still laughing. And big Gallen repeats, you got something you want to say? Like he should've kept his mouth shut when he was already in debt, but he says, the best woman never lets a man leave the house hungry or horny, plus she can drive your getaway car faster than any motherfucker. Well didn't everyone laugh at Ol Sexy and big Gallen got angry. As if that exists, he says. And Ol Sexy says, it does and it's living in my house. There was a cheer. Big Gallen says, sarcastic like, if that's the case then let's bring her here and let us see. She can race against Aleksi. And Ol Sexy says, why not? Aleksi Virtanen. She'll beat even him. And big Gallen said, if she wins, your debts are cancelled. If she doesn't, we shoot you in the legs. The crowd went silent then.

Macha put her hands on the table. She looked out of the window at where the arch was with its creepers and roses already taking hold. She cast her eye over the shining brass. Then she slowly got to her feet. Macha took their plates and washed them at the sink, then dried them, placed them in the dresser. As she put on her leather jacket, she took a final look around the room. Finny said that he was going too and there was nothing anyone could do to stop him. The man said that he didn't care who the fuck came just as long as the woman did because that's who he had been sent to fetch.

You could let him just lose his legs, Finny said to Macha.

The car was cold and dirty, with the eel sweat smell Finny recognised from Ness. Macha's hands were folded over her stomach, sitting in the back beside Finny. He knew that Macha would win the race. He was excited to think about their faces and how they would marvel at what they saw and then Ol Sexy Blue Eyes would feel ashamed and never speak of her ever again. They travelled, unspeaking, across bogland, scrub country, until in the distance they could see rolling hills, gentler land and then, eventually, the town. There streets were covered in papers, rubbish. There were flags and banners. A crowd of bikers had just arrived. Sprawling across the roads, tumbling onto the streets, were drinkers, revellers, men and women. There were stalls selling foods and a pig was being turned slowly on a spit. A woman was squatting in an alleyway while her friend ate a giant candyfloss. The young guy put on music like a building site as they drove out of the town, past rows of houses where some people were drinking, sofas pulled out into driveways. They were heading to the old airfield.

When Macha and Finny got out of the car, they followed the man over to a cluster of vans and cars. Big Gallen was there on a deckchair, as though it was a throne. He was surrounded by other men, other Gallens, and some who had married his daughters. Big Gallen looked at Macha's belly, let out a long slow breath. He shook his head. Eventually he spoke. Well what a fucking pathetic excuse for a man, what a sad little bantam cock needs a pregnant woman to rescue him. I don't think I have ever seen the like. Where's Ol Sexy Blue Eyes anyway? he said. Two men fetched him from one of the vans. He loped over, unshaven, frightened, his eyes swollen. He looked at Macha, then at Big Gallen, who had taken out his gun and was stroking it, tenderly, playfully, curiously, as if he had never seen it before. He held it out, trained it on a far-off point, then put it back in his pocket again. It almost seemed as though he might call the whole thing off. But then he said, let's start. Luck be a lady today.

Finny is on the next bottle. Bottle number two he regards as his friend, in the way that bottle one is not. That first one, hard to open on the journey, tastes harsh, chemical, even after all this time. Second bottle is more companionable, more mellow. Everything beginning to settle and the deadening starting, a little. Takes longer than it used to, that's for sure. When Ness was home that time, he suggested Finny should give up drink for something even stronger. No, Finny said. I go to Magill's and I get what I get. Mary already has it sitting out for me.

The race was to be two circuits, and as a courtesy to the lady, they would let her choose the car. The one she didn't want would go to Aleksi. Aleksi said he had never raced a woman, never mind a pregnant one. He didn't want to. Macha said nothing. But they both got into the cars. They had to adjust the seat so Macha could fit. The air shattered when they fired an actual gun to start the race.

They said there was something insolent about the way she drove. It was not one of those races where one car was behind and then came back in the final seconds. It was not one of those races where both cars were neck to neck the whole time. Right from the beginning Macha was ahead and she stayed that way until the car went over the line. There was silence from the onlookers. When Aleksi came to a halt, he got out of the car quickly. He was pale. That, he said, was some fucking voodoo shit.

Big Gallen from his deck chair said that, as a result of what they had just witnessed and god was his witness he had never seen the like, no further action would be taken against Ol Sexy Blue Eyes, the ridiculous old scrote that he was, and that all debts were cancelled. The woman could keep the car as her reward. Ol Sexy Blue Eyes went over to open the door for Macha. But Macha locked it. Macha did not look at him. She was bent over the steering wheel. He knocked on the windscreen, shouting her name. He blew kisses at her. He thumped his heart. But she didn't raise her head. Eventually he threw up his hands and walked off to a car full of compadres, heading back into the town.

Everyone left apart from Finny. No one noticed him leaning against the stunted tree at the edge of the airfield. When he went over to the car, he could see Macha's face twisted in agony. Her hands pressed against the windscreen. She struggled to open the door for him. Frightening sounds, like an animal, and a desperation of panting. He helped her get out of the car and she lay down on the tarmac of the airfield, writhing, tormented. There was no help from anywhere. He looked at the fields, the hills, the blank sky. He thought of Ness, hallucinating somewhere, Concho, loading up a van, driving to a handover. He imagined Ol Sexy Blue Eyes, already in a bar in the town, telling some woman a fancy story about how he'd got the better of Big Gallen. They were on their own.

Macha buckled and twisted, teeth bared. She cried out, screamed in agony, howled in anger. Her curses were blistering. They were ugly and disgusted and resolute, shapes of words, guttural sounds that promised that they would pay for what they had done to her, men, the men, the Gallens, Ol Sexy, the men, Concho, Ness, the men, they would know pain like this over and over. Finny had never seen a woman before. And now he had it shown to him how skin could split, how it could tear itself. And out came a head. An enormous shriek. The baby was slick with blood and green. And then came another. This time easier, quicker. Macha lay panting. Cut the cords, she said, just do it with your teeth. And Finny did that, once, and then twice, tang of pennies, the thick rope. Macha took a baby under each arm. Finny put the leather jacket over her and then his own coat.

It was dark when they headed back to the house in the car that Macha had been given as a reward. In the back, fastened by seat belts swaddled around them, were the two babies, one wrapped in a leather jacket and the other a coat. Macha had fed them, one to each breast, when they were on the airfield and now both slept soundly. They drove down the brae and then the Loanen. When they stopped outside the house, Macha said that she wanted back her

plus she can drive your getaway car faster than any

own black jeans. She told Finny where they were and, having picked up the key from under the smooth stone, he went in, found them and brought them out to her. She threw in the path the old tweed trousers that had belonged to Ol Sexy Blue Eyes, now covered in blood and shit. She said to Finny, you can come. He looked round at the two babies sleeping sweetly, heard their little puttering noises. And he looked too at Macha. Outside was the tumbledown house, a car on bricks, the kitchen table, his bedroom.

Finny cried in the kitchen when he watched the car drive away, slowly, carefully. She had waited for a full ten minutes before finally deciding to go. He looked down at her blood, still on his hands and under his fingernails.

That second bottle, yes, it's the one that is showing him most kindness. Finny sighs. The second bottle is his friend. But it's nearly finished. It's starting to rain outside and the ceiling in Ol Sexy Blue Eyes' room will be darkening even more. The water might even be running down the wall. Carrying the third bottle, he goes upstairs to his room, the little bed. It's chilly. Finny gets in, pulls the cover over him. But it is thin and he shivers.

Macha, you remember? My bed when you came? Please bury me in sheets, towels, dresses, curtains still with their hooks.

He thinks of her car, still outside on its bricks. Macha, please bury me.

WOMAN AND WAVE

Anne Griffin

Clíodhna's Wave

What puzzles me most about you, my love, is how you ignored everything I once told you about myself. Important morsels that might have helped with your goal.

Like how when young I'd asked my parents for a swimming pool (a full-sized pool, to be clear) for my birthday. Naturally I didn't get it. Not that it was a case of money or space. There was plenty of both in our suburban house on the hill, with our perfectly manicured lawn. I got a paddling pool instead. Poor Patricia, the childminder, was tasked with its inflation.

I insisted on filling it myself, standing in my Ralph Lauren pink-flowered swimsuit, despite the end-of-April chill, with the hose in hand. I watched the water breach that plastic wall at the same time as Patricia's frustration had breached her patience. She yelled – yes, *yelled* – that the water was making a mess of the lawn; that my mother wouldn't thank her *or me* when she came home to a mudslide rather than her gorgeous galloping green.

'But Mummy doesn't come home,' I'd retorted in calm confidence, ignoring Patricia's distress. 'And if she does, it's not till I'm asleep,' I concluded, as if that refuted the argument.

How I wish now that I had been kinder to Patricia over the years. I wasn't exactly what one might call a delightful child. Precocious and demanding, apparently. And too loud, by all accounts. So, delightful? No, not a word I never heard uttered about me. Had I been, let's face it, then surely my parents might not have abandoned me as they so often did. Working, holidaying, getting away from me. The ache for them burned bright inside of me, but I never found the right way to express it. I was forever damned to be the child who always wanted more.

And while I was right about my mother's, indeed my parents', timetable, Patricia was right about how my mother would baulk at her perfect world being mired by me.

In the end, Patricia wrestled the hose from my hands, drenching herself and me, not that I cared, loving as I did the feel of water, its cold sharpness on my shoulders, on my head, on my toes. And, oh, the goosebumps, tingling my skin! I simply loved it. My happiest of places.

I would play in that tiny spherical round of blue and white all day long for every summer that followed until I outgrew it. Me forever refusing to get out, no matter how much poor Patricia begged, even when the sun decided it was time to say its reluctant goodbyes to Cork City.

The important thing about that little tale was that you missed it, didn't you, darling? The bit about the water.

Silly, silly you.

And there you are now looking in that office mirror again. Five times in the last five minutes. Something you can't quite put your finger on is messing with that hair of yours, despite the effort you've put in this morning, back in the apartment. I watched, you see, as you dried and gelled that mane, making it sit as you so wished, even more meticulously than normal. Its height and pomposity exaggerated by the shaved sides. But that little strand, left of centre, will simply not comply, falling as it has all morning, to lie on your forehead. The fear that the rest will follow suit is too great. Again to the mirror. Again with the frustrated sigh.

Poor you.

'Is that window open?' you ask of your newest sidekick (the others, the Hectors, long gone by now). He immediately checks your clearly closed office window and door. He makes a racket of opening then closing them again, making sure you see him from the mirror, hear that he is carrying out your orders precisely. (It hadn't gone so well the day he said he didn't feel the chill you kept going on about. He learns quickly, this one. But then again, they all did, you made sure of it.)

Your hair repositioned with the little tube of gel you now keep in your pocket (due to this unseasonal inclement weather you keep going on about), you sit again at the chair, behind the desk where you think the big things. You check your weather app, again. Sunny skies. Calm, sunny Cork skies. You close your eyes and twitch your shoulders, as if the very action will somehow inject the warmth the summer-clad shoppers way down on Patrick Street are feeling.

You've been to the doctor. You've told him something isn't right. You are constantly cold. A feeling of dampness in your bones, your skin, your precious hair. But every test says you are perfect.

'It stinks in here,' you grumble now at Newbie.

But nothing comes in reply.

'Don't you smell it? Seaweed or something. For fuck's sake, it's everywhere.'

'Oh, that,' he says. 'Yeah, annoying.' He even tuts, poor petrified pet. It is, of course, a lie. He cannot smell the sulphur of the sea I wear as once I did Chanel.

Ignoring his deference, you bark your order.

'My coat.'

Newbie, in his tight black T-shirt, looks slightly lost. His reflexes slow. You point without looking up at the hook behind the door, where your woollen black coat, pulled from your winter closet this morning, now hangs out of place like a squirrel woken far too early from hibernation. Your index finger wags impatiently.

'MY. FUCKING. COAT.'

Newbie misses no more beats, grabs the weight of it and is quickly behind you, holding the coat out so you should easily be able to insert your arms, but you are shivering now, and fumble with the openings. You are twisting and turning and tutting.

'FOR FUCK'S SAKE.'

Newbie steps back, the coat still in his hands. You grab it roughly, jab it on, not bothering with the buttons, wrapping it like a blanket.

'Get out,' you say, but so quietly that Newbie must bend to hear you right. 'I said, GET. OUT.'

He is gone in an instant. To stand sentry on the other side of your office door, wondering if it's too late to take that job in Glasgow. You shiver in the sweltered heat of the June office, your bones aching. At the window now, you watch the pinks and yellows of skimpy outfits pass below. Your brain trying to make sense of the absurd. I can see your hand raise to the latch, thinking, if I open it, surely it will come, the warmth.

Do it, I will you, do it.

And, how wonderful, you do.

And there I am again. The spray of wave, landing on your cheek, your forehead, your eyelashes. Can you smell it, the brine? Is it not refreshing, my love? I swirl around you, dropping sea mist on your hair, those scarlet, raw fingers turning white with the cold and damp, or perhaps it's terror.

Don't you know me, my love? Don't you understand? It's me, your Clíodhna. Back to remind you of what you did, lest you forget. How you killed me.

Technically, of course, you succeeded. I am dead. But only in so far as I cannot pull my phone from my pocket to call you, or sit upon your knee once more to laugh along at your supposed wit. Or hold a gun to your head as you did me, before you rolled me – indeed, *rolled* me – like a striped beach ball, into the sea.

Dead, yes, dead in that way dead.

And yet I am not, am I?

Because here I am. Returned from whence you left me. I have travelled on the wind to find my way back. I can see you are finding it hard to take it all in. The power of nature was never your thing, was it? You are more a metal and hard-plastics man. Latest iPhone. Latest Audi. Latest semi-automatic. Pounding those Cork streets like you are the bees-bloody-knees.

Always about business.

Even when you fucked me.

Always an eye on not damaging the goods too much. The clients, back then in the early days when I still lived with you, didn't like it. I mean, they knew I'd fucked, been fucked, before, but they didn't like to bring that into the room, my room, where you dumped me, did they?

No, no.

We all pretended. In the moment. That I was pure. That I desired them and only them. That they were the best I'd ever had. And I was their best. I made sure of it. I earned every euro they handed you. It was why you liked me so much, wasn't it? I was both a gold mine and golden fuck. I was your special one. I knew it. The clients knew it. And, in time, the other girls I would meet would know it too.

No one quite like Clíodhna.

You called me beautiful.

Do you remember that? The first time you saw me and you addressed me so?

It was in Secret Kiss, the nightclub, crammed full of the young. And there you were, older. Stunning in your suit. Your head above the rest of the crowd, on the lookout. I was nineteen, worse for wear after the night of drink and drugs, and life. So young and yet so weary of the world. A well-spoken, precious thing, pretending she was perfect. At eighteen my parents had told me it was time to leave our mansion, their job done. And I was happy to go, to leave that empty, loveless place. They handed me the keys to a one-bedroom apartment on Pope's Quay. Blew air kisses and told me to keep in touch. My weekly allowance the stuff of dreams to most people. Money enough to gather a group of so-called friends around me who liked the life of oblivion as much as me. You had worked me out in under a minute. You read the recipe for my loyalty that I had hidden deep within my heart: simple, pure love. You shone your bright lights and promises at me, and I was yours, instantly.

How you courted me. (I like that word, don't you? Courted. It sounds stately on the tongue.) Jewellery and dinners and clothes, yes, but those things I already had. It was your attention, your apparent adoration of me that held my every breath. I was happy to drown in it, gorging myself on the very thing I had always been without.

Your apartment overlooked the city on all you owned, all you controlled. And yes, I am now ashamed to say, I did love the power you yielded. Basked in pride when we arrived at a restaurant or club, even the local newsagent's, seeing the deference. For a time, I was the queen and you the king. One can get dizzy on the power – no, not dizzy: arrogant. Like all the world and all its workers were there just for you and me. Was it wrong that I loved that too, for that short spell?

And then it turned. As all things do.

You filled me with your pills and powder until I was under your wicked spell, and you told me I should get with your friend in the spare room. I laughed, the champagne spilling from my mouth. He was a good friend, you said that night, although I'd never seen him before. But by then I was so out of it that I thought it might be my mistake, that I did know him. I did as I was told, thinking it some kind of quirk you had, wanting to watch me desired by another. Not that my brain was working at such speed right there and then, no, it was the day after I decided on this explanation. When I asked, I could see your eyes had lost their former spark and concentration, dulling, slightly, not shifting left or right, still looking at me, but there it was: the absence, the boredom with the subterfuge, with me. And yet, I doubted my instinct. Shooing it away. The fact that we still walked hand in hand that day was all the evidence required that I was still your queen.

Poor, silly me.

That hand in mine blinding me to the new order. How clever you were. Continuing the game. But there was something different now with those who surrounded you, your crew of men with shoulders wide; they didn't smile as broadly as before, and in time not at all.

Then came days when you did not come home but sent your messenger with more gifts of clothes and jewels and tablets. Attestation, I told myself, that you did still love me. That language so familiar from my younger days at home. And once or twice, another of your special friends (the boxroom totally mine now; how long had it been since I'd slept beside you?). And then another. And another. Until I understood what it was that you expected of me now. But by then I was so lost in what you had created around me, in me, that my very survival was dependent on your benevolence, my craving lost without the daily deliveries of those chemicals that bound me to you. And my love, still so desperate for you that I would have done anything. Your calculations all correct in how you snared me, making me believe that what we had was love.

Poor, silly me.

Was it weeks or months you kept me there? Me asking for you every day.

'Yeah, yeah, yeah, he'll be back later,' your messengers would say, closing the apartment door on me and the latest client.

But there was never really *you* again, was there? Late at night, maybe, or before I was fully awake in the morning there'd be the sense, the suggestion, of you. Only ever in the distance now, on the street below, a car window rolled down. Your hand visible on the door frame, the sparkle of that silver ring on your little finger. Your voice rising to me in the heat of the summer's day. And I'd close my eyes on its timbre, desiring you even still, wanting to let down my golden hair so you might climb your way back into my arms. To believe once more we were the blessed of this land.

Poor, silly me.

Two years I survived that hell. Twenty-one, and half dead. Was it a demotion when they moved me? Packed all my things, as I lay drugged on your velvet, royal blue couch. No longer your one precious thing. Sharing a house now that was tall and sleek, still on the right side of the River Lee. Perfect facade. The height of luxury. There were other women too. Elisa, Taylor, Missie, Flame. Four of us at any one time. None of them their real names. They christened me Clo.

We did your deeds. And for a while I was one of them, out of it. Lost in my misery. The endless churn of me. The endlessness of fucks and sucks and cocks and mouths and slaps and hands around my neck. And men's balls smacking against my molested skin. I smiled through it all. Praised and *oohed* and *aahed* and sighed at the right times, in the right places.

Drugged and drowning me, at the behest of powerful, handsome you.

The only cheer was when Flame sang. Sweet and high. She hardly knew she was doing it. Her tunes as instinctive and essential to her body as her eyes blink on waking in the fog of the afternoon. Even in that drug-induced state, her body, when not asleep or servicing a customer, would sing. This one day her chosen song was 'Three Little Birds'. She had to have sung it before; she had a limited repertoire. But to my ear it felt like my first time hearing it. Over and over it went, until the lyrics drilled their way into my heart. And there I was, back aged twelve in my parents' house. Me on my own, bar Patricia – Oslo, I think, that's where they were this time.

I never told you about Mr Felix, did I? The cat that wandered through our garden almost every day. I spoke with him. I fed him too, something left over from my lunch. I didn't particularly like cats, but he was something with which to pass the time when I got home from school, with which to feel connected. One day he brought me this beautiful, stunning goldfinch, red of head, black of back and gold of breast, in his mouth. Still alive, I noticed. A gift for my generosity, I supposed. I took her gently from Felix's jaw and thanked him and on he went. How I tended her that day. A small basket with a lid I stole from my mother's wardrobe, emptying out the neatly folded scarves she kept there, hiding them under my bed so Patricia would not suspect a thing when she surveilled the house. I lined it with a towel and put Tilda – that's what I christened my new little friend – in it. I brought her worms I'd dug from the garden.

Then I hid her in the shed, a place Patricia never went. But that night, when Patricia sat in the living room with the night-sitter, doing their 'handover' – a list of all the things I'd eaten, done and not done – I carried her to my bed. I whispered to her as I wrapped my body around the basket hidden under my duvet, hugging all the love I could into her, telling her not to worry, everything would be OK. At some stage I fell into the most restful sleep I had ever had.

'It's wrong to keep you, I know,' I told Tilda the following morning when she was recovered and tweeting her desire to go. I peeped in at her, opening the lid only slightly, and watched her jump about. 'It's best you go back to the sky, isn't it?'

I was naturally torn, wanting to keep prisoner this beauty I already loved, and hoped to be loved by. It was so early in the morning that the sitter was not yet up to make my toast. I tiptoed to the patio door and slipped outside. I looked up at the sky, a squint to my eye, distrusting that very thing that she called home. I cried as I lifted the lid and watched Tilda's escape. She circled, perhaps confused, or unsure, just like me, if this was what she wanted. But no sooner had I wondered if she might return, she was gone, out of view, back to freedom.

How I'd missed her over the years and years, that little thing that had entered my life for such a short time and yet had given me a true taste of belonging. And there in that tall house as Flame sang, the longing and loneliness returned, a solid ache in my bones, as if I had only just let

Tilda free once more. I went to the window to look outside, to try to find a passing Tilda to feel that love again. But none obliged.

And that is when I planned it.

Just three birds, I told Hector number one. By then we had christened all your henchmen, each one Hector, the other three following in numerical order. Not that we ever called them that out loud. Why we women chose that name, I do not know. Their actual names? No, we were never told those. Their anointment with those secret pseudonyms was the only power we held in this kingdom of yours. Hector number one, low in the pecking order, was there in our tall house most days and nights, doing your bidding, delivering food and drugs and men. He'd walk the hallways and landing, looking for signs of attempted escapes. What was it he expected the half-out-of-it might manage to do? We had no brains any more, or strength; had he and you not made certain of it?

Just three birds, I asked in the message I begged he send you from his phone – we were not allowed our own – the bravery for which came from nowhere, or was it more stupidity?

Just three birds, I wrote in a note to you that detailed how distinctive it would be. Three multicoloured birds adorning the rather stylish yet bland-in-colour sitting room, not that I mentioned that, with its white leather couches, and white furred rugs, and vanilla-smelling room diffusers, in which we 'welcomed' our guests throughout the day and night.

Something exotic, I enthused. A dash of colour. An edge. A difference. Setting us apart from the competition. And besides, it would shut me up. You liked that, didn't you, when we all just kept our mouths shut?

Imagine, I had wanted to believe that you said yes because of me, because somewhere in the deepest bit of you, I still meant something. But no, Hector number one told me, it was because you liked how my business brain was developing.

Poor, silly me.

And so, they were delivered. Three opaline Fischer's Lovebirds of the deepest, warming blue and green and orange. In a long cream-painted cage, quite elegant, that I placed in the window of the sitting room. I named each beautiful being: Azure, Emerald, Amber.

They were silent at first. Stunned by their transport and arrival. We four women gathered and looked at them looking at us. We circled. We poked fingers in their cage, wanting to feel the softness of their feathers, but pulling them out again as quick to save a nipping. The silent stand-off continued for a day or two until Flame, forgetting the new distraction, went back to her singing. And soon they answered her call with their chirps. The very air of the place losing its stale solidity and lifting so that it felt as if a wall had been taken down and we could feel the sun on our faces and the wind tickle our cheeks. We laughed. And then we laughed that we were laughing, so long had it been that such expressions were pure and joyful, no longer laden with sarcasm and false flattery. It brought Hector number one running from his daily search of our rooms, where he looked for burner phones, and weapons, and stashes of escapee cash, demanding to know what was going on.

'Oh,' he said, on seeing it was just the harmless birds, and left us to it.

Thereafter, in the mornings I got up early to sit and talk to them. Glad for their hypnotic spell that enchanted me so much that the horror of my life seeped away, lessening, quietening so it was almost a surprise when one of the girls entered and brought me back to the awfulness of our lives.

Despite these birds being the captured of the captured, their generosity and beauty began to change me. A mystical power healing the unhealable. Their song reaching into my cells and marrow, nudging gently, so that the abuse, usually blotted out by drugs, came firmly into focus. And I could see what I had become. And I did not want it.

Soon, I was hiding the pills. No longer needing their lure, their potency. The birdsong curing me. Ensuring no cold turkey, no pain. I was reborn, a new me, not wanting what it was you had endowed. My acting skills were put to the test, pretending that I was still the woman you had created. There was nothing to see here. I was the same. Your drugged and smiling Cork belle.

I was retching more, however, at the thought of who the Hectors brought to my door day after day, those I now had to face compos mentis. But I did it all, nevertheless. Everything they demanded. The birdsong rising through concrete floors and wooden doors, taking me away from myself as my body was twisted and turned, invaded, defiled and damaged.

The other women were unchanged. The world continued as before with only me awake, aware, afraid. It was unbearable. That is when I began to plot an escape. I had not left the house for eight months. In all that time, beyond the opened window, I had not felt a breeze on my skin, experienced the solidity of a concreted pathway underfoot, or breathed in the exhaust fumes of a passing car on a city street. In my drugged state I had waited for life to be brought to me. And now I was as a newborn, on wobbly legs, with a flaccid mind trying rapidly to regenerate, to find my way once more into the great outdoors.

In the early morning, when Hector number one was still asleep, I stared out my locked window onto the back of the property and the boundary wall and gate, to the alleyway beyond, lined with stately oaks leading downward to a small road. A way out. I tiptoed quietly to the basement kitchen to examine the back door's locks and push at its heft. It was no ordinary door. Of course it wasn't. A wall of solid wood with bolt upon unwieldy bolt. But there would be no tunnel digging, no calling from a window to attract attention. So, whatever needed to be done, needed to involve this door.

Over the coming days, in the early hours of morning when all was quiet save for the music of the birds, I crept down to the kitchen. With a belt buckle, a nail clipper and two cutlery knives, I twisted and turned the screws. It took days of untightening and retightening so Hector number one never suspected a thing. I was patient. I remembered years before, my father, on a rare Sunday in the house, was watching *A Man Escaped*. So surprised was I to see my father at home at all that when I had eventually wandered down from my room that morning, I slid onto the couch to watch it too, not even asking his permission or saying hello, hardly twitching, in fact, in case I drew any attention to myself and ruined this moment of family unity. For an eight-year-old it was a boring watch, but so besotted was I by my father's closeness, I watched Lieutenant Fontaine, the French resistance fighter, intently, spending his days and weeks and months preparing his escape from the Nazi jail. How ironic that that moment was the best parenting my father had ever managed. So, there I was, a captive, channelling my inner Fontaine. Steadfast, patient and resolute.

The morning came when I was ready. From my window, I looked out on Cork in winter. Frost settled on the ground. I imagined breathing in the sharp air, filling my lungs with promise. The traffic stirred below as city folk slept on in their beds. I wondered if my parents were too.

It was then I heard it, the raising of the shutters of the coffee shop on the corner to take in its deliveries. My signal.

My bare feet skipped through the thick fibres of the stairway carpet. Step after silent step. No ticking clock, no sharp intake of breath to disturb Hector number one, sleeping in his attic room. The cold tile of the hallway sucked at my feet. The birdsong chorus loud and glorious at morning's light. I stopped and waited. My head tilted upward, ensuring there was no bed-creak of a waking man. But nothing. On I went. The final descent. The wooden steps to the basement kitchen withholding its splinters, encouraging me on.

In the kitchen, I worked at speed, taking down the door with the tools I had hidden in washing powder. Four steps to the rickety back gate, a cinch in its dismantling at my now expert hands, and I was gone. Tiptoeing through the briars and refuge of the seldom-used lane. The distant sound of a 'good morning' called somewhere on a street beyond, carried to me on the morning air, making me smile at the normality within my reach. One step then two and I would be there, the little laneway that would lead me to that world of simplicity and kindness, to a blagged phone from the delivery man who might still be at the coffee shop, or a passer-by, or to a knock on a door through which I might step, never to return. My mind so lost in the many possibilities, I had not seen him.

Hector number four. Standing there, waiting for me. A prearranged date. He even smiled as he looped his arm through mine, as if lovers, and walked me to the end of lane, taking a left onto the wide expanse of city pathway, back up towards the house, where a car waited.

Your car.

The back door opened as we approached and out you stepped. You smiled at me as Hector number four stopped me right in front of you, handing me over like a bride.

'You always were so clever, weren't you?' you said, your fingertips lightly touching my cheek.

Was I? I thought, but said not a word. Instead, I looked beyond you, at the houses, the pockmarked concrete pavement, the painted railings. I was shaking though. Every bit of me jangling in fear.

'Did you think we didn't know?'

You gave a small chuckle.

'We've been watching you. All this time. We have cameras, you see,' you leaned towards my turned cheek so I could feel your breath, and whispered, 'everywhere.'

I did not budge. Kept staring ahead. But the buckle in my legs was winning. I squeezed my eyes shut on tears I had not realised had begun to fall while I willed the muscles of my body to keep holding me up.

'Silly, silly you.'

I imagined that coy smile of yours, the one I thought beautiful when first we met but soon realised was just for show. The slight up-turn to your lips shaping what you said next.

'You'll like this though.'

My peripheral vision let me know that you were bending into your car and pulling out something large and white. And that is when I turned.

It was their cage.

Amber, Emerald and Azure sat petrified and buffeted by the movement. You opened their little door and spoke to them, stupid baby speak pretending at not wanting to cause a fright. You took one after the other out and, with a smile and eyes that concentrated only on me, you crushed each one in your grip and dropped them to the ground.

You sent no one to my door looking for their satisfaction that night. Your guests wanted smiles and delirious delight at their very presence, not my darkened eyes and broken soul. But the next day, your investment cried out for its return. Hector number one was back, punching needle after needle into my body. Nothing worked. Those birds still sang on inside me, you see. For as long as their melody lived within my head and heart, it seemed your potions held no power. There was no upturn in mouth or spirit in this, your captive's body.

Instead, furious at your cruelty, I smashed windows and furniture. Pulled curtains from their poles. Tore the silken sheets. Hector number one called Hector number two, then he called Hector number three, then number four. Four Hectors holding me down, guarding the door, keeping the other women away. The takings were low that night.

You were summoned from your slumber beside your newest nineteen-year-old. You stood at the end of my bed where I lay pinned. The bed that I had savaged, its mattress innards on display from the gouges I had made with the sharp corner of the picture frame that only moments before had sheathed a painting of a bluebell. Until I broke it over my knee. You examined my face, closely, your indignant breath heaving. What was it you were hoping for? That you might see the why of my defiance? I spat at you. The spittle landed mostly on my chin, but one little droplet made it all the way to the end of your nose. And there it sat, that little gem. That's when I smiled.

You clicked your fingers as you righted yourself and your nose. The secret code for the Hectors to take me. Two at my side holding my arms, one ahead, one behind, in case somehow this one-hundred-and-twelve-pound prisoner could overpower them. I was bundled into the Hectors' car while you drove ahead in yours.

On motorway and country roads, we headed west towards a sun long set, replaced by the winter moon, hanging low and heavy. With city lights long gone, darkened fields and roadside hedging observed our cavalcade. Village after sleepy village lay in the wake of our speed and fury. I rested my head against the leather seat and imagined the window was open, and from that reverie there came the rush of wind on my face. And I was at peace.

On and on we drove until a turning that brought us up and up the steepest of hills, until the roar of wave below was in my ear. Down then. Descending to Glandore. I remembered it from our early days, the days in which I believed you loved me. Believed you were a man with a good heart. Kind. Honest. How I laughed at that now. Laughed so that three of the Hectors turned to look at me, the fourth, the driver, watching through his rear-view mirror, wondering at the depths of my insanity. But I was saner than I had ever been. In my final moments, the clarity of all that had happened brought a mirth that was inexplicable to the onlooker.

Under torchlight we walked, stumbled down the steep rocky edge. All of us. At the bottom, I stood facing you. Were you searching for it, the adoration that had once lived there? It was long gone, my love. You said no words and neither did I. Turned your head away eventually, nodding to Hector number four.

I will admit to fear, in those last moments. The stream of urine down my inner leg. Its heat a comfort, until it cooled with the night-time air and felt strangely more unbearable than the gun being held to my temple.

The shot, loud in my ear.

The ground, craggy as I fell.

My heart ceasing its rhythmic beat with surprising immediacy – I was not sure what it was I thought would happen with a bullet to the brain, that somehow it might beat on a little slower, lulling me into a peaceful death?

You returned then to squat beside me at the water's edge, to stroke my temple, until you had grieved enough, and you stood again, your foot finding the curve of my waist and you pushed, so that I rolled into the sea. And there I swayed: a little in, a little out. Did you worry that I wouldn't move at all, that the great Atlantic would reject your gift? I sensed your growing apprehension.

But you needn't have fretted. I could feel it, the oncoming roar that built and built until a wave of height and strength and anger rose up from the calm to claim me, to shame and frighten you for your betrayal. You ran, oh, how you scurried, knocking over Hector number two, to get to the safety of your car. It boomed so loud and long that lights went on down the coastline in harbour bedrooms. Curtains pulled to see the colossus hover in its beauty and its grief. To smash against the shore, as if it might be able to catch the fleeing cars.

Within the core of its fathomless deep, I was safe, cradled at last in a cocoon of peace.

Five months and three days, that is how long I have been here now, in the deepest of the deep. Swaying with the rhythm of the water. The in, the out. I never grow tired of it. I am contented. The weightlessness of bone and muscle in the arms of the sea bring solace. Its sway soothing, mellowing out what once was stretched and taut. My mind as fluid as our lapping at the shore on sunny days, when we cradle holidaymakers who swim and boats that stir out into the ocean.

I bristle only when another woman's life is taken. A warning arriving from nowhere, rushing through me so that I roar. It is then we rise and rise until the hills and mountains cower, and we crash against the shore, crying out for those lost souls. An intake of breath, a quick retreat, and then we scream again, breaking against rock and harbour. Raging against manmade walls and manmade ills. Spilling on roads. On and on until we are wasted and must retreat to rest, to grieve.

But when rebalanced, I shift in shape. The sea letting me go, its salty brine letting fly a mist that travels east, back over field and fence until I am there again, among city streets. Resting on park benches, or under the eaves of houses I no longer know the comfort of, until I am ready to sit outside the window of your apartment, where you once pretended I was your everything. Seeping through the cracks of your triple glaze, slipping across your underfloor-heated wooden slats until I rise and find your head, your torso, and I nestle in, my mist dampening that hair, that skin, until you wake with a shiver, bolting upright.

You know it's me, I know you do.

You have tried blankets and medicines and hoods and hats. And even gloves! The underfloor heating has been checked and rechecked, upgraded, no less, but I am still there to wake you every morning, to kiss you on the cheek at night, reminding you there is no solace now. Oh, the joy it brings to see you curl in on yourself, wizened and old, searching for the tiniest morsel of heat.

I am immortal now, forever to be by your side until your dying day. And it is coming, my darling, make no mistake. This little cloud of water, invisible to all but you, bringing low the great master, touching the untouchable. Woman and wave existing in simpatico.

DIARMUID AND GRÁINNE

Megan Nolan

The Pursuit of Diarmuid and Gráinne

It was awful the way Finn joked with the man on hotel reception when they arrived in Richmond. He was always able to do that, be funny with strangers even when in the deepest furrow of a fight. Back home in Kilmac he would be driving them into the village, Gráinne sitting beside him, rigid while he said terrible things to her, telling her what sort of girl she was and what would happen to her if she kept on the way she was. He would pass the Kielys' farm and the old Famine workhouse buildings, keeping his eyes forward or to the side to scan for passers-by even as he said the terrible things. Sometimes they would pass a neighbour and he would turn his face towards them and tap on the horn lightly in greeting and smile gently and nod, and the whole interaction would take five seconds and even though his mouth was as good as shut to perform the smile, it kept saying the words to Gráinne all the while.

Once they had been parked outside the school while he went through her bag, examining all the stray bits of paper in case they were notes passed between friends and even checking what she had written in the margins of her textbooks, face darkening as he got to the part of the biology book about reproduction even though it was mostly only stamens and pistils, and as he rummaged through it all there was a knock on the window and it was the sergeant saying hello. Finn opened the car door and all the tension of the previous moment evaporated instantly and he was jovial and casual again as he said hello to Sergeant Daly, who he had gone to school with and was great friends with.

'How's she cuttin', boss?' Finn had said, swinging one of his legs out onto the pavement to get a better vantage point to chat from.

'Arah, grand,' said the sergeant. 'Fine day. Won't we pay for that tomorrow?'

It wasn't a question that demanded an answer. He leaned down then to look in and smile at Gráinne. The sergeant was enormous – almost giant height, Gráinne thought – but gentle-seeming with it, his huge hands looking most at home coddling the cats he and his wife, the English teacher, kept. He would have been a comforting presence in life had he not been so close with Finn.

He tipped his head now and said to Finn, 'Look at this grown-up girl, I'd hardly believe it's her. You must be proud of her doing so well, Finn. I hear from the missus she's going to be great in the play.'

That was the start of the trouble proper. She hadn't mentioned to Finn that there was a play and that she was going to be in it, though she would have had to soon enough when the rehearsals started.

His smile didn't waver while he said to the sergeant, 'What's the play, Charlie? This one tells me nothing.'

'Ah. They're at that age. It's *Grease*, isn't it, Gráinne? I hear they're all making eyes at the handsome fella.'

'What fella is that?' asked Finn, still grinning like it was gas.

'That good-looking boy over from England, we were in school with his mother, you'd know her, she was only a few years below us. I hear he's causing quite the stir,' said the sergeant, and then, delivering the body blow, winked at Gráinne with knowing conspiracy.

Finn was thought of as a great man around the village for taking care of Gráinne despite not being blood. Her own father had never been in the picture, someone from Cork passing through, they said. Her mother had died in childbirth after. She was raised by her aunt Clare all her life, in Waterford city, until she was ten, and Clare met Finn when he was in town one Christmas night for a Twelve Pubs. They were married soon after and she and Gráinne moved out to Kilmac to live with him. Finn was born in the same house he still lived in, between Bunmahon and Kilmac, never having left it. His siblings had scattered and came back only occasionally at Christmas to sit in the kitchen for an awkward hour or two, looking at the photos on the wall and standing at the back door to face out onto the fields. They seemed to Gráinne to want to stay longer, to speak more, speak better, but it was clear Finn barely tolerated their intrusions. The house was his; he had made it so through never abandoning it, never trying for anything else.

Clare died when Gráinne was thirteen, and the village went mad. There was already the usual resistance to the new arrivals, the townies. Clare had a good job in the city council, which didn't help the mild but persistent suspicion of them as superior blow-ins. When Clare died, the faint hum of distaste that had already existed was concentrated now on Gráinne, who for her short life had been so inordinately blighted that it felt she was almost radioactive. Anyone, it seemed, who had a hand in making or birthing or rearing her was doomed to disaster. It was regarded with admiration then, when it became clear she would stay on with Finn.

'I'm the only father she ever had,' he had said to the women in the post office, who could scarcely believe a man who had just lost his wife would now have to be the sole parent to a girl who wasn't even his. 'What else would I do?'

When her aunt had only just met Finn, Gráinne loved him. In the pub on the day they told her they would be getting married, while Clare was flushed with pleasure up at the bar to buy drinks to toast with, Finn turned towards her with flattering seriousness.

'Is it OK by you, Gráinne?'

Nobody had ever asked Gráinne whether anything was

OK with her. All her life she had been a topic of discussion for others to deal with rather than a person with feelings and actions of her own. Clare looked after her but let it be known always that she wasn't obliged to, that she was doing her a favour out of kindness to her dead sister. Now things were being thrust upon her again – moving house, moving out to the country, moving school – but the changes felt good this time because Finn asked her so nicely about it. He had the air of a man it was easy to say yes to, a wiry, compact man with a handsome pockmarked face.

He had once been a carpenter, but now he seemed to have no need of a job, renting the fields all around the house, which was owned outright, to farmers. His life seemed to mostly involve the mastery of his surroundings, for everyone knew Finn and liked and minded him. When he met people on the street his eyes twinkled with pleasure and knowledge; he pleased them by recalling the details of their lives so well. At Christmas he gave presents to the priest and the priest's housekeeper, and the headmaster of the school. Once he drove Gráinne into Dungarvan to the cinema when Clare was sick, where they saw the second Lord of the Rings film, and even in that foreign terrain he was known by every second person they passed on the streets.

'I hope it is OK,' he said, taking her hand, shaking it briefly, as though in victory. 'I'm going to make it a lovely home for you, I promise that.'

*

The house was its own world and became smaller the longer she lived in it. First, as she was charmed by Finn, she was charmed too by the place, ancient but well kept. The outhouses, the open fire, the attic filled with religious pictures. It was like a film set she could poke about at will, and the sense of drama, of story, she had long comforted herself with in books was satisfied. She unpacked her things, her little library. She cared most for her diaries, with real locks, which Clare gave her each Christmas, and then her books. A well-thumbed copy of *The Illustrated Mum* by Jacqueline Wilson, a few Judy Blumes, the babyish ones she still treasured and returned to like *The Secret Garden* and *A Little Princess*. She had a poster of *Titanic*, the two beautiful faces etched in poignant longing; she had cried so hysterically when Clare took her to see it she had to be taken out of the cinema. She installed her small gallery of trinkets, pushing gently into the house to see if it was really hers.

Small things, then, as when she opened a cupboard and went for a particular cup and Finn shouted from across the room, startling her, telling her not to touch it. She jumped with the fright and dropped it and that was a dreadful few days. He had refused to speak to either her or Clare, his silence sitting fat and volatile in the centre of each room he occupied, and finally after three days Clare had made her write an apology card with a drawing in it and he had relented.

Another time not long after that he learned that Gráinne was friends with Deirdre Mangan in school and he sat her down at the kitchen table as Clare hovered in the alcove. He knelt down before her, crouched between her legs, and he gripped each bony white knee, squeezing them painfully.

'The Mangans are a nasty family. All those women are full of filth. You've enough of that in your bloodline already without adding more. You're not to talk to her again. And if you do, I'll know, because Mrs Daly is married to my friend the sergeant and she tells me everything that goes on.'

She refused to talk to Deirdre the next day and from then on, tears prickling as she turned away from Deirdre's shocked, gawping face. She and Deirdre used to meet up in the playground the day after *Friends* aired, to talk about their favourite parts and act them out, and now she had nobody to discuss that or anything else with.

Then it was the clothes. After her period had come and Clare had put some beginners' tampons in the bathroom, he accosted Gráinne after school one day to tell her he had seen them and she would have to take more care with her dress now she was a woman. She couldn't be running around in shorts and little vests any more. And she watched as he went through her drawers and wardrobe and threw half of it in the bin, leaving the biggest jumpers and jeans and longest skirts. When he was going through the room he found a few old copies of *Mizz* magazine and

J-17 that Clare would pick up from the garage on the way home the odd time, and flicking through them he binned those too.

Gráinne had always been a passive child by necessity, but she wasn't afraid of Clare and would ask her questions freely. Finn seemed to somehow arrest the questions in her throat, and it wasn't from shouting or beating, not most of the time. It was something else, something less measurable and therefore more frightening. He spoke in long unending stories, half murmured but as authoritative as though he was reciting the Bible. It was as though, she realised once, he had such total control over his surroundings, and the people who lived in his surroundings, that he hadn't the need to make himself clear. There was no mystery about who would decide things, no leeway, no reasons were required.

After Clare died it was worse. He insisted he had to sit in and watch while she had her shower, to make sure she was being hygienic. He pulled the stool inside the bathroom a few feet from the cubicle, humming. She was allowed to have the shower door closed over and the glass was clouded, so she told herself he didn't see anything. He would tell her when she had been washing long enough and she could finish, and he would leave the room, laying the towel on the stool for her to take. None of the doors in the house had ever fully closed. They had no locks, and the joints and hinges were misshapen, swollen so that they never shut completely.

In the evenings sometimes, when she sat in her room reading or doing homework, she would become aware of him crossing back and forward by the ajar door over and over again, until finally the creaking stopped and she knew he was out there in the dark looking through the gap at her. She gathered her will and kept at what she was doing, knowing that if she acknowledged what was going on or that she was frightened, they would have to enter a new and foreign territory, one she was hoping to stay away from until she was grown-up and could leave. When it was time, she turned off the lamp and to be safe got under the covers to remove her clothes and put on her pyjamas.

Often he made sure to tell her about all of his friends. He had friends not only in the school, and the police station, and the post office, but in the shop and all the farms around, and in the pub. These were people he had known all his life, people who would protect one another. The only person she ever met who seemed not to love Finn was the postman, Daithí, another fellow who had been in school with him. Daithí didn't meet Finn's eye when they crossed paths and he didn't smile when Finn launched into his yarns. A few times Gráinne had seen Daithí when he was delivering their post, or passed by him in the village, and he seemed to be looking at her with a curious intensity, staring straight into her with some unknown query.

Reading privately was no longer allowed. She could have her schoolbooks, but anything else she wished to read she had to read aloud in front of him at the kitchen table. He made her do this with an anthology of love poems he found out she had borrowed from the library, smirking at her as she cried with embarrassment, not allowing her to stop.

'Thank you,' he said. 'Thank you very much, Gráinne.'

She met Diarmuid on the first day of sixth year. He was the big excitement of the day, a transplant from England. Not only was he foreign, his parents were actors. The mother was originally from Kilmacthomas and had decamped to London when she left, a string of small but steady roles on soaps like *Hollyoaks* and appearances in McCains adverts under her belt. She met the father on set one day, the father who was a real actor, people said. Nobody, they had to admit, had actually heard of him, but he had starred in plays in the big theatres and had parts in actual films you could see in the cinema. He was a lot older, into his sixties already, and they had decided to move to Ireland to be close to the mother's ailing parents and to have a quiet, beautiful, big place to live after being in little flats in London so long. London was so expensive, they said, that you could be in films and on television and still only live in flats with no garden. It was just them and their son Diarmuid, who was seventeen and who had plans to study acting in the Lir school in Trinity.

Diarmuid was sitting in the classroom on his own when she arrived that morning, while the others chattered around him, pretending not to be looking at him while he took out his notebook and pencils from a brown leather satchel. It was the satchel that made her fall in love with him as much as himself in that moment. It was practical and beautiful and from a different time and place. The world it conjured was one of sturdy simplicity, gave a suggestion of things that were what they said they were and could be no other thing. He was like that too. He had a face from a long-ago film, dark skin and smoky, sad eyes and a wide, full mouth, which looked ready at all times to break into a grin or a song. He didn't look scared or defensive despite the alien situation he was in, and she felt calm looking over at him, still in the September sunlight, reading his book and licking his finger every now and then to turn the page.

During the first class the teacher asked them all to introduce themselves to Diarmuid and say something they liked to do. The class sniggered at this, the imposed formality, and most of the boys took the piss ('My name is Brian and I like the IRA,' shouted Brian Flanagan, at which Diarmuid smiled indulgently). Gráinne didn't know how to be funny but also didn't know how to be serious in front of others, and her heart was hammering as she said, 'My name is Gráinne and I like reading poetry and plays.' He smiled at her and said, though it wasn't his turn as he was supposed to go at the end: 'My name is Diarmuid and so do I,' and the class whooped and roared and her chest filled with an interesting new warmth it hadn't felt before.

He was so good at everything he turned his hand to that he should have been hated, but he bore his gifts with such good humour and lightness that the whole school, as well as Gráinne, was in love with him. Once when an essay of his won an inter-county prize, Mrs Daly referred to him in an attempt at mockery as 'the golden boy', but it was true, and after that Gráinne thought of him that way. He seemed to attract light and he emitted the soft warmth of a cat who had been basking all day, patient and slow and perfect. They only had school at first, before they found other ways, and at lunchtime he would take her by the hand and lead her down the field towards the old graveyard the nuns used to be buried in. There was a wooded area beyond it and he pressed her against the tree and leaned his full weight on her so there was no room for any intrusion, so she could think of no other thing.

The smell around his mouth made her know with certainty she was in love. It was so substantial a presence she could actually taste it, and gulped it inside of her when he lingered around her face between kisses. A few months in he knelt before her and raised her kilt and put his mouth between her legs, opening her up. She thought as it was happening, before she lost thought altogether, that this was a thing there was no name for, something she would never be able to let herself say aloud to any other soul. And that made her happy, that it was unrepeatable, happening only to her. When he stood back up he kissed her without wiping his mouth and she tasted herself and that she was good and bright and clean and suddenly she knew for certain that all the things Finn said about her, said about life, were not true.

She didn't conceive with intention, but nor was she as frightened and appalled as she should have been when she realised what was happening. Rather there was a cautious feeling of relief that something undeniable was taking place which would force things to change. There was a kind of spell Finn held over her that could not be explained to others – it was one of the few things she could not elucidate to Diarmuid. She knew he was a man like any other in corporeal terms, but this was also somehow not true. The web of his influence was everywhere, even if others couldn't see it all the time. There was nothing stronger than it, except this, now, the strength of life itself growing inside her. She knew also it was crucial he not be aware of what was taking place, for he would take the life for himself, he would destroy it or seize it and repurpose it into malignity. He would absorb it in one way or another and it would make him stronger.

It was still very early when she told Diarmuid. She had known almost immediately, a novel kind of tightness in her centre and the ancient ache of her breasts. Nobody had explained these matters to her but the knowledge was there anyway. They were a few weeks into rehearsals for the play, which Finn had allowed her to continue because it was Mrs Daly who was overseeing everything.

Gráinne had only auditioned because she wanted to spend time with Finn, but she was surprised to find the different ways in which she liked playing Sandy. Her singing voice was nice and clear, that was why she got the lead, but even the acting, which she had dreaded, had turned out to be exciting and illuminating. There had been times – many times, really – over the past few years when she longed to turn herself towards the other girls and acknowledge the strange, stubborn barrier that had been constructed around her by Finn and the sadness of her private life, which was too unusual and unspeakable to confide about. Small overtures had been made, here and there, but nothing substantial or lasting.

Now, with the plausible deniability of performance, she had access to the easy feminine intimacy she had never really known. When the girls brushed her hair in the sleepover scene, it was all she could do not to lean her head further into their hands and rub against them like a cat. The girls warmed to her too; they liked the life imitating art of it all, Gráinne becoming Sandra Dee becoming Sandy becoming New Gráinne. They exclaimed at her long eyelashes when they leaned over to doll her up, and her dopey shyness stopped irritating and bewildering them. It was as though now, in the final months of their shared girlhood, they could finally afford to be benevolent, accepting of her oddness, and able to see the qualities beneath it. The first time they ran 'Summer Nights' through, a whole different part of the feeling between her and Diarmuid came into being. It was suffused with the oxygen of others, for one thing, the oxygen of an audience their love was usually denied. But, too, there was an edge of hysteria, of genuine frivolity, that they couldn't afford to indulge in the narrow density of their stolen private hours. When they finished the song the whole group whooped and catcalled wildly, and Gráinne and Diarmuid caught eyes and both doubled over with laughing.

'I'll know everything you do in there,' Finn had warned Gráinne of the rehearsals, except he didn't know that Mrs Daly encouraged Diarmuid and Gráinne to go off and rehearse just the two of them when she was running other scenes. They had these windows now as well as the lunchtimes when they would go to the wood or to Diarmuid's bedroom, the house only a few minutes from the rear of the schoolyard.

When she told him she was pregnant, she cried a little, from the enormity not from sadness, and he was astonished but held her tightly and told her he was going to take care of her for ever, that she was not alone and never would be again, that he was going to make a plan and take them away from Finn and from Kilmac and everything she had been unlucky enough to know.

It was in her third month – when they had begun tentatively to discuss possible plans, places to go, ways to get there – when Finn found her out. He had been watching from outside the door as she changed that night – he must have got better at silence, she thought after it was done, as she hadn't heard a single creak or breath. The first thing she heard was a low dreadful moan from the darkness, which escaped him when he saw the curve of her belly. He threw open the door then. She stood stricken, naked, in the dim yellow light, as he stared at her. It was the first time he had ever looked at her full on, and the panic and disbelief on his face made him look almost human.

'It was him? You let him do this to you?' he said almost to himself. He was lost, baffled by the world at last. Never, she thought, had he lost control of his domain before. For a moment longer they stood there, suspended, looking at each other, both of them on the border of unfamiliar terrain. His power wavering in light of his ignorance and hers surging a little with the protection of a secret. She rushed to her clothes and covered herself and he began to breathe heavily, slowly, recovering composure. For a long time he didn't say anything, sitting on her bed and gazing up at the ceiling with an odd smiling grimace while she stood still and waited to see what his move would be. Finally he nodded, as though having settled something with himself.

'We'll get rid of it,' he said simply. 'I'll book everything tonight and we'll travel to London in the morning. Tell him to keep his mouth shut about it, and in a week it will be like it never happened.'

He was pressing on his temples with his thumbs, meditatively, and said almost as an afterthought:

'You'll never see him again. The whole family will have to leave.'

She knew he could make that happen. She didn't understand why or how exactly a man like Finn could banish a whole family, but she knew he could.

'I don't want to get rid of it,' Gráinne said now, and he smiled back, weary, mocking pity in it.

'You've no choice. The thing is, people would say all sorts of things. People might think it was mine.'

She sat in the room listening to him making phone calls the rest of the evening, booking flights and speaking to a woman at the Marie Stopes clinic in an area of London named Richmond. She heard him book a hotel called the Selwyn, and without knowing exactly what she would do with it yet, she wrote this down on a page of her notebook and tore it out and folded it as small as it would go and put it in her pocket. The next day, as the sky began to brighten in Kilmacthomas, one of the cows belonging to the Kielys began to scream and fell to its side, Gráinne dimly recalling talk of mastitis.

'She's riddled,' said Finn, as he was putting their bags in the car.

Gráinne had thought all night of what she might do, but no plan felt sturdy enough to counter his will. She could run, but running felt insufficient when she was alone and without money and pregnant. Finn went back into the house to fetch their coats and lock up and she heard Daithí, the postman, cycling up the lane, and knew what to do. *Hurry, hurry*, she thought as he got closer and she knew that Finn couldn't be very much longer. Checking the house behind her to see he wasn't coming out, she stood next to the postbox and when Daithí finally came into view close enough to make contact, she stayed silent but widened her eyes. As he stared back at her, she opened the box and put in the piece of paper she had folded with the hotel name written on it. She closed it and said, just audible enough for him to hear, 'For Diarmuid. The Chatwin house by school.' And Finn was behind her then.

'Good man, Daithí,' he called out cheerfully. 'Any good news for us today or only bills? I'll take them from you there.'

Daithí looked at them both for a moment, then nodded at Finn.

'Ye look like you're on your travels. I'll just put them in here and you can get them when you get back,' and before Finn could respond, he had opened the box and pushed some letters inside with one hand and secreted the scrap with his other. 'Are you away anywhere exciting? Is it not still term time?'

Finn, a little confused by the postbox pantomime, frowned and said, 'Someone belonging to Gráinne died in England, a relative of Clare and her mother's, so we'll go over to the funeral.'

'Ah,' said Daithí. 'Sorry for your loss, Gráinne,' and looked her straight on and nodded so she knew he had heard her.

Late that night in the hotel in Richmond, though she knew she ought to be panicking, Gráinne felt calm. They had gone to the clinic to have a scan but it wasn't possible to do anything else on the same day, they had booked too last minute for that. They would have to stay for another night before she could return and take the drugs, and she knew Diarmuid would come for her before that. The hotel was yellowed and maudlin – she thought she could feel the accumulated vibrations of anxiety from other girls who had stayed here before going to the clinic. She wondered if the staff all knew what they were doing there, if they cared or thought about it at all.

The room had twin beds only a few feet apart and she refused to sleep that night. There had been spurious codes Finn had abided by to do with the realisation of his ownership over her, she knew. She couldn't have said exactly what defined them – was it a certain age she would turn? A signal he was waiting for? – but there had been a private logic he obeyed. Now the fabric of their coexistence had been torn and she wasn't sure what he was capable of, so she remained awake though breathing with gentle regularity to make him believe she wasn't. After some time he himself slept while she found herself praying in the darkness, and it wasn't God but Diarmuid she felt herself beseeching.

In the morning he left her alone in the room while he went downstairs for breakfast, and she quickly put her things together in the rucksack, knowing the time had come. Diarmuid knocked softly and before she opened the door she felt his presence, clarifying and cleansing, waiting there. When she opened it they grabbed one another in silence. She put her hand to his neck and felt the boyish softness of where it led down to the clavicle. She loved this part of him and it was joyous to have a single moment of remembering they were children together before they had to begin this next part of life, a part where they would never have the dubious luxury of childhood again.

On the way to central London she asked if he knew where they were going.

'My godfather lives in Deal, by the sea. We'll go to stay with him until we know what to do,' Diarmuid said.

'We can't ever go back there,' she turned to him and said, taking his jaw in her hand and fixing her face to his so that he would understand and believe her. 'He'll kill us. Or something worse than killing.'

Diarmuid began to say something and she interrupted.

'I don't know what's worse than killing, only that he knows how to do it. You have to trust me. There are things I can't explain but I know them anyway.'

'I know you do,' he said, and gathered her to him. At Waterloo he bought them tickets with a credit card his parents had given him for emergencies. He had written them a note before he left, saying he would be at Geoffrey's in Deal and that they weren't to worry and he would explain as soon as he could. Then he had turned off his phone, not wanting to have to handle them until he and Gráinne were fully safe. On the train, she slept finally, tucked under his arm, coat around them both, and she dreamed it was a broad sheltering wing instead of an arm, that the two of them were birds about to take flight.

Deal had a long, dark pier that crept eerily into the ocean and made Gráinne think of Gothic churches in foreign countries she had seen pictures of in the art history textbook. It was March, not yet time for the holidaymakers, and the town was muted. They walked arm in arm along the beach for two miles before they reached Geoffrey's cottage. He was expecting Diarmuid when he knocked, his parents having phoned to tell him the little they knew of what was going on. Geoffrey was another actor, once remarkably beautiful.

He had played a bewitching young gay man in a famous play about the AIDS crisis, and then he had been cast in another gay role, and another, and then as he entered his late forties his career was over before it had fully begun, too well known as one thing to play anything else, and no longer pretty enough to continue doing so. The beautiful boy was still visible there, Gráinne thought, as she looked around the small home at pictures of him in his prime. You could see him trapped beneath the contemporary face that had expanded and blurred from booze and time.

'What sort of trouble have you got yourself in, young man?' he asked Diarmuid after they had all sat down around the kitchen table. 'The usual sort teenage boys get in, I take it?' and indicated Gráinne, whose arms were cradled over her middle.

'In a sense,' said Diarmuid. 'But – worse.'

They tried to explain about Finn, but Gráinne could tell it was no use. Geoffrey nodded along as though he knew, but it was clear he thought Finn was simply a strict parent and Gráinne a hysterical girl frightened of him.

'You can stay here as long as you like – my home is your home, you know that. Gráinne, you too, but tomorrow we will have to speak to your father' – she bristled at this description of Finn – 'and your folks too, naturally,' he said to Diarmuid. 'I know this all seems like the end of the world, but it's an old story. Everything will work out in the end.'

People often said things like this to Gráinne, and it had never proved true. Geoffrey showed them to a spare box room with an air mattress and a pile of blankets and they huddled together, pressing forehead to forehead. The exhaustion came over her fully then and she wept into him both with relief for his presence and apology for having embroiled him in her existence.

At dawn she woke from bloody dreams and shook him awake. 'Turn on your phone,' she said to him.

When he did, there was a message from his father's number, but what it read was: 'I know where you are. I'm coming.'

Diarmuid frowned at it, and she put a hand on his arm, trembling, and said, 'It's not your father. It's him.'

She could not think of it now, there was no time. She could not think of that house, which had been witness to her life's only joy, its only privacy; which had been host to their love and their creation, being violated. She could not think of the door kicked in, nor of Diarmuid's parents and what might have become of them, of what violence against them he would have been capable of if it was required, what was stolen or rifled through, information he now had. Now there could only be movement, swift and decisive and in the direction of a place Finn had no knowledge of. She could feel him now, could feel the monstrous, relentless engine of his possession moving in their direction.

They packed their bags again and went out on the street before they spoke, to avoid waking Geoffrey.

'We'll walk now,' said Diarmuid. 'In case he can see what I'm doing with the card, so he doesn't know where we're going.'

'Where are we going?' she asked.

'Dover is three hours from here. And then, ships on from there.'

'Where do they go, to France?'

'Not only. They go to different islands, and Norway, and Spain. If we don't decide where we'll go until we get there, then there's no way he can know. He can't know what we don't know. It has to be only us, only what happens together, in real time.'

She knew he understood now what it was they were running from, that whatever Finn was couldn't be quantified by the boundaries of the everyday world, that if it wasn't magic or something not of this earth, it was also not explicable with ordinary logic. That he could find his way seamlessly into things other men had no purchase on. And they reached the cliff. And on they ran.

*

Norway. When he said Norway it stirred something in my mind, and as we went on I tried to think what it was. It was calm and fluid whatever it might be, and after a while it came, slowly. I had read about it once when I was small, before Clare met Finn and we still lived in town. The library in Ballybricken was a temporary one while they did up the main one on Lady Lane. It was chaos up there, the shelves falling down and disordered, so that the adult books were mixed with the children's ones. I was looking for a Roald Dahl book one afternoon, there were stacks of things only loosely in alphabetical order and I was stepping over the piles, picking through them. I found one, only it wasn't a title I recognised, and when I opened it there weren't any pictures. Still, I sat down with it, put my back to the cool wall – in my memory the strewn, stray piles of the library and I were alone, nobody else among them, though that can't be. I opened the book and tried my best to read and all I really recall was the feeling of peace when he describes the water near his grandparent's house, how it felt to be a child alone in an expanse, reckoning with space and air and time like that. I sounded out the word, incorrectly – fjord – and filed it away in my child's mind for future things, places to go and things to see and people to be. That was Norway, I remembered. A brief muddle of other images, gathered from nature programmes and geography textbooks. A sky that didn't darken no matter what the hour. The sky was overlooking a terrific bridge that seemed to cross an area bigger than the whole of Ireland. An illustration of a very old theme park, everything made from *wood and the rides as beautiful as sculptures. But more so when I spoke the word Norway inside my mind, what I liked, what felt safe, was that it was a place I knew nothing about, a place I couldn't even almost imagine, and if I could get to a place which had never existed concretely in my mind – if I didn't know it then he didn't know it either – that was a place I might make a life.*

DIRTY LAUNDRY
Salma El-Wardany

Deirdre of the Sorrows

Sorcha

She has never given much thought to heaven or hell, and she thinks the idea of God is a little far-fetched, but here, in this room, steam curling above her head, sweat running a river down her back, her hands blistered red, she thinks maybe hell does exist and prays to God. Any god. She'll take whichever deity is going.

She shifts her weight, hoping it will calm the kicking in her stomach. She pulls the sheet from the vat, hauling the wet material onto the wringing board, the water soaking her apron, the smell of detergent and damp hitting her in the face. This sheet is nicer than the one she lay on with Felim the day they snuck into the empty house on the outskirts of town. It's softer. Sometimes, when she is on the colander station and no one is looking, she holds the dry sheets she has just ironed to her cheek, and remembers the best day of her life. Staring into Felim's eyes, the whole world rolling around their mouths, their laughter echoing off the walls of a family home that was not theirs, but in the aftermath, in the newness of her own body, she could believe for a second, was theirs. It only lasted the day.

By the time she saw Felim again, their fathers talking shop above their heads, her nervously whispering about a baby in her belly, the dream had turned to dust. His face ashen, his words quick, panicked. She had been standing in a new place, one she thought they had arrived at together, but she had the sudden feeling he had been here before. Knew the lay of the land. Where to go. What road to take next.

When he suggested that his father would make arrangements to give the baby away, she felt something quicken in her womb. A ripple. A sudden pain. Almost a yawning chasm that she likened to a scream. In the end, his father had made the arrangements anyway. Her own father said nothing. Wouldn't even look at her. She had been a thorn in his side since her mother died. With no other children, he was finally a free man and had no objection to Sorcha being sent to the Sisters of Mercy.

Like lightning before thunder, she sees the sharp crack of the stick before she feels the sting bloom across her thighs.

'Idleness will not be tolerated, Sorcha,' rasps Sister Fergus.

'Sorry, Sister,' she mutters. 'The baby is kicking again and I was just—'

'I am not interested in the details of your sin, Sorcha,' Sister Fergus interrupts, 'but I am interested in hard work.

Which, incidentally, is the only way to shake the devil out of you.'

Sister Fergus, her face twisted like bitter lemons, makes the sign of the cross over Sorcha and moves to the next girl in the line.

'Repentance, hard work and prayer are your only options, ladies,' continues Sister Fergus, 'and by the power vested in me by God himself, I am here to help you. I will pray with you. More importantly, I will pray for you. I will ensure that you have work to fill your wandering hands and keep you in the eye of the Almighty, but I will not tolerate idleness.'

Sorcha feels a pop between her legs but doesn't realise her waters have broken. She is already soaked skin deep, and there's no telling what liquid has come from her body and what has been pumped out of the pipes. She only knows she's in labour when she hears the voice of Sister Lebarcham calmly easing an enraged Sister Fergus off her body, which she now realises is curled in the fetal position, the pain so blinding it had brought her to her knees.

Over the next nineteen hours, she floats in and out of consciousness. The edges are fuzzy. Occasionally, people enter and leave the room. The only constant is Sister Lebarcham. Her voice is a lighthouse in the storm, her kindness a buoy keeping her afloat.

When the baby finally emerges, a wet slippery thing, Sorcha pulls her out of her the same way she hauls the laundry; with a firm grip but gently so as not to stain or mark. It is the first time she is fully awake, her life screaming into focus with her daughter's first gasp.

'Good God,' murmurs Sister Lebarcham, staring down at the baby.

'What?' asks Sorcha, panicked. 'Is she OK?'

'Fine, fine,' soothes Sister Lebarcham. 'I've just never seen a child born so bonnie.'

Sorcha has never seen a newborn. She stares down at her daughter's emerald eyes, her linen-white skin making them seem brighter, the flop of silky gold curls crowning her head like roses, and her lips perfectly red. 'Don't they all look like this?' she asks.

'No, child,' replies Sister Lebarcham, 'they certainly don't.'

'I'm going to call her Deirdre. I'm allowed to name her, aren't I?'

Sister Lebarcham smiles softly and places a cool cloth on her sweat-drenched forehead. 'You can name her, yes, but you know how this works, Sorcha. You're one of the clever ones. You know she won't be here for long and the family she goes to will name her themselves.'

Sorcha has the sudden urge to howl. To hold her daughter tighter. She kisses her quickly and breathes in her scent, her eyes flashing with anger. She starts to argue but Sister Lebarcham waves her away.

'For now, name her. It will be between us.'

'Then Deirdre it is,' Sorcha replies stubbornly.

Sister Lebarcham tilts her head to the side. 'Are you sure?'

'Why?'

'In old Irish it means broken-hearted.'

Something hardens. Sorcha nods. 'Yes.'

'Well, by the looks of her she'll certainly be a heartbreaker.'

A few hours later, as she lies staring at her whole world gurgling beside her, the door bangs open and Father Conchobar steps into the room, another priest she doesn't recognise at his side. Neither of them looks at her. They stare, slack-mouthed, at her daughter, and Sorcha can taste iron in her mouth. Something curls up the base of her spine and for a moment she feels more animal than woman. The instinct to aim for the jugular claws at her.

Father Conchobar picks up her daughter, holds her up to the light. 'What say you, Father Cathbad?'

The priest nods slowly. 'Yes, the child is certainly blessed with beauty, but as said in Ezekiel 28:17, beauty corrupts.'

Father Conchobar nods. He places Deirdre back and they leave. They don't acknowledge Sorcha.

Hours later, when they have taken Deirdre to the nursery with the other babies and her heart feels lead-like, she creeps along the corridor to Father Conchobar's study. It is the only door with light snaking out beneath it. She is about to knock when she hears voices. Father Cathbad mentions Sorcha's baby and her panic fuels her bravery as she raps quickly on the door.

Father Conchobar opens the door, annoyed to be interrupted. Surprise crosses his face when he sees Sorcha. She steps into the study before he can close the door, the words falling out of her mouth on top of each other.

'Please don't send her away to a family. I promise I'll look after her and work twice as hard and do whatever it takes. But please let me raise my daughter here. She needs me. I'm her mother. It wouldn't be right. I'll take extra Mass with the sisters and do extra errands, but please, Father, I can't be separated from her.'

Father Cathbad's face plumes red. 'How dare you. Barge into Father Conchobar's office and make demands. Let alone naming the child. This baby is born in sin. In our keeping and charge. Father Conchobar has every right to—'

'There, there,' interrupts Father Conchobar, stepping between them. 'Let us remember our merciful Lord and try to turn the other cheek to those who wrong us.'

He holds up his hand as Father Cathbad attempts to speak. 'Do not worry. Leave this with me, I have a plan.' He gestures to the door. 'It has been a long night.'

Father Cathbad nods in deference, closing the door softly behind him.

'A plan, Father?' she asks, nervously.

He ignores her, calmly walking to the front of his desk, leaning on the edge, a hand pensively placed on his chin. Sorcha's legs begin to tremble. The lack of sleep. The pain. The labour. It is all coming home to roost. She swallows. Gathers the courage she has left.

'Please, Father, let me keep her here.'

Father Conchobar waves away her pleas soothingly. 'Come now, enough of that. You shall get what you want. Your daughter will stay here, under the care of Sister Lebarcham, with the Sisters of Mercy, in the mother-and-baby home. You will be permitted to visit her once a week.'

She opens her mouth to argue but Father Conchobar frowns. 'Would you prefer she go to a good family across the sea? There are many Catholic families in America praying for a child.'

Her legs buckle. She grips the back of the chair, shaking her head slowly.

'Well, then.' He nods. 'She will serve our Church here.'

'Deirdre,' she mutters.

Father Conchobar looks annoyed to be interrupted again.

'Deirdre is her name,' she continues.

'Fine,' replies Father Conchobar, standing up to walk closer to her. 'You can name her, although mothers in our home are not allowed to name the children they birth in sin. You know the rules. I, however, on this occasion, will be compassionate and allow you to name the child.'

She is weak with relief. She doesn't know how long her legs will last.

Father Conchobar stands behind her, his breath inching along her neck. 'You will have to work hard, Sorcha.'

She nods.

'You will have to work exceptionally hard for this Church, which has given you so much. Has saved you.'

Father Conchobar lifts her dress as he speaks, slowly and deliberately pressing down on her back until she is bent in half. She feels him slip into her, mixing with the blood and the afterbirth, the cavity inside her becoming a wreckage and a ruin all at once. Her knuckles on the back of the chair shine white and desperate up at her.

Deirdre

She stands as still as she can, her small legs trembling with excitement and fear. She can hear Sister Lebarcham getting closer.

'Where are you? Come out, come out, wherever you are,' floats through the cracks in the wall. She stuffs her dimpled hands over her mouth, catching the giggle like a butterfly.

'Could Deirdre possibly be in here?'

A cupboard door opens and closes. The rustle of clothes. The drag of a chair.

'What about here?' exclaims Sister Lebarcham, pushing open the door disguised as wood panelling. The light bursts across Deirdre's face and she runs out of her hiding place, squealing in delight, into the arms of Sister Lebarcham. Her four-year-old legs dangle against the nun's tunic and she buries her head in her habit.

'Again, again.'

Sister Lebarcham nods. 'Yes, again. You hide, as best you can, and I'll come and find you. One . . . two . . . three . . .'

She runs out of the room and down the corridor, as quietly as possible, like a little mouse. Just like Sister Lebarcham has taught her.

She lays her head on the cool table next to her and daydreams about her mother. Her memories mingle with the snippets Sister Lebarcham has told her. The word 'misneach' floats through her mind. Take courage. A whispered bedtime command from her mother. Sister Lebarcham always tells her that her mother was determined, so she has decided that she will be too.

'Come now, Deirdre,' says Sister Lebarcham, gently tapping the ruler against her head, 'back to your sums.'

'But why do I have to do so many sums? Sister Fergus says I've learned too many for an eight-year-old girl.'

'Did she now?' murmurs Sister Lebarcham, turning her back to Deirdre to stare out the small window, the bluebell sky attempting to push its way into the room through the metal bars.

'You must have a skill, Deirdre,' she continues, 'and since you've shown a natural ability with numbers, we will turn this into your skill. Wouldn't you like that? To have something special you can do?'

Deirdre shrugs her girlish shoulders. She wants to please Sister Lebarcham. 'OK.' She bends her head back over her books, quickly and easily working through the sums. The afternoon light shines on her golden hair. Sister Lebarcham mutters a prayer under her breath and remembers the promise she made a dying woman: to protect her daughter. She feels angry at being bound to an impossible task. How was anyone supposed to protect a girl, let alone one as beautiful as this.

She walks through the thick woods behind the laundry, the hem of her dress attempting to meet the tips of the grass. The snowdrops flash white among the green, the sweet violets peer around trunks, and the smell of wild garlic is everywhere. With the laundry hidden from sight by the dense trees, she is free and unbound. Anything might happen.

She once overheard the men with the vans, the ones who pick up and drop off the sheets, talk about the woods and how a monster with one eye lived within. When she'd asked one of the Sisters about it they gave her ten smacks with the cane for believing in fairy tales and sent her to the isolation room for three days. She wasn't allowed dinner during that time, but Sister Lebarcham came every night and snuck her bread and cheese. Deirdre loves the woods. She walks in them whenever she can sneak away, when the nuns are distracted and the other women are doing the work. Sister Lebarcham says she should walk every day to be strong, and because soon, on her twelfth birthday, she will be expected to work in the laundry with the other women and there will be no time for long walks.

Spring is beginning to push life through the earth, but for now the air is still cold. She starts to run to keep warm and can't help but laugh at the freedom of it all. She wants to be a bird today and so she jumps and hangs on a nearby branch, her legs swinging back and forth. Eventually she pulls herself into the tree, to the furthest branch she can go, and lies down, staring at the wide open sky.

She is moving her arms side to side, just like a bird, when she hears muffled voices and the snapping of cold twigs underfoot. Father Conchobar walks with a young boy carrying an armful of logs. She instinctively draws back, the muscle memory of hide and seek with Sister Lebarcham taking over. She watches as Father Conchobar indicates for the boy to put the logs down, while he lifts his cassock and unbuckles his trousers. He murmurs a prayer of obedience while pulling the boy's trousers down. Deirdre clutches the branch, her knuckles as white as the clouds above her. Father Conchobar continues his prayers as he sweats and heaves over the boy, muttering about God and the glory, the glory, the glory.

She pulls the sheet onto the colander, stretching it taut. She tucks a small corner between the table and her hip to keep it in place. She knows every trick. The younger women often ask her for help and it irritates the nuns. They don't say anything, however. They know she is under Father Conchobar's care.

Once the sheet is ironed, as she folds it in half, she rubs the corner quickly over her cheek. A small tick developed for comfort. Something she saw her mother do. She wishes she'd had the chance to ask her mother why she did it, what it meant. On the nights when everything feels awful and she misses her, she rubs her own bedsheet across her cheek while falling asleep, the rough starch scraping along her smooth skin.

The bell tolls for dinner and they all tidy their stations. Deirdre quickly folds the final sheet and moves against the flow of women heading to the hall. Instead, she slips through the hidden door beneath the staircase, through a small passage she barely fits into any more and up the back stairs to Sister Lebarcham's room.

'You should be going for your dinner,' Sister Lebarcham says, without turning around, her back bent over a writing desk.

'But it's my birthday tomorrow,' she replies, hopping from foot to foot. 'I'm going to be sixteen and you said that's my special age.'

'And what of it?' replies Sister Lebarcham drily.

'Well, surely that means a special present?' Deirdre replies.

Sister Lebarcham laughs loudly, deep from her broad belly. She stands up and moves around the desk. She takes longer than she used to. Her face is more crinkled. It doesn't occur to Deirdre that Sister Lebarcham is getting older until the slow crawl of her body reminds her that the years are passing.

'Well, since it's not your birthday yet, I couldn't possibly say. But go on, hurry to dinner and we'll see what tomorrow brings.'

Deirdre kisses the old woman on the cheek quickly, before Sister Lebarcham can bat her away. She leaves her office, a spring in her step, her shoulders back. The days at the laundry and in the church are relentlessly similar, the foreverness of it sewn together into one never-ending horizon. But Sister Lebarcham always said things would be different when she is sixteen, and she only has one more day to wait. She is on the cusp. Sitting on the lilting edge of change. The delicious promise of tomorrow.

Sister Lebarcham

She takes a long pull of the cigarette and lets it dangle between her fingers while the smoke floats out of her. The night is thick around her, the saltiness of the Atlantic Ocean occasionally cutting through. She leans her back against the old coal shed and looks up at the blackness. The edges of the mother-and-baby home, and the church next to it, are just visible in the distance. She doesn't know why anyone would build a coal shed so far away from the intended buildings, but she is grateful for the sanctuary it has given her over the years. The only person to ever find her here was Sorcha, and occasionally, in the blackest part of the night, they would stand side by side and enjoy their bad habit together.

Sorcha had once asked her why she had become a nun, and in the middle of the night, when the truth was easier, she had replied, 'I hated the idea of marrying a man.'

Sorcha had snorted in disbelief. 'So, what, you decided to marry the ultimate man instead?'

She had laughed at that, always entertained by Sorcha's quickness. 'Yes, but it's one man I don't have to see, or share a bed with.'

The young woman had sighed, something flashing across her face as she put the cigarette to her lips for another drag. 'Aye, that might be the right way to do it.'

'We all choose a path, Sorcha. One way or another, it seems to involve men.'

'It's 1965.'

'So?'

Sorcha had shrugged. 'Just thought it would be better than this.'

'It might still be,' she replied.

Sorcha had nodded, something resolute in her face as she ground the cigarette out beneath her heel. 'Deirdre is going to have better. I'm going to give her something better.'

'Good lass,' she had replied, watching as Sorcha picked her way through the darkness, sneaking through the side door.

She didn't have the heart to tell her that plans for Deirdre had already been laid. She remembers the day Father Conchobar had charged her with Deirdre's education and care, explaining that the child's beauty was a blessing for their order. That at the age of sixteen, Deirdre would be married to Ewan Mac Durthacht. Their parish didn't have any real money and nothing much flowed in and out of the place, but if it did, and if there was coin to be found, it was in Mac Durthacht's pockets.

She had tried to ask Father Conchobar if that was wise, but, like most of them, he was not a man who took well to being questioned. Her own forensic tracking of the books told the full story, however, and the debt that Father Conchobar owed to Mac Durthacht. But word in the parish was that Mac Durthacht's previous wife didn't die of natural causes, and while there was absolutely no evidence to prove this, she wasn't going to let Deirdre go to one of the most violent men in the town. She takes a final drag of the burnt-down stub before crushing it beneath her heel, lifting her tunic to do so.

She places her hand over Deirdre's mouth before shaking her awake. The girl's eyes spring open to meet hers and she places a finger to her lips. Deirdre nods, her complete and unquestionable trust making something ache inside her.

She leads her to the church and lights one solitary candle by the altar. Deirdre looks disappointed.

'Don't tell me that my birthday surprise is prayers, Chammy.'

The use of her pet name from when she was a baby fans the ache inside her. She remembers Deirdre's gurgling face shouting 'Chammy' over and over again, in a way that so often sounded like 'mammy', and for a fleeting moment she thinks about another road she might have taken and what it could have looked like. But there is no time for sentimentality, so she pulls Deirdre down to her knees next to her. If anyone comes in, all they will see is two women praying at the altar of Christ.

'Listen to me. Tomorrow morning you are to be married to Ewan Mac Durthacht—'

'But I don't want to get married,' interrupts Deirdre.

Sister Lebarcham smiles. 'Let me finish, child. You know you are so like your mother.'

Deirdre smiles at that, her chin a little higher. Before she can interrupt again, Sister Lebarcham continues.

'You will one day, and when that day comes, it will be a man of your choosing, but Father Conchobar has promised you to Mac Durthacht since you were a baby.'

'That's his plan for me?' whispers Deirdre, horrified.

'Yes, but it's not what your mother wanted, and I wouldn't wish Ewan Mac Durthacht on my worst enemy. Take this and put it on.'

She hands Deirdre an old habit and helps her pull a tunic over her head. 'You've got to be out of this place by the morning, do you hear?'

'But where do I go?'

'Go north and then take a ferry to Scotland. Once you're there, go wherever you want, child, just make sure it's not here. Mac Durthacht will turn over every rock in Ireland to find you. Keep this habit on – people will be more likely to help you. Keep the veil down, until you're well on your way, for God's sake. Your face is too recognisable.'

She pushes some notes into Deirdre's hands. 'The first laundry van will be out the back, dropping off the sheets any moment. Get in the back and say nothing. I've arranged it. He won't ask questions. Get out when the van stops in Belfast. Save your money for the ferry and a room.'

Deirdre's lips begin to quiver, her eyes full. 'But I don't want to leave you here.'

She runs her fingertips across Deirdre's cheek and brings her forehead to her lips. 'This is where I belong.'

'Come with me,' Deirdre urges.

'No, lass. I'm too old to be running around like that.'

Deirdre swallows and then nods, first light catching the movement through the window, illuminating the tears that are beginning to run down her face.

'Go on, you'll miss the van. Quick, get away with you.'

Deirdre kisses her cheek quickly, just like she used to as a toddler, and runs from the room. She turns back to the altar, head bowed, prayers falling from her lips.

Later that morning, Father Conchobar bursts into her office, Ewan Mac Durthacht behind him.

'Where is she, Sister?' he asks through gritted teeth.

She takes her time standing up, her old joints on their own schedule, and walks around the desk.

'She'll be in the laundry, working, Father.'

He slaps her so hard the blood pools in her mouth, the force of the blow bringing her to her knees.

'You know fine well she's not there, we've already looked.'

She looks up into his eyes and thinks, as she often does, how weak men are. Their only resolution and resort lies in their fists. Father Conchobar sees the disdain in her eyes. He clenches his own fist and brings it firmly down on her mouth. The splintering of teeth bounces off the walls.

Deirdre

Twelve years later

She sits in the back garden and watches her husband pull the dry sheets off the line, spinning them over their daughter's head. Aodhamair squeals in delight, her six-year-old legs scurrying to catch her father. It is a perfect spring day in Stirling, the morning a slow crawl. She tilts her head up to the sun and dismisses the list of things she still has to do: the accounts for the pub, the order for the kitchen, the suppliers to be paid, the wages for the staff. It can all wait a few moments longer while she savours the taste of happiness, rolling back and forth over her tongue.

She feels her husband bend down and place a kiss on her lips and opens her eyes to meet his.

'Thanks for bringing the laundry in.' She smiles.

'You won't ever fold sheets again, my girl,' Naoise replies.

Deirdre feels her hips go soft. She takes her husband

by the hand, leaving their daughter playing outside, and leads him to their bedroom. Still, after all this time, she is surprised by the strength of her own desire for him. It is untamed. Hungry. Dripping. She becomes a wild creature with him, a wolf out of its den, an animal that is both hunter and prey, a screaming thing.

Afterwards, she lies facing him, rubbing her cheek softly on the pillow. Naoise looks at her as if she is heaven-sent.

'Do you remember when we first met?' she asks him.

'How could I forget?' he replies. 'You grabbed me by the ears and shook me. Told me to mind my manners.'

'Well, that's what you get for talking about a lady behind her back.'

'If you remember, woman,' Naoise says, his eyebrow raised, 'I was commenting on your beauty to my brothers. I was hardly being rude.'

She laughs and leans into him. 'I know. I just wanted to get your attention.'

'You already had it, love. It was always yours.'

He sits up and pulls Deirdre on top of him. She licks her lips. It is another hour before they return outside to meet the picture-perfect day once more.

The pub is full and the night air is sweet. The band plays a reel in the corner and the chairs and tables have been pushed to the side. People are still clamouring to get through the front door and the staff can't pull the pints quick enough. She sends a prayer up for Sister Lebarcham, as she always does, a quick thanks for all those evenings bent over the maths books that allowed her to take a dress-washing service and turn it into their first lease.

As she leans over the counter to pass a drink, she sees it. Today's copy of the *Irish Post*, sprawled open on the obituaries. Her eyes cling to the words 'Sister Lebarcham passed away peacefully on Thursday morning, surrounded by the nuns of the Lady of Mercy.' The world disappears as Deirdre picks up the paper, easing the soggy pages from one another. She is back in the mother-and-baby home, her childish voice calling for Chammy over and over again. She tries to swallow as the realisation sinks into her, but it is suddenly difficult to breathe. The man opposite her is looking at her expectantly, his mouth moving again and again.

'What?' she asks.

'How much, love?' he repeats exasperated.

She waves him away. 'On the house,' her back turning before he can finish thanking her.

Naoise is suddenly beside her, steering her out the back of the pub.

'What's wrong?'

She holds the paper out, her breathing becoming faster. 'Sister Lebarcham. She's . . .'

He quickly scans the page and swears quietly under his breath, pulling her into his chest.

'I'm so sorry, Dee.'

'She's dead, Naoise.'

'Yes.'

'She can't be dead. I haven't had a chance to see her.' Deirdre pulls away from him. 'I should have gone back. I should have seen her.'

Naoise just stares at her sadly.

'What have I been doing over here all this time?'

'Surviving,' he replies bluntly.

She snorts, angry at herself. 'I didn't even know she was ill. I should have known.' She shakes her head, as if clearing it. 'I'm going for the funeral.'

Naoise swears again, this time loudly. 'Like hell you are. It's not safe, Deirdre.'

'It's been over ten years since I left.'

'So what! We both know Mac Durthacht holds a grudge.' He scratches his beard angrily. 'He hasn't forgotten you slipping out of his fingers, and he sure as hell hasn't forgiven you. Or me for marrying you. Everyone back home says as much.'

'I don't care,' she replies, clenching her jaw and meeting her husband's angry stare.

'But I do, Deirdre!' shouts Naoise. 'You don't know what he's capable of.'

She softens slightly at the fear in his eyes. 'We're married. In the eyes of God and the world. We have a daughter. A life here. No one can take that away from us.'

'Ewan Mac Durthacht doesn't care about our life here. It's not worth the risk or the hassle of going.'

She hardens. 'Sister Lebarcham saved my life. It's only because of her we have this life. I'm going.'

Naoise opens his mouth to argue, but whatever he sees in her eyes stills him. He snaps his mouth shut stubbornly. 'Then I'm coming with you.'

She shrugs. 'As you like.'

Homecoming

The ferry ride over the channel is stormy and dark, the waves seeming to rise in tandem with the rage that rolls through Deirdre. She is sick to her stomach at her own cowardice. For staying away this long, ignoring the nagging voice that has been quietly urging her for the last three years to go home. If she can call that place home. There's always been a reason to put it off, something else to pay for. Now she will never get the chance to wrap her arms around Sister Lebarcham again, press her face to her weathered cheek and whisper what she did with her life. What Sister Lebarcham's final sacrifice bought her. How she took every sum and equation she taught her and made a living from the knowledge. How she had fulfilled her mother's whispered dream of a better life. She wanted to be able to tell Sister Lebarcham that she had done it for them all. For her mother, for herself, and for Chammy.

She clenches her teeth to stop the nausea overtaking her. She knows Chammy is dead, but she also doesn't know how she will arrive back in that wretched place, stand on the steps of her old home and not find her there, arms wide, mouth curving upwards in a small smile.

The boat arrives in Belfast along with the driving rain. It might be summer, but Ireland never really cared what season it was supposed to be, and she prefers it this way. Hood pulled up, shoulders braced against the wind, something to push back against. She cannot scream or yell or weep, but at least the sky was releasing its own misery down on them all.

Naoise walks by her side, suitcase clenched in his hand, his mouth a tight line. They find their way to the bed and breakfast, ready to travel to the home in the morning. In bed that night Naoise doesn't say much, just pulls her to him and holds her in a vice-like grip till morning.

The next morning dawns bright and clear, as if the rain had washed any bitterness out of the sky. As if Sister Lebarcham had ordered the perfect day to be laid to rest. She always liked sitting out in the sun when it happened to come around.

She clasps Naoise's hand as they step off the bus in town, her thumb rolling a pattern over his palm.

'Are you sure you don't want me to come with you?' he asks, worry making him look older.

She smiles, stroking his face, as if she could smooth away his fear. 'I have to do this by myself. Plus, it will be easier this way. Go see your mam. Send her my love and tell her I'll be up after the funeral.'

He nods and kisses her hard. Before he can say anything she says, 'I know, I'll be careful.'

He nods again as she turns to walk down the hill. She doesn't need to look back to know that Naoise stays standing at the end of the street, watching her fade into the distance.

Before she rounds the corner to the church, she pulls Sister Lebarcham's old habit and tunic out of her bag. The same one she wore to flee this place, she now wears to come back, hoping it will help her once more. Keep her hidden out of sight. She fixes the veil over her face and slips in with the other nuns, walking slowly past the mother-and-baby home and into the church. She sits at the back and clasps rosary beads she does not believe in, hoping people mistake her desire to hide for grief or piety.

A young priest leads the funeral, speaking about Sister Lebarcham in a way that tells Deirdre he did not know her at all. She wants to claw his eyes out. Grief and rage roll around her stomach and as she glimpses Sister Lebarcham's lying in the open casket, her face devoid of life and the woman she used to know, she chokes back the urge to howl.

Then she sees him. Father Conchobar, sitting in the front row, nodding along, a pained expression on his face that she imagines is supposed to be grief but looks more like a smirk. He stands at the end to say a few words about 'the sister he has served alongside'. It takes everything in Deidre's body to keep her head bowed. To not meet his gaze.

It's not until she walks with the congregation to the graveside that the first tear begins its slow journey down her face. She doesn't need the empty words of priests to grieve her own Chammy, but seeing her coffin lowered into the ground breaks some part of her. The urge to run, to flee the pain, pulses through her limbs but she holds still. She won't leave Sister Lebarcham now. She will honour her until the last clod of earth has landed on her grave. She will stay with her in her darkest moments, just as Sister Lebarcham had always stayed with her when she was a child. She won't fail her now.

As the last people leave, the gravediggers begin their work, the rhythmic thud of their spades the only sound. Eventually they too leave, and she bends down to take a handful of earth, gently placing it on top of the fresh mound. She lets her hand linger, stroking the mud as if Sister Lebarcham can feel it. As if it matters now. She looks up to the mother-and-baby home and knows there is another version of her life in which she is still there, and another one in which she is the one underground. But instead, she is here beneath a blue sky with a blue-eyed daughter waiting for her at home, a husband who folds the sheets so she doesn't have to, and money to feed them all. All because of one woman who kept a promise to another woman. A chain of them extending through the years and beyond the grave. 'Thank you,' is all she manages to mumble through her tears.

She doesn't know how long she stays like that, one hand on the mound of earth above Chammy, head bowed, the sky changing colour above her, but a sudden yell jerks her upright. She peers into the woods beyond the graveyard looking for the sound, and it's only when she hears Naoise scream her name that she begins to run, cutting through the trees, the muscle memory of her girlhood pulsing through her body as she dodges roots and branches. As if she never left.

By the time she arrives at the source of the noise her veil has been lost and her habit hangs around her neck, hair sprawling across her face. Naoise is slumped by the old coal shed, his face bruised and swollen, two men she doesn't know standing over him.

'Jesus Christ,' she gasps in horror, moving towards Naoise.

'I wouldn't take the Lord's name in vain if I were you, Deirdre,' says Father Conchobar, stepping out from behind the old oak she used to climb as a child.

Trembling, she moves back. A thickset man stands next to Father Conchobar and grins at her, his smile lopsided and empty.

'Allow me to finally make this introduction,' Father Conchobar continues. 'We're twelve years too late, but patience is a virtue. Ewan Mac Durthacht meet Deirdre, your new wife.'

Naoise lets out a strangled yell and tries to fight off the men. They punch the air out of him.

Deirdre feels the air leave her own chest. 'You must be out of your mind,' she gasps. 'I'm married.'

Mac Durthacht steps forward, pulls a knife from his pocket and runs it, quicker than it takes to draw breath, across her husband's throat. 'Not any more, you're not.'

There is a single second, a sharp intake of breath, a slow blink, before the world swings into motion. Deirdre thinks she screams, but the noise that comes from her is not human.

'No, no, no.'

She reaches Naoise, placing her hands to his throat, as if it could change anything.

A slow smile spreads across Mac Durthacht's face.

Father Conchobar makes the sign of the cross.

The light leaves her husband's eyes.

The world ripples.

Deirdre leaps at Mac Durthacht, her blood-soaked fists cracking across his face. He laughs.

'You bastard,' she gasps between breaths. She wants to tear the flesh from his bones, but she barely touches him before he throws her to the ground as if brushing lint from a jacket.

She stumbles to her feet, trying to catch her breath. 'God forgive you, what have you done?'

'Stop whimpering, woman,' replies Mac Durthacht. 'I will not be made a fool of, and a man has a right to defend himself.'

'Defend?' she splutters.

Father Conchobar steps forward. 'Yes, indeed,' he nods. 'Your husband viciously attacked Mr Mac Durthacht first. A tragic and unnecessary act of violence. I'll be calling the authorities, but in the meantime—'

He doesn't have the chance to finish the sentence before Deirdre lunges, catching the priest by surprise and knocking him off his feet as he stumbles over the root of the tree. She tries to make contact, her nails frantic and desperate, searching for the sockets, the mouth, anything to sink her fingers into, but Mac Durthacht pulls her easily off him by the back of her habit, holding her close to his face. His grin smothers all the light out of her.

'You're going to be a real handful, I can tell,' whispers Mac Durthacht, leaning into to her mouth. 'We'll have a lot of fun together. You're even more beautiful than they said.'

She smiles slowly, looking up beneath her lashes, before lifting her knee and slamming it into Mac Durthacht's crotch. He folds like paper, a small puff of air escaping him as he wilts to the ground. For a split second she takes in the scene around her. Father Conchobar rising, inching closer towards her. Mac Durthacht's face slowly turning purple. Tiny spurts of blood still gurgling from her husband's throat. A jet-black raven standing next to his unmoving head, beginning to peck at the blood-soaked ground. Life stubbornly moving on around death. Time still ticking.

She turns, just as Father Conchobar lunges for her, and runs. The same way she used to, hair whipping behind her, arms furiously propelling her forward, just like a bird.

She hears Conchobar's footsteps behind her, but she is quicker and knows these woods better. She makes it up the hill and falls breathlessly into the church, rushing to the seventh pew from the front, running her hands along the wood-panelled wall as she goes. She finds the slight indent and pushes. The panel swings open and she curls into her childhood hiding place, trying to steady her breath.

Some wild part of her wants to believe it's Sister Lebarcham who is searching for her. That she is still a girl and the man she loves isn't lying in the forest beyond the coal shed, eyes wide open, the shock still in them.

The church door swings open. Father Conchobar's slow footsteps echo off the flagstone floor. 'There's nowhere to hide, Deirdre. You're in my house now.'

She clenches her teeth to stop from screaming.

'Ewan will give you a good life. While the death of your husband is tragic, there is no need for you to fall into hardship and trouble. There is a clear path for you here, my child, but you must be reasonable. You must see sense. Sister Lebarcham would not want this for you.'

At the mention of Chammy, fury licks in her belly, overtaking fear, and she pushes open the panelling and steps out.

'Don't you dare mention her name.' He swings around to face her. 'You have no idea what she wanted.'

He sneers at her, the sing-song quality to his voice disappearing. 'I know she was insolent, disobedient and more trouble than she was worth. Like you. And your mother. All of you, unable to simply do as you're told.'

He walks towards her, and for a moment she is a child again. Frozen. Fixed to the spot. Breathless with fear. Trembling in his office during Bible study while his hands inched their way across her body. She had always been saved by Chammy, who seemed to know when to burst in with a message from the Mother Superior or an emergency that required Father Conchobar's attention. She would wipe Deirdre's tears afterwards and remind her that she must never be alone with him. That she has taught her to hide for this reason. But Chammy is gone. There is nowhere to hide.

'After the kindness of this parish,' he continues, 'this Church. After my personal protection, this is how you repay me.'

She hears the crack of the back of his hand across her cheek before she feels the throbbing pain in her mouth.

'And look at what you have done,' he continues. 'Look at the chaos you have caused. A good man gone, killed in his prime because of your wilful disobedience.' He strokes his hand across the red bloom of her cheek where a bruise is beginning to form. 'Naoise is dead because of you, Deirdre. Had you stayed, had you done as you were told, that man would be alive today. All the better off for never having met you. His soul rests on your conscience.'

He pushes the hair back from her forehead and tilts her face to the light.

'Such beauty,' he murmurs, 'and yet such destruction in your wake. Are you proud of yourself now, Deirdre? Are you happy with what you have done?'

She tentatively steps back. Her legs feel boneless. All the fear of her childhood winds its way around her throat as she slowly begins to back away.

He sneers at her, his eyes raking their way up and down the length of her body. 'There is no running this time, girl. You will marry Ewan Mac Durthacht and fulfil what was promised. Your mother is long gone. That ungrateful bitch is dead. There is no one left to protect you.' He grins in a way that makes her blood run cold. 'It's just you and me, Deirdre.'

Images flash through her mind. Naoise's gaping throat. Sister Lebarcham's sunken cheek as she lay in her coffin. The handful of earth she had pressed on top of her grave. The blue sky in Stirling. Her daughter laughing. The billowing sheets of laundry. Sister Lebarcham's face of pretend surprise when they played hide and seek. The mound of earth. Her husband's sweat-drenched body. Her own body on top of him. Her mother laughing. The tree she would climb. The boy in the woods.

Father Conchobar slowly begins to unbuckle his belt as he inches closer to her, never taking his eyes off her face. There is nothing but confidence in his posture, decades of being obeyed in his every step. 'You know something, Deirdre?' he whispers softly, his voice as low and gentle as a lover. 'Your mother loved you very much.'

She chokes back a sob as she feels her back hit the church wall. 'It's why when I called for her,' he continued, 'she came willingly. She did her duty. Repaid my kindness. Paid her debts. Gave herself to me whenever I wanted. It is time for you to do the same. To sacrifice, as your mother did.'

She shakes her head quickly. 'She wouldn't,' she gasps. 'She would never.'

He laughs. 'But she did. You know, I think she even enjoyed it, but that's to be expected from a whore like her. After all, that's the reason she ended up here with us.'

He finally reaches her and places his hands on either side of her arms, stroking gently. 'Come now. It is time.'

He turns her around, his weight heavy behind her, and slowly laces his fingers through hers, placing their joined hands on the wall. She stares at them, just like the hands of any lovers you might pass in the street. He untangles his hands from hers and they begin their slow descent down her arms, her ribs, her waist. They linger for a brief second before they crawl over her hips. She rests her hot cheek on the cool stone. Hears his trousers thud softly to the floor.

'That's right,' he murmurs, 'good girl. Just like your mother.'

There is a pop, a small click inside of her, a lighter springing to flame. She sees her mother's bright face, the steam of the laundry a sheen across her features. She can so clearly see her mother rubbing the sheets against her cheek, as if she was standing next to her in this godless church. The mischief that twinkled in her eyes always present. She hears her mother's voice, '*Misneach, a chroí.*' *Courage, my heart.* The words she would say every time they were separated, her mother to the dormitory with the other women, Deirdre to the nursery with the children who were still waiting for families to claim them while their mothers wept down the corridor. She had stood by her mother's unmarked grave as Sister Lebarcham took her hand and whispered those same words to her and she in turn has whispered them to her own daughter. Now here, Father Conchobar on the cusp of taking everything, those words whisper to her once more: 'Misneach, a chroí.'

Deirdre sobs again, but this time she forces it out between her teeth. She feels his body go slack as he positions himself. She breathes slowly, mustering as much force as she can, and throws her head back, her skull colliding with Father Conchobar's face.

The pain floods her, but she whirls around in time to see him stumble backwards, shock laced across his features as he trips over one of the hassocks, tumbling down, arms flapping furiously, reaching for her as if she would stop him. The crack of his head connecting with the pew reverberates through the church, his body sprawled awkwardly between two rows, his eyes firmly shut.

She clasps her hands across her mouth in shock. Steps closer and peers at him, noticing the slow rise and fall of his chest, and she exhales, weak-kneed and gasping for air. The pain comes screaming back and she grabs the back of her head, her hand immediately wet. She pulls it in front of her to see the red blood, her heart stopping in fear, before tentatively prodding the back of her head again. She finds nothing and exhales again, suddenly noticing the blood oozing from Father Conchobar's face, his nose bent at a grotesque angle. She crouches down close to the priest and sees red beginning to bloom across the flagstones.

She swallows down the grief that threatens to break her if she thinks about Naoise – *not now, not now* – and shakes her head. She moves the two pews and grabs Father Conchobar's arms, hauling him to the altar. Bar his breathing changing slightly, he doesn't stir. She has to stop twice to catch her breath, and by the time she has him where she wants him, she is dripping in sweat, the priest's blood smeared down the front of Sister Lebarcham's old tunic.

Looking around for what she can use, Deirdre spots the pew ropes and grabs two, tying one to each of the unconscious priest's wrists and the other ends to the altar. It is a massive, ugly, golden thing, part marble, part wood, with gilded gold on it, that Chammy always said was an arrogance for any church to own when people were starving in the parish. She smiles wickedly. Wishes she could tell Chammy it's finally being put to good use. She licks her lips. Something has taken over her. The fear has hardened into something she does not recognise. It feels wonderful.

She stands back and cocks her head, surveying the scene. *Still not right.* She takes two more pew ropes and ties them to his ankles above his trousers, joining the other ends to the railing at the entrance to the altar. The distances are not symmetrical and so he is splayed out oddly, like a misshapen Vitruvian Man, blood rolling from his nose slowly into his ear. His trousers are still gathered at his ankles, so she pulls them off and throws them to the side. She leaves him like that and rummages in the sacristy, finally emerging with a blunt bread knife, the only thing she could find, a glass bottle of holy water and a stole. She sits next to him and hums to herself as she begins splashing the water on his face to wake him.

After a few minutes he blinks his eyes open, staring straight at her, and then wildly around as he realises his constraints. Before he can say anything, she slams the stole into his mouth, tying a tight gag. He tries to choke out words but she shakes her head. 'Come now, Father, it's time to pay your debts.'

His eyes flare wide in fear as she drags the bread knife against his cheek.

He shakes his head wildly from side to side, bucking up and down as she begins to pull down his shorts. Time hangs suspended above them, the darkness of night closes around them. She thinks about her mother, playing in the laundrette, the babies she cuddled before they were gone, the kids she made friends with before they too were gone, Chammy chasing her through sunlit woods, Chammy's smell as she crawled into the old nun's lap in the evening, the bright lights of the pub and the brighter smile of her daughter. Naoise folding the laundry. The sheets. Those starch-white sheets. Yes, she murmurs to herself, there are debts to be paid.

An hour later, she strips off the habit and takes a fresh one from the wardrobe in the sacristy, grabbing a veil alongside it. She hurriedly steps into the new outfit, the same way she once had done with Sister Lebarcham, and strides out of the church, heading for Belfast and a ferry that will take her across the sea. Home.

Before she catches the bus to Belfast, she stops at a telephone box and calls the authorities. She quickly explains that they will find a dead body in the woods at the bottom of the hill by the church, and that Ewan Mac Durthacht killed him. They can also find Father Conchobar inside the church, but if they want to find him alive, they must hurry. The operator asks her to stay calm. To stay on the line. To answer some questions. How strange, she thinks. She feels calmer than she ever has. Everything has slowed down. Life has become grainy and fluorescent in its detail. She gently places the receiver back in its cradle and, like a bride on her wedding day, slowly lowers the veil across her face. This time, Naoise won't be the one to lift it. He has gazed upon her face for the last time. Her legs tremble. The bile rises. She knows that in the not-too-distant future, she will hate herself for leaving the man she loves to rot at the bottom of the forest. For not bringing him home. She will hate herself more for letting him fall in love with her. For not keeping her wretched beauty away from those she loved. Like a disease, it has infected everyone around her. It has altered the course of her life. Painted a target on her back. Made a mockery out of her.

She steps out of the telephone box and into the night. The darkness nearly swallows her whole. She would like to sink into it. Drop to her knees. Tear her throat out. Peel the skin off her face. Anything to let the grief claw its way out of her. Naoise is gone. The world has been cleaved open. Nothing will ever be the same. But there is still a blue-eyed little girl who waits for, beneath a cornflower sky. There is still a life worth living. She unbows her head. 'Misneach, a chroí,' she whispers.

WOO
Sarah Maria Griffin

The Wooing of Etain

I wrote it off at first. You see these posts online, shared over and over, strange and unexpected things children come out with. Things about seeing women at the foot of their beds, about being watched over by someone they know – someone you don't know. Imaginary friends, imaginary lives. The creative nodes in their growing brains unburdened, somehow, by anxiety, so they have a freedom that adults can't quite afford – children can just make things up, can't they? It's their right, the absolute psychic freedom they have, or, well, that they're supposed to have. If it's your first time on the planet, you have nothing to mull over, nothing to carry.

Even from when she was very small, her father and I would just listen to her babble, her narration of her life. She spoke first at such a young age, so even when her language was made up of only fragments, she used them to paste together a rolling monologue of the things she saw, as she saw them. Puddle. Tree. Doggy. Cloud. Sunshine.

Banana. Toast. Moon. All of these singular words one day just latched together with a kind of grammar, her sentences full and fast and her talk literal. Until it became the other thing, and eventually, she told us the things she remembered. Memories that we had no place for in any life we had witnessed her having – so we assumed she was just a born storyteller. We come from a strong oral tradition and all that. We told her stories from the moment she was born, just how we were told stories ourselves. Her stories felt like recollection though. Never stalled with the pauses that one takes when creating something new. It felt as though she was simply recounting memories to us, when she was too little to have many memories at all.

When I think now of how we rationalised it, I am shocked still that we didn't bring her to be seen by someone earlier. Not that having her seen did a single thing to help, in the end. Not that I listened, not that I could listen. There was only one way this was all going to go, and if you believed Etain, it was the way things had gone for her time and time again before.

When it happened first, it wasn't from another life. It was from the very start of hers. She told me, from her place across the little white table in the corner of the kitchen, that there wasn't enough water in the place she grew in for her to turn and make her way out, but that was all right, because a nice woman with white gloves lifted her out with ease. She went to a place where there was bright light and music and then she met me, and I was warm and good and very big, the biggest face she had ever seen. I asked her if she remembered what I said, and she threw her grubby, buttery hands in the air and said, 'I feel love!'

When she said this, barely four years old, in crisp sentences that had presumably been honed from my constant chat and ceaseless playing of podcasts, she looked at me over her plate of toast triangles and into a part of my eyes that made me feel like I was being operated on, again.

There had been no point in explaining to her that she had been a caesarean birth – she simply knew she had been made inside my body, and that she came out to meet us. You could frighten a child – or an adult, frankly, with too much description of exactly how a child enters the world via scalpel, spinal block and luck. I certainly didn't tell her about the loss of amniotic fluid, about the week's confinement in a hospital room, about being watched around the clock by baffled midwives who could not place where the water that should have been in my womb was going to, or why it was diminishing and rising so quickly. How a woman can become a tide, alone in the white of a maternity suite, while the medical team stand at the shore with no answers. How nothing was certain until she was out of me.

I didn't tell her about her position, breech, her head inside my ribcage, making it impossible for her to turn the right direction. I didn't tell her that in any other time of history we both would have died, that she and I were miracles of science. Our survival, our healing, our forward march into life after the event horizon of birth, such a glorious thing.

Not really a chat you can have with a toddler, you know? I was saving it, perhaps, for someday when she was an adult. Perhaps when she had a child of her own. She had no way of knowing – even though she was, technically, present for the event. So when she looked at me and described the diminishing pool, the white latex hands of the consulting ob-gyn, as casually as though she was recounting an afternoon at the soft play, I did feel frightened. Not of her, but of what she knew. Of the chance that she was something other than the girl I had borne, or that something other lived inside her. An awareness. A knowledge.

'I feel love,' was not what I had said though. It was what Donna Summers sang, over the speakers in the operating theatre. This welcome anthem. These heavy, metronomic beats, her stride into the world, this outrageously simple statement. I feel love, I feel love, I feel love, I feel love, I feel love. We listened to it in the car, we listened to it in the kitchen, it was a song that we decorated the air of our life with. I could, at least, write this off as coincidence. She was as likely to screech a lyric from that song as she was to say, 'Let it go,' or 'I am Moana.' So silly, if a little spooky.

The next time she talked about life just before her birth, she audaciously told me she was there the night she was made by me and her father. We were en route to the big wooden playground in the park by the seaside, near where I went to secondary school. The park that had, when I was young, been mostly a site of mitching off class and illicit consumption of naggins of coconut rum. The park that had somehow shed adolescence with me, and now was a hub of mothers, overseeing their feral young caper around bright Technicolor installations that were designed to challenge their kinaesthetic learning and not, somehow, break any of their collarbones and wrists. The height of the slides made me feel ill, but made Etain laugh like a brook in the woods.

She laughed like this when she told me that we had been in the hot country. I asked her, Like on a holiday? Yes, a holiday, she said, I love holidays, to the beach! I nodded. She said that me and Daddy sat in the hot air and the moon was big and the sea was loud and she was flying through the sky with her tiny wings and her different eyes and then a gust of wind blew her into the red drink I was drinking.

'Mm-hm,' I said, my stomach tight. 'Red drink.' Wine. Merlot. From the Carrefour.

Her father and I had been trying for a year and had all but given up. We'd been told to take a holiday, relax, as if the spectre of what we couldn't seem to manage didn't rise terrible and cold at the same time every month. As if a holiday would help. The expensive, invasive app on my phone let me know that the window of time was open, and the pair of us shrugged and said might as well see what happens. The night was almost ruined because the heat of Palma had laden the air thick with bugs, but the more we drank, the less we cared. I worried it was the smell of the sun lotion, and we both smoked our way through two boxes of cheap, misbranded cigarettes to try to keep the insects away. I all but gagged when I discovered one, had, too late, dive-bombed into the last of my drink. I choked, swallowed, a little wine came out of my nose. Etain's father laughed and patted my back and held back my hair while I retched and told me it was like the good old days, us at a house party somewhere, me unable to hold my drink, him minding me while I tried to evacuate my stomach – at the time, to make room for more drink. We'd been fools, in our twenties, but fools who adored each other. Fools who made each other somehow stupider and more capable, at once.

The next morning her father had said to me, soft in the white starch of the hotel bed, 'There was an old woman who swallowed a fly' – and I pulled a pillow from under myself and hit him with it and he laughed so hard and we had sex again. Why not? There wasn't much chance for us, we thought, the diminishing time slot of fertility closing in around us by the second.

But that was it. That fly, I supposed, and somehow in the park, sunny and leafy and alight with the laughter of other children, she looked up at me with that same blue gaze she had a year before and said that she remembered. Airborne, prism eyes, the heat of Majorca, the thick red liquid of supermarket wine. The passing into my throat. Into my body. The wine spilling her into the water, the tiny sea in my belly. And in that cocktail she transformed. She became who she was, again. I smiled down at her and did not betray my horror at her knowledge. I told her to run ahead, show me how fast she could go. The little lights on the soles of her sneakers pinged pink and white and green off the path. I felt as though my bones were turning soft.

Perhaps telling my aunt was the mistake – once you speak a weird secret aloud to another person it becomes real, like a raw tooth taken out of the darkness of your mouth. My funny, gentle godmother, my mother's oldest sister, Evelyn, stood in my kitchen with her jacket still on, her hands on her hips, light glinting off her hoop earrings and the rail of dense gold rings on her fingers, and said through her cigarette-grey teeth, 'Hun, you're to come with me to see a medium. Your ma and the rest of them always said Etain had an old soul and I agree, the eyes on her aren't the eyes of a small child. I know a reliable one. Up in Kildare. Near the shopping outlets. We've all been to her, she's very good.'

And perhaps I was more the fool to bring little wee Etain to the potpourri-dense living room of a mid-fifties Kildare woman with my mother and three of my aunts in tow. I certainly felt like one, but the sincerity with which my godmother led the affair helped take the edge off the absurdity of bringing your highly imaginative daughter before a suburban mystic who best specialises in communicating with the dead and aura readings at hen parties.

My cynicism was not kind, especially given how warmly she treated us, the mugs and mugs of thick milky tea she served us as she observed my child playing politely with a box of oracle cards and pastel crystals on the shag carpet, as we sat around her on the plastic-coated suite.

My mother took Etain to the car after half an hour of this, and I sat with my aunts, and Evelyn held my hand for support as the mystic – Breda, her name was Breda – gave a deep sigh and averted her eyes from mine and said, to the window, 'She's a ticket. A joy. Beautiful, too, you can see the start of a remarkable fairness in her. But look, I'm sure someone has said this before – she's about older than the wheel, girl, you can see it in her eyes. She has seen many shapes, many lifetimes. She's been a great traveller, but not of her own choice. Over her lives on this earth, again and again she finds herself with two spirits in pursuit of her. A king who loves her, and his queen, scorned, who hates her so much that she casts terrible, terrible spells down on her. She is caught in the push and pull between them, and her fate is marked by their argument. His love for her, and his wife's jealousy. Though her path through time has been dictated by the violent tides of this acrimony, it has led her to you, for one of her lifetimes. And aren't you lucky to have her?'

As Breda spoke, the stiff, perfumed air of her living room fell dense and silent. I thought I was going to be sick. The dried plants and oils cloying in on me were matched by the weird gravity of what this woman was telling me about my child. Evelyn's eyes were on the floor, pouring tears. My other two aunts clasped each other's hands, their eyes closed, listening as if at Mass. We kind of were, I suppose, at a Mass, and this priestess, this preacher, was unfurling a litany of little Etain's life, lives, before.

We paid her almost a thousand euros for the privilege. It was as much as my last payment to the office of the doctor who brought her into the world. Three heavy zeroes. What was I to do with this? Only file it away somewhere in the back of my head and move on? Was I to be frightened out of sending her to Montessori, or to school, or on into the world? Was this, this tale, this yarn spun by an eloquent charlatan, going to define how I engaged with her? Was it a secret of her existence, or a story told for a high fee to a room full of vulnerable women, spooked by the wise eyes of their tiniest family member? I could not carry that day heavily for long. There were things to do. Foods to try for the first time. Parks to stomp in, supermarkets to browse, letters to learn and songs to sing and animals to enjoy. Life to actually be lived, rather than be read through the prism of some strange destiny. I couldn't do it. I had to let Etain be a child. And, when I think of how it all ended, I am glad I did. I am glad I did not become another captor.

She wouldn't tell me another new story of her lives before for some time, after we had seen Breda. Sometimes she would say, 'Oh, when I was a fly I saw the whole world from way, way up. Everything was so big! And I was so small!' or things of that nature. Sometimes she would say she was a fly for a very, very long time and she travelled very, very far. But there were no new memories. She was, in many ways, a straightforward child in the world. She cried and she danced and she spat out food she didn't like. I blinked and she was ten. I blinked again and she was sixteen. I was over half a century old, the scar from where they cut her from me still numb, sometimes, my gait a little funny.

There were no other children, as we had guessed, but she was enough. More than enough. Central. Hilarious. And, as Breda had asserted, beautiful. Though I assume every mother feels like this in some way or other about their child, awed at their singularly perfect face, full of resonance and hereditary detail – I really must tell you, Etain was beautiful. Her beauty didn't make her less kind, less silly, less sweet. It never calloused her to others. There was a tremendous grace about her, and her friends were assorted types from cross sections of social groups. She had mates from cross-country running, from camogie. She had mates from speech and drama. She would go to the art-house cinema in the city a couple of times a month with a clutch of well-meaning goths. I felt somehow as though I was observing perfection in motion, some kind of socially complete savant. Good grades, good friends, good health, good heart.

So, when the first night eventually came that Etain stumbled home drunk, eyes mad, yellow hair tangled, reeking of cigarette smoke, I handled her standard teenage misstep with grace. She was just about to be seventeen, of course there was a rebellion brewing inside her.

In the bathroom she knelt over the toilet bowl and I held back her hair and petted her back, a big glass of water and a cool washcloth for her head ready for her when she was finished heaving. The mascara stains on her soft cheeks flung me into my own past, my own teens, and ricocheted me back to her tiny cheeks as I held her in infancy. I rubbed my thumb across them as she lay back against the side of the bathtub, making the shushing sound that had soothed her back then. The shush comes from the womb, the noise the placenta makes, the pulse of it, whoosh, whoosh, whoosh. Something carnal and old in us finds it soothing, the first watery music. I was almost tempted to turn on the shower – that used to settle her when she was in her bassinet too. But there was no noise of motherhood that could soothe her. She had something to tell me, slurring, but definite.

'I was a pool of water,' she said, 'Before I was a fly, before I fell into your wine and into your womb and out into this life,' and I said, 'Go on?' and petted her, like she was a frightened animal.

'I was a pool of water in a green field and I dried up. I felt it, I felt myself shrinking, I felt myself changing, growing limbs I had not had, losing the truth of myself and shifting into something I did not know, something awful. I felt myself fade and disappear and just when I was almost gone, I was the fly. And when I was a fly, he found me, and kept me in a little glass case as his companion, wherever he went. A tiny prison. We were happy, I think, like that – me and him. He never loved anyone else but me – never needed anyone but me, even though I was a little red fly and he was a man and we couldn't even kiss each other. But she – the woman – his real wife – found me again and she shouted so hard that she blew me away to the hot country, and that was when I fell into your wine. I would probably scream bloody murder if I found out my husband was in love with a little red fly.'

Her eyes had fallen closed and her head lolled back and I made the whoosh sound to her, hoping that the tide of my calm would wash away this strange recital. The chords of it so similar, but these new grace notes made my own stomach lurch, made the tiles on the bathroom floor feel unreliable and soft.

'I would love you even if you were still a little red fly,' I said to her. 'I would love you if you were a puddle in a field. I would love you no matter what you were,' and she sobbed, mouth crooked in a way I had only seen the time when she sprained her wrist coming off a slide the wrong way.

'That's the problem,' she said. 'I can never just be a girl. I can never just be a person. No matter what I do, he loves me, she hates me, and even when I am water I am not safe. Even when I am a horrible little bug, I am not safe. Even when I am a tiny baby, the water dries up around me again. She hates me, so I can't just be a girl. He loves me, so I can't just be a girl.'

And a part of me that wanted this to be mere teenage melodrama wondered, is it the goths she's hanging around with who are bringing this triangle to her table? Has she caught herself up in some polyamory nonsense for which she is not emotionally equipped? Has she taken up with some poor girl's boyfriend and made her furious? I'd done something similar myself as a teenager, and I'd had it done to me; been both corners of that triangle in my life. Was there a healthy, kind way to parent her through this moment – what would the forums suggest? Govern, garden, guide, isn't that what they say about kids? When they are tiny you are the mayor of their every moment, when they are a little bigger you treat them as though you were tending to a precious plant – helping it survive and thrive but allowing it to take whatever shape it needs – and then, when they are bigger again, say, on the crest of seventeen, all you can do is be the lighthouse that casts safety through the dark, be a point for them to return to. Isn't that what you're supposed to do, when your child is almost an adult and is falling apart? Beam light down on them so they can find the path? They might as well give you all these metaphors before you leave the hospital, along with the instructions to hold their head up and make sure they're always wearing one layer of clothing more than you are. When you have a child you find yourself saying these things to yourself, and then to them, hoping that something works. Metaphor doesn't work, not in the clutch of things. Not when all you want to do is mould reality to fix their problems. You don't want to be thinking in the abstract when your daughter is crying at half two in the morning over a situation you don't understand. It is not the time for poetry.

So instead, I stuck to the truth. I told her that even though her imagination is one of my favourite parts of her, that I could be more helpful if she gave me a very literal description of what exactly is going on with this girl who hates her and this guy who loves her. I assured her that I would never be angry at her, and I would always be on her side, but it would help if she left the metaphors behind, for now. In the crawl space behind my eyes I could see Breda the medium telling me the girl was older than the wheel. Telling me about the pursuit. Warning me. It's easy for your mind to go to these places rather than to face the problem at hand – the problem being, one very drunk and sad teenager.

She didn't say much else then, just thanked me, told me she loved me, nestled her face into my shoulder, leaving mascara stains on my nightshirt and a sort of miasma of tobacco smell that I could still pick up in the morning. It made me want to smoke, though I hadn't in years. It made me never want to be young again too.

I stood with her while she washed her face. I made her drink the whole glass of water and eat two slices of toast. I watched her brush her teeth in her pyjamas, more sober, sadder, more tired. Her father slept through the caper of it all, and when I told him about it the next day he said, 'Well, the apple doesn't fall far from the tree,' and I was annoyed, a little. Etain was not an apple, and I was not a tree. Etain was not a fly, nor a pool of water, and I was not some strange vessel that harboured her briefly during some long journey through time and space, I insisted this to myself. We were both just women. We were both just girls.

That night was just a blip. Etain was unchanged by it. In the cold light of day she never mentioned the triangle again, not at breakfast the following morning, not in any of our quiet evenings on the sofa thereafter. An experimental night of rebellion didn't bode poorly on the rest of her academic and social life. There was never even a whisper of a vape, let alone cigarettes about her. Sometimes I'd observe her and wonder, was she too good to be true? When was the trapdoor going to open inside of her, like it had with me when I was her age? I kept waiting for her to turn into a pale, mute, occasionally hissing thing.

And you know, silly as this sounds, she was all set up to smash her Leaving Certificate. I was so proud of her. The sheer work ethic she had, the quiet, determined ambition. I hadn't the head for it all myself, but she was going to do international politics and history at Trinity College; she was captain of the camogie team. No interest in boys, or girls, that we knew of, but as far as we were concerned it was safer for a girl who looked like her to be kind of a late bloomer. Fine enough if they paid her attention, but if she had no interest in them herself it gave her more of her own time to spend on growing, cultivating her own self, rather than living in some intense teenage tandem with a lad or a girl who would be gone by the time she turned twenty. Selfishly, it was nice to still feel like she was mine. Like she wanted to spend time at home between the gold stars of her schedule. Plenty of nights, rolling up to the end of her schooling, the pair of us would sit on the couch with hot drinks, warm in the glow of the television, narrating our opinions to one another. Her father would join us from time to time, and on those nights it felt like there was true balance in the universe. Her figure in the doorway from the kitchen, her hair in curlers for school, soft grey sweatpants, an old camogie jersey. She was committed to Christmas slippers, year round, and often wore cooling eye-bag patches like crescent moons on her face, even though she had never even had a whisper of a purple shadow under her eyes. I can feel the way the shape of the sofa redistributed itself when she would sit down beside me. That big red sofa a quiet island, and we a perfect population of three. Though there was a storm on the horizon, I couldn't – wouldn't – be able to feel it until it had passed the threshold of my door and it was too late.

The night she left us came just as she turned eighteen. To talk of it now feels like madness. Our girl, standing with a man in the window of her lavender bedroom. Walking to the door of the room at precisely the moment in which she unbecame our Etain and became something else, at the hand of this man she had memories of since her very first childhood. This man who had been chasing her. This man who severed her from her body time and time again. Transformations, time and time over. He did not look like us. He looked old, and young, and not from here. He looked alien and ancient. He looked like he knew her, and she beside him looked like she knew him too. A stranger making Etain a stranger to us.

I don't even think I screamed.

To watch a human body become something else, unbecome, is not something the eyes can manage, let alone the brain, let alone the heart. Both of them at once shrank and stretched, there in the light her laptop gave off, still running, still humming. They made no sound but the odd crackling of bone and flesh, like kindling. The whiteness all over them was immediate, but it took me a moment to realise what was growing all over them was feathers. Feathers on the floor, in the air, on their bodies, which were no longer the shape of my body or yours but long, their wings archangel and terrible and risen in violence.

Their necks were the worst thing, giraffe in their stretching, serpentine suddenly in flexibility, white and tubed with feathers. Thick, terrible cords before the face of my daughter became a bird of orange beak, and the man matched her, the pair of them all but identical, wild, terrible. I searched for my daughter's eyes in the mess of things – where was my baby in this disaster? – and she was lost in it, like in a kind of rapture. This is what it was to witness an exit from reality. This was the fading and the disappearing. This was the growing of strange new limbs. This was not Etain's first time in this wretched dance of body becoming.

She had changed and transformed and drowned and undrowned. She had travelled all this way to meet me, and her travelling was not yet done. I looked for her body but it was evaporating. How dry feathers are, they might as well be bone. How there was no blood. No tears. I watched her mutate and transform. I watched her disappear. He loved her, so she could not just be a girl.

What is it they say about swans? Their wings are so strong they could break your arm, if they wanted to. Swans hiss like snakes, and mate for life. Swans should be left alone. I thought there was a myth, an old story about a queen who turned some children she did not care for into swans. I had never heard a story like this, though, before. A girl beloved so darkly and despised so entirely that she was turned again, and again, into something that was not what she wished to be, which was just herself.

In these stories you don't hear about the mortals they left behind, standing in the room they decorated so tenderly, polite little heaps of clean laundry by the wardrobe, make-up influencer chatting inane nonsense on the laptop screen, the jasmine of body spray still hanging around the vanity, the hairdryer still plugged in as the girl elopes out the open window, all terrible violent wings and mute in the eyes, behind a creature, a man who has loved her since before the wheel. You don't hear about the humans left in the white, feathery wake.

How the clock kept ticking. How the silence fell on the house. How the police eventually had to be called, some strange lie told about kidnapping, how that made you look, how that made your father look. How nobody could explain the feathers.

My husband had been standing on the stairway when it happened. He was at a slight angle to the room and offered a mere snapshot of the horror, but saw enough to be changed by it. He himself was transformed into a grey, boneless thing. He allowed me to design the lies and agreed, softly, with every delicate lie I embroidered around our horror, our private loss. I would say he became someone I didn't know, but that wouldn't be the truth at all. He became no one. He dissolved. When a job offer opened up for him in Dubai, he simply told me he was going. Plenty of Irish over there, he said, numb, refusing to meet my gaze. I told him to go, holding the private hope that whatever happened to him in the sun would cure him, but also understanding that he may never come back. And if he needed to take flight himself to survive, so be it. If I could have grown wings and fled myself, I would. But someone had to stay and protect the story. Someone had to stay and wait for her, in case she appeared again one day.

After the storm passed – the media, the police, the investigation, the endless circulation of her picture on social media, the remarks from strangers on how they had never seen a girl who looked like her, such a beauty, what a terrible shame, the essays by women broken by the mere idea of the abduction, the loss – I went to Breda.

My mother, my godmother, my other two aunts flanked me like a grey procession. There was no little girl by my side, only a Ziplock bag full of white feathers I had gathered before the police got to our house that night. Though the police had searched our home high and low – the fridge, the freezer, dug up our back garden – the little bag of feathers in my knitting bag hadn't even caught a stray glance. Girls go missing all the time. They are stopped on their walks home from work, their evening runs, and they are ended there and then and the world gasps a second, then continues, and then a man kills another one, then another one. Etain's surreal, eldritch disappearance hid in the rot of this ordinary, terrible cycle. Feathers were the least of anyone's concern. Only mine, sitting at night, staring into the white of the bag, wondering where my child was.

Breda flung the door open wide and her arms around me and I broke into pieces in her embrace. She had pointed to the bomb and I had packed it away where I could not hear the ticking getting faster, could not see the timer running down.

In her living room, still the same as it ever was, we sat on the floor, the heavy carpet maybe only changed in that it was a little stained by a decade or so of sunlight. Breda emptied out a bag of quartz. I emptied out my bag of feathers and I told her the thing I had not said to anyone, the women of my family horrified as I spoke, assuming I was having some kind of psychotic break, instead of merely speaking the truth. Breda listened, stoic and patient, as I told her of my daughter made swan, of how the tale of the water and the fly and being chased through time was true and I was merely a rest stop for Etain on her way through the universe, being pursued by a man who loved her and a woman who hated her.

Eventually, Breda leaned forward and ran her hands through the feathers and said to me that Etain was free. That there were transformations and adventures ahead of her still, thousands of years of them. That she was a high queen in her way. That she was part of a story so far out of our hands that we could never assume to hold her. That it had been a privilege to be visited. She was gone, but she was loved. She felt it. In my body, in my home. She felt love, she felt love, she felt love, she felt love, she felt love. And among the feathers and stones, I, alone and without my child, for the first time since she left, felt it too.

Further Reading

If you want to learn more about the myths and legends featured in this collection, here are a few good places to start – a mixture of (readable!) academic texts, folklore and retellings for children.

Tales of the Elders of Ireland (Oxford World's Classics)
Trans. Anne Dooley and Harry Roe

Early Irish Myths and Sagas (Penguin Classics)
Trans. Jeffrey Gantz

An Irish Folklore Treasure (Gill Books)
John Creedon

Thirty-Two Words for Field (Gill Books)
Manchán Magan

The Big Book of Favourite Irish Myths and Legends (Gill Childrens)
Joe Potter

Acknowledgements

Thank you to my wonderful, tireless agent Juliet Pickering, who didn't even flinch when I told her I wanted to commission and edit an anthology (most agents would run a mile screaming). Thank you to my editor Christina Demosthenous for trusting a journalist to edit fiction, and to Abigail Scruby for taking this over the finish line. A special thanks to Aoife Crowley for her breathtaking work designing the cover of this book, and to the indefatiguable Eleanor Gaffney, who slotted all the puzzle pieces together. Thanks to our copy editors and proof readers, as bearla agus as gaeilge – Talya Baker and Gráinne Ní Mhuilneoir.

Thank you to all the authors within this collection for taking these stories and twisting them into something new, yet ancient – and a heart-felt thank you to all the authors who expressed interest in contributing to this project when it was not even the size of a poppy seed. To my parents, who gave me the gift of these stories when I was growing up.

Thanks obviously to my husband, Chris, who shouldered two years' worth of laundry and childcare while I worked on this in the mornings, evenings and weekends around my (beloved!) day job at *New York* magazine's the Strategist. And thanks to Aoife, for being as patient as a three year old can be when I told her, once again, that I can't go to the park because I'm working. I hope you're all proud of this collection, I certainly am.

RAISING READERS
Books Build Bright Futures

Dear Reader,

We'd love your attention for one more page to tell you about the crisis in children's reading, and what we can all do.

Studies have shown that reading for fun is the **single biggest predictor of a child's future life chances** – more than family circumstance, parents' educational background or income. It improves academic results, mental health, wealth, communication skills, ambition and happiness.[1]

The number of children reading for fun is in rapid decline. Young people have a lot of competition for their time. In 2024, 1 in 10 children and young people in the UK aged 5 to 18 did not own a single book at home.[2]

Hachette works extensively with schools, libraries and literacy charities, but here are some ways we can all raise more readers:

- Reading to children for just 10 minutes a day makes a difference
- Don't give up if children aren't regular readers – there will be books for them!
- Visit bookshops and libraries to get recommendations
- Encourage them to listen to audiobooks
- Support school libraries
- Give books as gifts

There's a lot more information about how to encourage children to read on our website: **www.RaisingReaders.co.uk**

Thank you for reading.

---

[1] OECD, '21st-Century Readers: Developing Literacy Skills in a Digital World', 2021, https://www.oecd.org/en/publications/21st-century-readers_a83d84cb-en.html

[2] National Literacy Trust, 'Book Ownership in 2024', November 2024, https://literacytrust.org.uk/research-services/research-reports/book-ownership-in-2024